"YOU NEEDN'T LOOK SO GUILTY, MR. REILLY ..."

". . . it's not as if I caught you in a seduction."

Seduction? Chagrin chafed at Maggie. Why had she blurted out such a telling remark, especially as the image of a very shirtless Devin standing in the lamplight the night before rose to taunt her?

Since her carriage had careened away on the docks, her whole world seemed tilted beyond her control. Fair or not, she laid the blame at a certain Irishman's feet—or, more accurately, in his hands.

She had stood at the barn's side door for a full five minutes or more, mesmerized by the play of Devin Reilly's hands on the gelding's sleek black coat. His long fingers, made for sketching or playing a musical instrument, stroked the animal with an intimacy that warmed her far more than it should.

She'd never planned on allowing a man to invade her life so thoroughly, never expected the flash of lightning or riotous clamor of a daring embrace to linger and intensify, never thought to be haunted by the lilt of a voice or the knowing sparkle in a green gaze.

Unsettling feelings at best, especially unwanted and unwelcome in the scheme of her life, no matter the tales of chivalrous knights, courtly romance, and tragic fates her grandmother had used to lull her to sleep on sultry summer nights.

Devin stopped his grooming and favored Maggie with a look that sent sparks shooting through her. "Seduction is one means of ensuring cooperation, Miss Brownley."

Dear Romance Reader,

In July, we launched the Ballad line with four new series, and each month we'll present both new and continuing stories set everywhere from medieval England to the American West—the kind of passionate, romantic stories you love best, written by the most gifted authors. At the back of each book, we'll tell you when you can find subsequent books in the series that has captured your heart.

This month beloved author Jo Ann Ferguson completes her riveting *Shadow of the Bastille* series with **A Sister's Quest,** as a French schoolteacher embarks on a perilous—and passionate—adventure with a Russian count. Next, talented newcomer Elizabeth Keys offers the second book in her *Irish Blessing* series, **Reilly's Gold.** What happens when a man determined to find his fortune in America meets a spirited woman instead?

Beginning this month is a series from rising star Kathryn Fox. In 1874, three men—loyal, brave, and true—ride into the Canadian wilderness to fight for justice as *The Mounties*. In the first installment, a recruit trained as a physician will capture a bootlegger—yet *she* will claim his heart for **The First Time.** Finally, new favorite Shelley Bradley presents the second book in her breathtaking *Brothers in Arms* series, as a Scottish knight bent on revenge finds the power of true love with **His Stolen Bride.** Enjoy!

Kate Duffy
Editorial Director

Irish Blessing

REILLY'S GOLD

Elizabeth Keys

ZEBRA BOOKS
KENSINGTON PUBLISHING CORP.

http://www.zebrabooks.com

This book is dedicated with our thanks to the Wild Ones—our electronic lifeline and support—Denise Agnew, Debra Lee Brown, Sherri Browning, Jenni Licata, Tess Mallory, Linda Opdyke, Carolyn Rogers, and Sally Walker; and to our parents, John and Edith Mayberry, and James and Edith Proctor, who believed in us from the start and gave us the courage to pursue our hearts' desires.

Prologue

Beannacht Island, Western Ireland
1842

Three pairs of troubled green eyes stared down at the party below. Three young chins rested against three pairs of fists that gripped the stair rails on the landing.

"Why are they all laughing?" asked Devin, the youngest. "Ain't you 'posed to be sad when someone dies?"

"Only if you loved them," Quin, the eldest, answered with the authority of his superior age.

"I loved Granny." Devin sighed.

"Everyone loved Gran, you ninny." Bryan, who would have been the eldest if only he'd been born a year before Quintin, cast Devin a withering glance.

"So why are they all laughing?" Devin asked for what seemed the dozenth time in the past half hour.

His brothers ignored him, intent on their contemplations.

The clink of glassware and the crack of cutlery on plates underscored the general hum of voices rising in animated discussions and punctuated by merriment from the packed reception rooms below. The worst tragedy the three Reilly brothers had ever faced was being celebrated in grand style.

Almost as one they rose from their crouched positions to file down the hall. The door stood open, as it had each evening of their young lives, awaiting their arrival.

The rocking chair, with only Gran's green shawl to occupy it, stood sentinel by the cold brick hearth in the too-silent room. They lit the lamps and coaxed a meager flame in the grate, trying to restore a little normalcy to this hallowed place, breathing deep, comforting breaths of the lavender and crushed rose scents that lingered in the air.

Bryan cracked the window. "Let out what needs ta go out, my dears. And let in what needs ta be in." He whispered the instructions she'd given each night before she'd begin.

'Tis a wise man who learns to set free what is not his to keep and to accept what is freely offered him, she'd add sometimes, though that part Devin didn't truly understand.

"Let's have at it, then." Quin sat on the hearthstones beside the rocker, as he always did.

Devin hung back for a moment, sniffling. Rolling his eyes in disgust, Bryan pulled him down to join them on the hardwood floor. Devin rubbed his sleeve across his nose, but held his peace.

"Ye must be ready fer The Blessing at any time. And ye must heed it, fer a blessing missed is a curse indeed."

Quintin's voice echoed across Granny's room as the brothers huddled together. He was charged with the telling this night, and he recounted the oft-told tale reverently, with all Granny's inflections, missing not a word nor glimmer of magic.

"But how will we know?" Devin asked in a hushed voice. This time his question formed a necessary part of the ritual.

"You'll know," Bryan answered.

"We'll all know." Quintin shot his brothers a quelling look. " 'Tis a sound once heard that lingers on. A sight once seen and never forgotten. A feeling once felt, always remembered. 'Tis in the blood of all Reillys."

He ruffled the dark curls on Devin's head. "Aye, you'll know, young Devin. And it will be up to you to make of it what you will. Capture The Blessing or suffer The Curse."

The distant rumble of a storm over the ocean deepened the night's gloom. A hint of lavender puffed by on the breeze from the window. Devin shivered, his eyes round with wonder, though still red-rimmed from a day of tears. "I wish Granny could tell us the story."

His tone was hollow with the loss keening through them all. As one, their eyes flew to the empty rocker. Devin loosed a shuddering sigh.

Bryan elbowed him in disgust, though his own lip trembled a bit. "We promised we'd remember, Devi. Don't start now—we promised."

"Aye." Quintin's tone returned to that of the boy he was. "And you promised Gran you'd not mewl like a babe."

Tears dripped over Devin's chin. "I'm trying, Quin. But . . . I miss her." The last came in a watery whisper.

A gust of wind burst against the window, rattling the panes. Quintin and Bryan exchanged a look. The image of a windswept hillside and a freshly dug grave seemed to hover in the air between them.

With a sigh, Quintin knelt next to Devin. "We all miss

her, Devi, and we always will. Gran knew we would miss her. Why else do you think she made us promise to retell The Blessing?''

"Because it is important?" Devin hiccuped.

Quintin grinned. "Aye, boy-o, but it is also a way to stay close to her." He lightly cuffed Devin on the chin. "Now, buck up will you? We canna get through a telling if you're going to blubber.''

"Aye." Devin wiped his nose on his starched Sunday jacket and struggled to smile. "I'll not cry."

"Much," Bryan muttered, earning a halfhearted kick from Devin for his efforts.

Before they erupted into a full scuffle, Quintin continued. "The Blessing has been in the family for generations. Nine unto nine.''

"But won't that mean it stops with us? We could be the ninth generation." Devin had whispered, his anxiety fueling the atmosphere Quintin had created.

"No, you dolt," Bryan shot at his younger brother, "nine unto nine means eighty-one generations."

"Nine unto nine," Quintin repeated, ignoring the interruption. "Reillys take heed and Reillys beware, for unto ye is delivered a great gift—a token of esteem, a promise, a fearsome gratitude." The firelight flickered over his solemn face. "For nine unto nine, ye must make the choice. Only ye can direct the course to joy or sorrow. Only ye decide if it is Blessing or Curse."

"I hope mine's not a curse." Devin shivered.

The older two ignored him.

"It can roll in with the thunder or seep in like the dew. It might fly past in a flash or dance by on a song. The knowin' is up to us. The doin' another part."

"Aye." Bryan's reverent agreement lingered in the air. He sucked in a deep breath. "The joy of yer heart, the wish of yer soul, the direction of yer life, the path of yer choosing.''

"The choice, once made, cannot be undone," Quintin intoned.

"The decision, once forged, cannot be altered," Bryan and Devin returned in urgent half whispers.

"Blessing or Curse for all time."

"For all time." They repeated the last together, three pairs of mirthless green eyes glistening with new tears.

Their voices died away, leaving only the solemn tick of the clock on the fireplace mantel and the murmur of the adults from the parlor below.

Chapter One

"Never again," Devin Reilly growled through gritted teeth for at least the dozenth time. They'd reached harbor almost a full week later than anticipated. Pride alone held his spine erect. No Reilly had ever crawled from the deck of a ship or collapsed in an ignominious heap upon reaching landfall, and he'd be damned if he'd be the first.

"If ye've any prayer of making that ship, ye'd best hurry. She's the last one bound fer San Francisco fer more than a week."

The ticket agent's words spurred Devin's course along Boston's crowded dockside as he fought his way back toward the wallowing implement of torture that had brought him to this land of opportunity a mere hour earlier.

The *Sweet Rose Marie.*

He shuddered, wondering what type of lecture the literature professors at his university in Dublin would have made out of that misnomer.

His stomach quivered anew just thinking about the roil and pitch of the extended voyage from Limerick. He'd never felt so wretched in his life, yet here he was, forcing what little speed he could manage from his protesting muscles as he hastened up the ship's gangplank for the last time. He needed to gather his belongings and board the magnificent clipper ship just two berths away. He could only hope the trip to San Francisco aboard her would offer surcease from the relentless nausea that had plagued his Atlantic crossing. His stomach clenched in mutinous rebellion as he crossed the deck.

"*Diabhal.*" Devil curse the weakness in his limbs.

No matter how many times he made the transition between motionless earth and moving ship, he would never get used to it. Right now he didn't have time to linger over his miserable reactions to something that should be as inbred and soul-deep as his very name, but he'd give his left arm—and possibly a good portion of his right— for a hot cup of Granny Reilly's special ginger tea, the one thing that had ever granted him relief from his detestable seasickness. Only California's easy gold and the urgent need of it back home had prompted his hasty travel aboard the *Sweet Rose Marie.*

"After this I will never cross so much as a pond on any other than a Reilly vessel," he vowed as he slung his bag over his shoulder and tucked his sketchbook under his arm. "Ever again."

Struggling to keep a tight clamp on his weakness, he left the ship for the last time. Boston's dockside bustled with activity. People, carriages, and horses darted in every direction in a startling collage that stung his senses no matter where he looked. This New World was brighter somehow than the one he'd left behind, the colors crisper, the lines of the buildings straighter, and the sounds sharper.

Welcoming land breezes ruffled his shirt, carrying the distant scents of damp earth and green grass mixed with the pungent evidence of human habitation from the city before him. His stomach heaved again. No relief here. He moved aside on the quay, biting back a self-disparaging groan as the men behind him jostled past.

He rested his hand on a rough-hewn crate and took a deep breath. His legs still felt like melted India rubber instead of strong Reilly muscle and bone. He could almost hear the derision in his older brothers' voices as they taunted him for being the only Reilly unable to put to sea. Quin and Bryan never suffered the slightest twinge, even in the heaviest seas.

"Hey, Reilly."

The hail forced him to turn back toward the ship.

"Ye forgot this, mate."

A worn envelope fluttered in the assistant purser's hand and then came flying toward him. He caught the missive and waved his thanks.

The sailor had proven to be a friend during the crossing, the only good memory Devin would take from it.

"Good luck, Reilly. I hope ye find yer gold."

Devin winced as the man's hearty shout voiced his intentions to all and sundry. He offered a farewell salute and tucked his mother's letter away in his waistcoat next to the ticket as he turned to rejoin the throng and make his way to the clipper.

Another grass-scented puff of breeze teased him, promising relief from sea air and harbor stench. He forced himself forward and tried to take his mind off his continued queasiness. A young woman glanced his way as she stepped up into her carriage. Like the scent of greenery in a city, she seemed out of place—a soft and pretty refinement in pale green taffeta, at odds with the bustle and noise on Boston's waterfront.

Devin lost his grip on the tablet and charcoal he carried under his left arm as a bulky shoulder thumped him from behind.

"Hey, you," a deep voice growled as the drawing supplies clattered to the dock.

Despite his rubbery legs, Devin managed to remain standing. Turning, he faced the shoulder's owner, a rough character with a dark beard and a filthy bowler angled over greasy curls.

"And what might I be able to do you for, sir?" Devin strove to remain polite, although he longed to smash his fist into the man's sneering face. Not a very auspicious beginning to his American adventure.

The man's eyes widened as Devin spoke, and he poked his cumbersome companion in the side. "Here, Henry, he's one of them Irish."

Henry, a scruffy-looking chap with a scraggly blond mustache and patched trousers, frowned and narrowed his eyes. "Took our jobs away from me and my brother, them Irish did." His breath reeked of whiskey and he bunched his formidable fists.

"You damn foreigners, takin' over everythin'." The first man sneered as his companion advanced. "Go back to yer slimy little island and stay there. We don't want yer kind here."

Seeing the blow coming didn't help. Devin's sea-worn muscles couldn't react fast enough. Henry's meaty fist sent him flying backward into the path of an oncoming carriage. A shrill scream rent the air.

"Whoa!" The harsh shout came as Devin hit the ground hard. His breath whooshed out of him, and his rucksack of belongings tore free from his shoulder.

He twisted to avoid the sharp hooves thrashing in his

direction and gained his feet as the carriage horses reared
and bolted. A quick assessment revealed the anxious face
of the driver and the panicked expression of the lovely
young woman who had caught his eye only a few moments
before. Her deep brown gaze locked with his for a fear-
charged moment before the carriage zigged along the
quay at a frantic pace toward the water.

"*Diabhal.*" The curse tore from him. He took off after
the carriage, the terror in her eyes spurring his actions.
Pain jolted up his limbs, but he ignored it, dodging the
gawking populace in a desperate race to catch the carriage.

The driver's garbled commands carried back to Devin.
The man's efforts to control the runaway pair managed
to slow the carriage a small bit as the horses struggled
betwixt the training of the whip and the instincts of nature.
Devin could see the driver's efforts would not be enough.

Evaluating his few options, Devin snagged the reins of
a fine black mare being held by a ragtag lad. "I'll bring
her back, boy-o."

He swung up into the saddle without breaking stride,
ignoring the shouts from behind him. Devin clucked his
tongue and leaned far over the horse's neck.

"Come on, darlin', show us what you've got," he
coaxed, his breathing harsh. His heels dug into her sides.

With a responsive flick of her dark ears, the animal
launched into a champion gallop. Devin gained quickly
on the careening carriage as its horses battled each other
and their driver. He wheeled his own mount in front of
the carriage, cutting off the end of the docks as a possible,
but all too deadly, escape route. The carriage teetered
ominously for a moment and then tore free of its inter-
twined harnesses like a ship losing its mooring.

The carriage team screamed their fear and distress. He
snagged their reins and coaxed them to a steaming halt
as the carriage continued its inexorable tilt, landing with

a solid crash and resounding shudder against the side of a tall warehouse.

"Hold these." He threw the reins to a seaman who had jumped from their path at the last moment.

Devin slipped from the mare's back and rushed toward the carriage, his first concern for the hapless occupant whose frightened gaze had forced him after the vehicle. He braced one foot against the wheel and levered himself up enough to reach the door handle and jerk it open.

"Are you all right?" he called into the darkened confines. He couldn't make out anything for a moment until one pale hand extended up from the gloom.

"Yes, I think so." There was a slight rustle of petticoats and a whisper. Although he couldn't make out the word, it sounded distinctively like a muttered curse. "Could you help me out?"

Devin stretched out to grasp her gloved hand, locked his fingers with hers, and pulled. Awareness sizzled up his arm like jagged lightning. Sweat prickled the back of his neck as thunder pounded against his ears in a wild storm only he could hear. His breath locked in his throat, and he fought the instinctive desire to release his grip as the contact shot into his heart and hurtled straight through his soul.

The Blessing.

He grimaced and pulled her into the sunlight as Granny's words echoed through his mind, clearer than ever before. *'Tis a sound once heard that lingers on.*

"Not now." The words groaned out of him as he pulled the girl to safety. The Blessing signaled life-altering events. "I don't have time for this now."

The knowin' is up to us, the doin's another part.

She slid against him as he helped her down. The touch of her body against his echoed through him, a relentless summer storm circling around and through his being without mercy. Thunder and lightning. *Blessing or Curse?*

He set her on her feet and held her for a moment longer and a heartbeat closer than necessary. His mind's frantic signals to release her somehow did not quite make it to his hands as they tightened on her trim waist.

'Tis a feeling once felt, always remembered. The Blessing signaled the need to make a decision, to set a course for his heart's desire, but all he could think of was the overwhelming urge to gather her to him and never let go. Impossible.

Her dark gaze, wide and immeasurable, trailed across his face before locking with his own. Her eyes were smoky amber, fathomless, and eternal. Her lips parted in a small oh, as if she felt something of the power surging between them. She smelled of ginger and chamomile, and he couldn't shake the certainty that despite the distance he'd traveled and the journey he had yet to face, he had just come home.

A sight once seen and never forgotten.

Unable to release her, he seemed just as unable to breathe or to move, other than to lean forward and cover her parted lips with his own. Home indeed. Who was this woman?

"Mo chroí." The Gaelic endearment echoed from deep inside. *My heart.*

Longing swept through him in a heady, unstoppable torrent at the taste of her mouth. All vestiges of sanity and purpose vanished as the need to gather her to him crested and broke over his common sense, drowning all rational thought. Her lips seemed frozen beneath his for a fraction of time. Then she melted against him like water rippling along a shore. She tasted as sweet as rain on a summer afternoon, felt as soft as a breeze floating in from the back meadow at home.

Home. Beannacht Island. A sharp reminder of his objective in traveling to America pierced the haze. As if this entire adventure would not be enough to explain, the vision of Quin's frowning censure over such a public display as he was creating with this woman swooped in.

Devin tore his mouth away and stepped back. Gratitude for the abrupt cessation of the sensations touching this lass evoked warred with a wild yearning to gather her close yet again.

A cheer from the small crowd that had gathered brought her chin up and forced a determined glint into her eyes. She straightened her shoulders.

Devin glanced over the heads of the leering crowd. Sure enough, the clipper's short sails were being unfurled. She was about to sail without him. Whatever he'd just imagined happened, The Blessing could not possibly intend for him to miss his ship. Not now. He needed to retrieve his pad and clothing and board that clipper before it departed with all his hopes and dreams.

"I don't have time for this," he repeated, returning his gaze to her and struggling to shove unbidden longings away. Some introduction to a new country—barely off the boat and he'd set about seducing the native women.

Her straw bonnet angled askew across her back, and her hair, a wild tangle of tight sandy curls, had come loose beneath the touch of his fingers. She took a deep breath and blew it out slowly, as if gathering her composure. Untying her bonnet, she freed her curls still further. They framed her face and trailed over her shoulders. Longing to bury his hands in their silken depths swept him anew.

"I'd ha' stopped that coach meself if I'd knowed a kiss like that was the reward." A gap-toothed sailor saluted them with a half-empty rum bottle.

She squared her shoulders and raised one slim brow at

the sailor. Her dark eyes snapped fire above the rosy glow
in her cheeks and the slight swelling of her well-kissed
lips. The sailor shrank away, and she turned back to
Devin. "I'm sorry you've no time for this accident. It
was not in my plans, either. But could you help me find
my coachman before you rush off?"

Her tart tone stung. So much for the rescued maiden
heaping grateful praises on his head. "And you are most
welcome, Miss . . . ?"

"Brownley," she offered with a lift of her stubborn-
looking chin. She extended her hand in greeting, then
halted, leaving her gesture dangling in the air between
them. "Margaret Sylvia Worth Brownley."

"I see—"

A groan broke into Devin's reply and slashed alarm
back into Margaret Sylvia Worth Brownley's glittering
brown eyes.

She swiped a mass of curls back over her shoulder and
knelt beside the carriage, heedless of the dirt that would
surely stain her dress.

"Marcus? Where are you?" Concern edged her questions as she peered beneath the vehicle.

"Here, Miss. My leg." Another groan. "I'm caught."

"Oh, dear." Margaret stood. Her gaze flew to Devin's,
worry etched between her brows. The need to be on his
way tore at him, but he could not ignore the wordless
entreaty he saw there.

"Move back," Devin directed as he grabbed for a solid
hold on the carriage. Several men from the crowd lent
their assistance. Devin strained with every bit of strength
he could manage and the carriage slowly rocked back
onto all four wheels, giving a slight bounce on its well-
oiled hinges.

Margaret Brownley didn't waste time with thanks as

she disappeared around the other side of the carriage. "Oh, Marcus."

Her cry of dismay forced Devin to follow. She turned her dark glance toward him as he rounded the corner.

"We've got to help him."

We? How easily she swung back and forth between tart miss and maiden in distress. Devin bit back a sigh as sympathy for the coachman's plight seeped past his annoyance with the volatile and far too attractive Miss Brownley.

"I'll help the little woman fer ya, mate," the drunken sailor offered from right behind Devin.

The ticket agent had said almost an hour. Surely he had a moment or two left to spare. He couldn't leave her to the likes of the sailor, not after he'd helped cause the situation by kissing her so soundly.

He knelt beside the older man, whose left leg was cocked at a funny angle. "I can get you into the coach, but I'll wager 'tis going to hurt more than drunken pride on a bright Sunday morning."

The coachman managed a slight grin that turned into a pain-filled grimace. "I think I can manage that."

"All right." Devin slid his arms under the other man's torso and tightened his grip. He nodded to Margaret. "Open the door, lass, and stand away."

She did so without comment, though her teeth tugged at her lower lip.

Devin lifted the coachman, who struggled valiantly against the pain he must be feeling, and slid him into the coach with as little wasted movement as possible. The man's face was white and drawn when Devin released him against the soft leather padding.

"Thank you, Mister—" Margaret Brownley began.

"Just what do you mean by stealing my horse?" A

voice Devin recognized from his abrupt misappropriation of the mare a few minutes ago blasted him from behind.

Devin turned, clutching his fast waning patience by a slim thread. He really did not have the time for any further delays. " 'Twas not a theft, sir. Your horse was the nearest. I borrowed her to save this woman from an even more unfortunate accident than the one she just suffered.''

The tall man's eyes narrowed as he ran his gaze over Devin from head to toe. Painfully thin, with a pallor befitting a prisoner, he managed to puff his chest out with inbred superiority. "Fresh off the boat, are you?" Under his wispy mustache, the man's lip curled in a derisive sneer. "How dare you put your filthy Irish paws on my property? I'll have a watchman over here to arrest you immediately.''

"Please." Margaret broke into the gaunt man's tirade, coming forward to stand beside Devin as if he were a nursling in need of a champion. "This man saved my life and that of my coachman," she continued. "The entire Brownley family are in his, and your, debt.''

The sight of the clipper sliding backward from its berth snagged Devin's attention and left him speechless as the two Bostonians prosed on. So much for The Blessing. The thought twisted pain through his stomach. What was he to do now? Cool his heels for a week or more before he could book another passage to California in a place that looked upon Irishmen as lower than the dirt? Cursed indeed.

The man peered at Miss Brownley for a moment and then raised his brows. "Brownley, did you say? Are you related to William Brownley?''

"Yes, he is my father.''

Recognition dawned over his face, swiftly followed

by a calculated gleam sparking in his eyes. "Oh, Miss Brownley, I do apologize. I'm Horace Milford."

Tipping his hat, Milford bowed slightly before continuing. "I have a great respect for your father. I . . . do you, by some chance, *know* this . . . man?"

Milford's gesture toward Devin made it clear he hesitated to name him as such. Anger roiled through Devin in a hot red haze. He'd had all he could stand. He would have advanced on the man, but Miss Brownley stepped into his path as though she'd read his mind.

"Why yes, I do. He is—"

"Devin Reilly," Devin said through gritted teeth before Margaret Brownley would be forced to lie further.

"Mr. Reilly is here to help at my family's . . . estate," she finished smoothly, "so I can vouch for him completely."

Milford looked skeptical. "Help on your family's estate? Are you sure?"

"Quite." Margaret Brownley nodded, sending her curls dancing over her slim back. "Now, if you'll excuse us, Mr. Milford, I really must get my coachman home and send for the doctor. Thank you for the loan of your horse. I'll be sure to mention your assistance to my father."

She turned her back and locked her gaze with Devin's. "You will help me get Marcus home, won't you, Mr. Reilly?" she asked in a low tone. He recognized the light of desperation shining in her eyes. Although most of the crowd had dispersed, the overeager sailor still eyed them from close by.

Devin nodded, not trusting himself to speak when all he wanted to do at the moment was drive his fist through Horace Milford's smug face. After all, he had no other plans for the next week or better.

"I must fetch my belongings," he told her. "I dropped them."

He couldn't help wondering how his elder brother Bryan would have handled the situation. With his solicitor's acumen and cool logic, no doubt. And Quin? The eldest Reilly would probably have clapped the man in irons for daring to speak so disrespectfully to a Reilly captain, and then kissed Miss Brownley into a daze rather than allow her to defend him in public.

"Mr. Reilly?" With a start, he realized she was awaiting his response.

"Aye, Miss Brownley?"

"Will you help me up?" She extended her hand.

Devin held back for a moment, hesitating to suffer the wild, shattering contact of The Blessing again so soon, but with no excuse to give her, he took her hand.

Warm and soft, even through her gloves, her fingers sent a cascade of yearning into his palm. But no thunder, no rush and tumble rolling through his depths. Just the faintest hint of ginger and chamomile lingered in the air around her. He almost sighed with relief. Perhaps he had imagined the whole Blessing episode.

Margaret Sylvia Worth Brownley? What on earth had possessed her to spew her entire name to her rescuer like that? As much as she loved her Grandmother Worth, Margaret generally avoided using her full name, given the avaricious circumstances under which she'd been saddled with it.

She settled onto the carriage's front perch, steadying herself with one hand against the roof and wishing she could as easily bring a small measure of balance to the emotions running riot within her.

Devin Reilly's daring rescue and the liberties he'd taken on the docks had loosed feelings inside her she'd never dared dream existed outside the realm of the romantic bedtime stories with happily-ever-after endings her grandmother used to tell.

She reached for the reins to untangle them as she awaited her escort, considering the scandal of driving her coachman home by herself as opposed to spending any more time in Devin Reilly's disturbing company. The fastest route home would surely lead to a dozen sightings by the tabbies her mother considered friends. Taking the reins herself was not really an option.

Mr. Reilly swung up onto the perch beside her after checking the horses to be certain they had not been injured. He'd also checked the fastenings with what appeared to be an experienced eye, alleviating her worries over having to explain any damage to her father.

As the Irishman settled on the seat, his thigh wedged tight against hers, bringing heat to her cheeks even through the bulky layers of petticoat she wore beneath her gown. It had been far too long since she'd demanded to drive the coach, she thought. In her childhood, the seat had appeared large enough for three. Now two seemed a stretch.

Her lips still tingled from the intimacy of his kiss, and her thoughts seemed intent on cycling through her head in an unending and senseless rotation. If only Tori had come along, she'd have been more than a match for Mr. Reilly's dangerous charm. The soft burr in his voice wouldn't skim straight through her if her friend were here to provide some distraction.

She waved politely to Mr. Milford and bit back a groan, hoping the man would not report the whole of this morning's incident to her father. William Brownley had enough eyes and ears throughout Boston as it was.

"Do go slowly, Mr. Reilly." Margaret touched his hand atop the reins and then pulled back as his vivid green eyes glanced her way for a moment. Her breath caught in her throat as she remembered the demands of his lips on hers and the dizzying response that had thundered through her.

"I don't want Marcus to be any more uncomfortable than necessary," she explained, biting her lip and wishing she'd told him to hurry along instead.

"You're a lass given to direction, are you not, Miss Brownley?" He lifted a brow and clucked to the horses. "Have no fear. Growing up around a shipyard, I've seen injuries worse than your Marcus is suffering. He'll recover right enough."

So he'd grown up around ships, had he? He didn't have the hard, weathered look of most of the sailors she'd seen on the docks.

She watched Devin Reilly's hands as he led the horses through a smart turnaround on the quay and then back the way they had come. She could imagine those strong hands capable of many things, but they were not as callused and ragged as those of most of the men who loaded her supplies after a buying trip like today's. She wondered what he was doing coming off the ship just docking when she'd arrived. What had caused him to leave his homeland behind?

It came to her that she was riding along Boston's busy dockside with a virtual stranger wedged tight against her side. She knew nothing about him save his ability to stop a speeding carriage and start the wild racing of her heart. Dismay lodged in her chest. At least she was in a very public place.

What had become of her staid requisition trip for the Brookline Daughters of Grace? Her usual thrill on such an excursion was being able to bargain down one of the cargo masters as she sought the most foodstuffs for her money.

The carriage halted near a ship called the *Sweet Rose Marie,* where the entire incident had begun. *That's right, he needs to fetch his possessions.*

"I'll be right back, lass." Reilly alighted with a speed

that both surprised her and left her feeling oddly bereft. She scanned the dockside crowds as they went about their varied business. At least the spectacle she had made of herself just now seemed to be over. No necks craned in curiosity to study her.

"Marcus? How are you faring?" She twisted around and called into the carriage interior. "I'll send for Dr. Raymond just as soon as we reach the house."

"All right, Miss." His reply was muffled, but steady. "Don't fret yerself."

She tried to shove her hair back into a semblance of order, wishing for the tenth time today that she possessed her sister's more orderly locks. Just as she tied her bonnet into place with what she hoped was a perky bow, Devin Reilly swung back up beside her.

"Where are the things you went to fetch?" she asked before getting a good look at the scowl on his dark brow.

"Gone."

His terse reply knotted her stomach. "Gone? What do you mean gone? Did someone send them on ahead to your lodgings? Are you certain you checked the right place? Perhaps one of your friends is merely keeping them safe."

He looked at her straight on then with a trace of sadness hardened by a glint of anger. "I know no one in this great land, with the exception of you, Marcus, and that Milford. I have missed my ship. I have no lodgings and now I have none of my belongings—not my sketchbook, not my clothing, not even my pouch which was to see me to California. I am as good as marooned."

He turned back to the horses and chucked the reins, clicking softly. "Walk on."

Guilt suffused her. He'd lost everything saving her. "We shall report this theft to the authorities. I'm sure they will launch an inquiry immediately and track down your property.''

"Aye, lass," he answered on an exasperated sigh. "It is quite certain the authorities will be most concerned over my small bundle of clothing and whether I have the means to get to my destination. Though how I shall eat their concern is beyond me."

His sarcasm chafed, but she would not be deterred. He'd rescued her, and she must return the favor.

"Turn there." She pointed ahead. "I belong to a small charitable organization in my parish. I'm certain the Daughters of Grace will be able to give—"

"Know this, Miss Brownley. Reillys are not partial to accepting charity, no matter the grace with which it is offered." He stared straight ahead, but the set of his chin and his tone indicated her offer appeared far less than gracious.

She gulped a breath. "Then I shall ask my father to reward—"

"I'll not make money from merely doin' what any man should."

She exhaled in exasperation. "No one else did, though," she grumbled. "Whatever will you do?"

"I'll escort you home as I agreed and then seek my fortune as best I can."

"Without money? Without a job? Don't be ridiculous!"

No answer. Sometimes men seemed the most unfathomable creatures on the planet, no matter their origins. Devin Reilly was bereft and alone all because of her, and bent on refusing any assistance through stubborn pride alone.

As if her conscience didn't have enough to bear given Marcus's injury and her own commandeering of the older carriage for her errands this day. Her mother heartily disapproved of her trips to the docks, barely sanctioning them even when Tori, the rector's daughter, accompanied her.

Just imagining the row that was sure to be raised if—*when*—that grand dame learned she was to be deprived of her coachman as he convalesced following her older daughter's solo mission to aid the riffraff made Maggie shudder.

"How could you do this to us, Margaret? Why can't you behave as a genteel, refined lady like your sister?" the august Alberta Brownley would no doubt say, relishing her favorite remonstration. "How am I ever to get on without a proper driver?"

Maggie chided herself for wishing Marcus a speedy recovery almost as much for her sake as for his own. The carriage jostled for a moment as the wheels on one side passed over a missing cobblestone on State Street. The motion pressed her against the able-bodied wall of Irish arrogance beside her and she bit her lip at the warm thoughts that sprang to mind.

Perhaps he would prove the answer to all their troubles. She slid him a brief sideways glance and nodded to herself. Best not to broach the matter until they'd arrived home and Devin Reilly was faced with the actual choice of going back into the world, hungry and penniless, or availing himself of a hot meal and some gainful employment. Surely she could convince Papa to offer at least that much.

Chapter Two

Weariness mantled Devin's shoulders like autumn moss on the leeward outcroppings of Beannacht Island.

The enormity of his situation—penniless, adrift in a hostile city, a heedless land—spawned daunting prospects too immense to bear in one sitting. They seemed almost insurmountable against the backdrop of the hopes he'd nursed across the churning Atlantic.

Pressed tight against Margaret Sylvia Worth Brownley's pale green skirts, his leg was the only part of him that felt truly alive as the sights and sounds of Boston Harbor passed by the carriage as if in a long, tortured nightmare. Even through the layers of fashionable cloth, his thigh jangled with enough warmth to scorch through the sense of futility clinging to him.

Mo chroí, he'd called her. His heart.

More like a delusion brought on by weeks of dehydration due to seasickness. Yet in her arms he'd found sanctuary, on her lips he'd tasted home, and in her eyes he'd glimpsed laughter and promises. If he dropped the reins and gathered her to him once more, perhaps he could halt his jeering doubts and self-loathing.

His stomach clenched. He could not afford such a distraction. He needed to clear his thoughts, not clog them with lustful desires or childish fantasies of The Blessing. Being guided by delusions from the heart meant only disaster. Margaret Brownley had cost him enough already. Once he'd seen her and her coachman safely home, he could set about righting his sorry situation.

Somehow.

At least she had subsided into silence once he'd disabused her of the notion he could be her latest charity recipient. He stole a glance at her profile as she chewed her lower lip and studied the bustling intersection they approached. The last thing he needed was a well-intentioned but misguided savior, no matter how beautiful. No, make that especially one as beautiful as this girl. The one lesson Seamus, his friend from the University of Ireland, had taught him was that if a fellow allowed his hopes to center on a lass, destruction was sure to follow.

The sunlight gleaming against the horses' shining coats dimmed as they passed beneath shadows from the warehouses lining the street, just as his foolish dreams of only a few hours earlier had grown dull beneath the onslaught of his current situation. So much for making his fortune.

He no longer possessed even a change of shirts or the price of a loaf of bread. He was indeed a pitiable creature. A likelier candidate for the charity she'd offered he'd never known. Still, the offer rankled.

What had prevailed upon him to board the *Sweet Rose Marie* so many weeks ago? How had he convinced himself he could land in America, strike it rich, and save the family? Quin would surely share a good horse laugh with Bryan over this misadventure—*after* they'd both blistered his ears for even trying to come up with a solution to the island's problem on his own.

A fleeting phantom of The Blessing could not alter his course. He'd have to get himself out of this to prove to himself, and to Quin and Bryan, that he could. He'd have to. But how? He had no clue. He only knew that he wanted—he *needed*—to do this on his own, without help from Reilly Ship Works contacts in the city.

"Diabhal."

As soon as he could, he'd seek out those devil's minions who'd greeted him with a fist and landed him in this predicament in the first place. A satisfying thought, even if not quite accurate. He'd arrived here of his own accord.

He headed the horses in the direction she pointed, trying to ignore the slender elegance of her fingers and the fine bones of her wrist. This was no time for mooning over a lass he'd never see again after the next hour or so, Blessing or no.

"Diabhal," he swore again as his thoughts circled back to the catalyst of his problems.

"I've no idea what you keep muttering to yourself, but I'm quite certain it is not the sort of language your mother or mine would consider suitable for polite conversation."

He cast another sideways glance at Miss Brownley. Small wispy curls escaped her bonnet to dance around her face in time with the carriage's jolting rhythm. The lively motion, in opposition to her still posture and prim words, betrayed the vibrance he'd tasted in her kiss.

With her gaze cast down toward her gloved hands, clasped tight in her lap, the thick fringe of her eyelashes nearly brushed the hint of color edging her smooth cheek. She appeared the very essence of demure propriety.

His gaze lingered on her lips and he could almost feel them beneath his again. Summer rain and soft breezes, wild thunder and jagged lightning. She'd returned his kiss in anything but a proper fashion. Her carefully crafted facade surely hid a wanton's heart. His condemnation reeked of injustice, but nothing of the day's events thus far seemed justified to him, least of all his present ties to this lass. Perhaps he could begin to comprehend The Blessing's portents by learning more about the woman it seemed bound to.

"And what would yer mother consider a suitable conversation between a destitute Irishman and a grand lady such as yerself?" He rolled his words to emphasize his brogue the way the students at college did around stuffy English visitors.

She glanced over. The soft color in her cheeks heightened, but her chin rose and she held his gaze for a long moment. She was truly not the timid, demure miss she seemed wont to portray. The sparkle of intelligence in her eyes begged for release as she appeared to consider her response.

The deep amber of her eyes nearly swallowed him whole before she turned her attention ahead and left him bereft of the harbor he briefly envisioned there.

"We need to turn to the left at the next intersection," she told him over the din of the crowd. "And my mother would most likely disapprove of any conversation we might have. Still, I wanted to divert your attention, and I have."

Despite a clipped smugness that should have rankled, her speech was low in tone and soothing to his ear after weeks in the company of sailors. Soft traces of chamomile laced with ginger tantalized him as she pointed the way. His breath snagged.

"To what purpose did you seek my attention?" He guided the team around the corner. "And why bring my mother into it?"

"I have noticed that men frequently bluster when they

are frustrated, or feeling on the lower end of events.''
She tossed him a look that twinkled with conspiratorial
mischief. ''Mentioning their mothers seems to draw them
back to the matter at hand.''

''Which would be?''

''You must stop dwelling on the past and concentrate
on the future, as my grandmother would say. When the
goal is big enough, or the choices few enough, it is worth
the risk of a little personal discomfort. Use the past for
guidance, not blame, while you look ahead. She nodded
in emphasis. ''Cursing your fate, Mr. Reilly, will not
change it. Only action will.''

The truth of her advice startled a chuckle from his
depths. ''Your grandmother sounds very much like my
own. Then, to emphasize the point, she'd no doubt spin
me a fine tale about a brave Fian warrior who spent so
much time thinking of his lost battle he failed to plan for
the one ahead.''

''Fian warrior?'' Margaret Brownley's eyebrows knit
together as she wrinkled her brow over the phrase.

''Ancient tales for a different day, lass, when I've less
to consider regarding my immediate needs.''

Mercifully, she accepted this and left him to his redi-
rected thoughts. What was he going to do once he'd seen
Miss Brownley home? Most likely those scurvies had
disappeared into a tavern to swill away his savings. He
needed to find employment and shelter. The *Sweet Rose
Marie* was set to leave for Charleston this evening, but
he doubted her master would be willing to take on a
crewman who'd spent the better part of the crossing with
his face in a bucket. Besides, his gut told him he needed
to stay here in Boston where he'd experienced The Blessing—if that was truly what he'd felt.

What possible portent had The Blessing conveyed when
he'd drawn Margaret Brownley from the carriage straight

into his arms? Had he missed his boat in more ways than one by delivering her, delivering himself, into a curse? Or was there a reason he was being forced to stay in this city?

He hadn't thought of Granny's tales about the family's ancient gift in a very long time. Her face had become a blur through the years—a wide grin of greeting and twinkling blue eyes. What he remembered more was the smell of her lavender perfume and the love that rolled through him when she rocked him by the fire and spoke low and soft of magical things that once were and of wonderful things yet to come.

The Blessing had been the story Granny always saved for last. It was the turning point for all Reillys, the benchmark of their lives. Quintin and Bryan might have earned the right to claim a Blessing, but what had he ever done to merit one?

The knowin' is up to us, his brothers had told him long ago, *the doin' another part.*

Surely this strange manifestation only proved his hasty decision to journey to this land heralded a curse, evidenced by the loss of all his possessions and money.

Only ye can determine the course to joy or sorrow. Only ye can decide if it is Blessing or Curse. Echoes of his Granny's tales answered him from across the years.

He needed to find his own way out of this predicament, no matter how tempting it might be to seek assistance from one of his father's or Quin's many business associates in this port.

"But what exactly am I to do now?" The true enormity of the odds against him struck home with discouraging blackness as he navigated the small carriage around a dry goods cart standing by a corner.

"Do? Why we'll stay fairly straight on this street all the way to Brookline," Maggie informed her makeshift coachman in between gnawing her lower lip. Fine one she was to be giving Devin Reilly advice when she had so little idea of what she was going to do herself once they arrived home.

She tried to force her churning thoughts away from the distraction of watching the Irishman's hands expertly guide the horse and carriage through the city. Her arms still tingled from the pressure of those hands when he'd pulled her from the carriage—tingled not in pain, but with a strange awakening pleasure that rippled inside her to twine with the elation of his scandalous kiss.

Diabhal. What a satisfying curse, whatever it meant.

She could not afford the distractions this man too readily provided with his dark curls, dimples, and stubborn male pride. His quick thinking had saved her at great cost to himself. How infuriating of him to flatly refuse all consideration of a reward for what he'd done—what he was doing. She'd never have been able to manage the trip home on her own, not without jolting poor Marcus to pieces. Yet his continued assistance would bring the censorious wrath of her parents squarely on her shoulders.

While no one in her family would most likely learn of the shocking display she'd made of herself on the docks, Milford not withstanding, the enormity of the scandal broth that could be brewed over her riding side by side with a stranger—an Irish stranger—grew the closer they got to home. She pressed her lips together. She should apply her grandmother's advice as easily as she dispensed it and concentrate on how to smooth the ripples her unconventional homecoming and the upheaval the loss of the family coachman was sure to create.

Her gaze came back to his hands and the easy way he handled the reins. An idea shivered through her and she gripped her hands tighter in her lap. Perhaps Devin

Reilly's expertise would pose a solution to both their problems—at least the more immediate ones.

"You're doing a fine job with the horses. Do you have much experience with them?" Hope made her question more than a casual inquiry, but he seemed not to notice.

"I've some experience with both riding horses and teams," he answered, without giving her any particulars.

A scowl creased his brow. He looked as if he'd rather be anywhere on the earth than here answering her questions. That expression would never do. Anything but the bland face of a true coachman would be sure to draw more attention from the increasing numbers of carriages and riders they would pass, any one of whom could be Papa or Mama's acquaintance.

"This is called The Common." She raised her voice a trifle and gestured toward the large field they were passing, where urchins played and couples strolled. "It was used in colonial times for grazing. Most of our New England towns have a common or village square."

"New England? As if *old* England wasn't enough to plague the earth?" His frown lightened just a bit as he took note of the rolling expanse of meadowland amidst stone and granite edifices.

She smiled at him. "This group of northeastern states may bear the name of our former country, but that is the extent of our connection. America is a democracy now."

"Aye, liberty and justice for all." He nodded. "We studied your Declaration and your Constitution in great depth at university in Dublin. Though it was outside our sanctioned curriculum—the British are still a might touchy about such things." A smile chased over his lips.

"You've been to college?" Her mouth dropped open in surprise. Why should that news seem so unexpected? Devin Reilly's speech was more refined than the average sailor she'd encountered on the docks, and his hands were not the callused ones of a laborer. Obviously, she'd paid far greater heed to her father's rantings than she'd thought.

Her astonished reaction raised Devin's eyebrow.

"I beg your pardon." She could feel heat creeping across her cheeks. "Of course there's no reason why you shouldn't have an education."

His brow smoothed, but he offered no comment to ease the moment. She ventured a smile and tried to skirt back to their previous conversation. "I don't suppose the British are at all enthusiastic about anyone in their empire discussing our revolution. Might give them ideas."

"Exactly so." His lips actually twitched into an answering smile. "The horrified look on the chancellor's face last spring when he interrupted a heated discourse on the wisdom of the Continental Congress was something to see indeed."

He shook his head and fixed a pointed green stare at her. "Though from the prevailing winds that greeted my arrival, 'twould appear *New* England mirrors the old in its belief that the Irish are an ignorant lot."

Before she could answer, Maggie noticed the approach of an open carriage gleaming with brass fittings and drawn by a pair of matched chestnuts. Her heart sank. The occupants were unmistakable. For a moment, she wished she could slide below the seat for the rest of the journey home. Anyone but Jonathan Adams Lawrence III's mother.

The older woman, who wore a large black hat adorned with a drooping purple ostrich feather, nodded. The feather bobbed in the breeze, oblivious to the disapproval chiseled on Mrs. Lawrence's features. Her companion, a younger woman with sleek dark hair and skin the color of fine porcelain, dipped her head ever so slightly as they passed. Jonathan's sister, Amelia, kept her speculative gaze fixed on Devin.

Maggie's own mama would be doubly furious over this

afternoon's adventure if she'd ruffled Mrs. Lawrence's sensibilities. Her stomach twisted. The battle over her mother's hopes where the younger Mr. Lawrence was concerned was one Maggie was not ready to face. Not today.

Squaring her shoulders, Maggie returned their frosty greetings with a dazzling smile that collapsed as soon as the occupants of the other carriage whisked past. She prayed she'd appeared for all the world a carefree young lady out for a drive on a sunny afternoon—prayed with a fervency she had not experienced since wishing her sister would be struck with the spots for all the mean things she said about Tori.

"Miss Brownley?"

"Oh." She started, then attempted to continue their conversation as though nothing were amiss. The censure she faced for riding up front with such an unconventional driver should not be laid at his door. "You must pay no attention to the blustering of the Know-Nothings."

"Know-Nothings?" He frowned at her.

"A group of politicians and businessmen who seek to make themselves greater by denigrating others." She detested her own father's role in the organization. "They think they are terribly clever with such a name, but they just betray the smallness of their own minds."

"By others, I take it you mean the Irish."

He obviously had no intention of ducking the issue of prejudice against natives of his country. Chuckling mirthlessly, he met the speculative look she cast him. Her cheeks burned with embarrassment for the actions of her countrymen toward his.

"Perhaps these know-nothings fail to realize most of the boats that dock in this and other harbors also return across the sea"—sarcasm laced his tone—"carrying tales of your streets paved with gold and the . . . er . . . generosity of the welcome you Americans extend?"

"But you came here anyway?" She studied the set line of his jaw and the directness in his gaze. Strong. Determined. Undefeated in spite of losing everything he owned.

"Did you not say to me that sometimes, when the goal is big enough or the choices few enough, it is worth the risk of a little personal discomfort?"

Intrigued, she couldn't stop the questions his predicament prompted. "What about you, Mr. Reilly? Is your goal big enough? Or were your options so limited you were forced to leave home?"

She envied him the freedom he'd found to strike out on his own, the spirit of adventure that must have brought him across the ocean—answering to no one, possessing the confidence to declare, despite the odds, that he'd take no charity, that he'd earn his own way.

"I'll tell you my story, Miss Margaret Sylvia Worth Brownley, if you'll tell me yours first." The keen intelligence in his eyes promised he would brook little in the way of dissembling.

"What is it you'd like to know?" She stalled. She had learned through her life in Boston society that few people wanted to look beneath another's outer appearance and see the person within, and those who did were often dissatisfied with acquaintances made on that level.

"Anything. Have you lived in the city all your life? What sort of work does your father do? Do you have any brothers or sisters? What are your goals? Your choices? What was a refined lady such as yourself doin' amidst the hustle of a busy harbor?"

He chucked to the horses as they deftly avoided a carriage stopped at the corner of Charles Street. The shift in the wheels pressed Maggie tighter to Devin Reilly. She inhaled a whiff of balsam mixed with the earthy musk of the deep forests that turned her thoughts immediately to Maine, her true home.

Perhaps a little personal information would gain her the same from him. "My father is interested in investments, but would be horrified to consider his dabbling work. Someday, I'd like to run a lumber mill. And I visit the docks every week to arrange for goods and foodstuffs for the North End Mission supported by the Daughters of Grace."

She caught back a gasp as her own words echoed in her ears.

"Whoa now, Miss Brownley. What was that nugget you buried in there? A lumber mill?"

The corners of his mouth quirked.

What had possessed her to declare her secret dream so openly? Most of the men she knew would not only find the idea of a woman running a business ludicrous, but scandalous as well. If he laughed at her, she'd shove him off the seat and drive herself the rest of the way home.

"My Grandmother Worth has run her lumber business in Maine on her own for over thirty years." The explanation tumbled out despite her best efforts to hold it back.

Devin Reilly didn't laugh. Instead, his questions and observations prompted her to tell him a great deal more than she'd told anyone besides Tori. Her summer visits to Maine, her admiration for her Grandmother Worth, her impatience with the shallow life expected of the young ladies of her acquaintance, all spilled out.

She realized only as they reached the gates to her parents' home that she still knew next to nothing about her rescuer. The enormity of what she, of what they all, would face in the next few minutes settled on her like a granite boulder.

"The gates are open. You can turn in there and proceed to the back of the house." Even to her own ears, her voice sounded like the hollow thudding of Marbury's footsteps on the back stairs, devoid of the spring and life telling Devin about Maine had added.

Squirming, she twisted around to call into the interior of the carriage. "We're here, Marcus. We'll have you set to rights in no time."

"Aye, miss. I'd prefer not to worry Jenna about this until the doctor arrives, if possible."

"We'll pull around to the kitchen and get you settled there before I send for her. But as your wife, she'll want to make you as easy as possible while we await Dr. Raymond."

The tree-lined drive broke right toward the circle in front of the house. The small curricle and brown mare tethered there proved a welcome sight. If The Reverend James Carlton was paying his weekly visit, her mother would be far less likely to raise a scene over her eldest child's unconventional homecoming. And if Tori had accompanied her father on his call, they could put their heads together and see how best to make sure Devin Reilly's good deed did not go unrewarded. It was the least she owed him.

"If you go round to the left, we can take Marcus straight into the kitchen. Timmy, our stable boy, should still be here to take the horses." She touched Devin's arm to flick his gaze back to hers. "Marbury, our butler, is too old to handle bringing Marcus in on his own."

"I've come this far, lass. I'll stay 'til the job's through." The green flint in his gaze softened a bit before he turned to the task of steering the rig to the back of the house.

The kitchen door sprang open before the carriage reached a full halt.

"Miss Margaret, where have you been?" Mrs. Marbury puffed out the door in a blur of black and white. "The Reverend and his daughter have been here near half an hour, and your mother's rung three times to see if you were back from the library. You were supposed to be here to help set the plans for the big tea next month!''

Maggie's stomach twisted as the housekeeper halted by the drive. The annual Daughters of Grace tea.

''I forgot—''

''What are you doing on top of the carriage instead of inside?'' the elderly woman scolded as she fixed her attention to where Devin Reilly tied the reins off. ''And with a stranger, no less! Who are you, young man?'' She squinted up at Devin, a disapproving frown creasing her round face. ''And what have you done with our coachman?''

''Marcus was hurt,'' Maggie answered before Devin damned her with the truth. The last thing she needed was for him to reveal the circumstances of their meeting. ''This gentleman was kind enough to bring us both home.''

''Hurt? How?'' Mrs. Marbury's skepticism dissolved into concern. ''Where is Marcus?''

''He's right inside, madam.'' Devin slid from the seat to stand beside Mrs. Marbury. Odd, the burr in his accent was barely discernible. ''The mishap occurred . . .''

Maggie gasped, apprehension filling her throat. Marcus stood in enough danger of losing his position just from his injury without her parents learning he'd been assisting her in her unauthorized expeditions.

Devin's gaze flashed to hers for the barest second before he continued, ''. . . on the street as I was passing by. I rendered what little assistance I could.''

Thank goodness he hadn't betrayed them. ''It's his leg,'' Maggie told the housekeeper. ''If Mr. Reilly will help us bring Marcus into the kitchen . . .'' Maggie glanced at him and caught his nod. ''We must send Molly to fetch Dr. Raymond at once.''

''Of course, Miss. I do hope it's not broken.'' Mrs.

Marbury stepped over to the carriage door. The woman sent Maggie a look filled with worry. "Will we need to lie poor Marcus down right away?"

"I think he can sit in a chair with his leg on a bench." Maggie turned to climb down. "He doesn't want to frighten Jenna."

Devin Reilly's strong hands circled her waist and lifted her before her foot reached the step. Just for a moment she was whisked back to the docks and the feel of his hands as he plucked her from the overturned carriage then pulled her into his embrace. Never had she expected a kiss to send such a cascade of fire and longing coursing through her—not that she was an expert in such matters.

Echoes of the thunder he'd awakened in her veins still reverberated in her limbs, heightened by the closeness of his body as he set her on the ground. Probably just a reaction to the excitement of the accident and the anxiety of the trip home. She forced herself not to turn around and look up into the shelter she imagined in his eyes. Getting Marcus settled and smoothing their homecoming needed her full attention.

"If you ladies will open the kitchen door and clear the way, I will endeavor to deliver your coachman into your care," Devin directed. Mrs. Marbury turned an appraising look on him, then nodded ever so slightly.

"But you'd best hurry. He appears ready to let himself out, and I don't believe his knee can take the strain." Devin pointed to Marcus, who was struggling to pull himself over to the carriage door. His face was blanched with the strain, and deep lines of pain etched his brow. Maggie knew her coachman was trying to show he was not as seriously injured as they all feared.

Mrs. Marbury opened the carriage door and peered inside. "You just stay put, Marcus Watson. This nice young man is going to see you get inside. There's no sense in making a bad situation worse by trying to do too much before the doctor has a look at you.''

"What happened to Mr. Marcus?'' Timmy Fletcher huffed up to them from the direction of the stable, his face burning with all the curiosity a twelve year old could generate.

"Never you mind,'' Mrs. Marbury scolded the lad. "You take this rig back to the barn and spruce it up best you can. The mistress has a reception she'll need it for tonight.''

A soft groan from Marcus twanged through Maggie's guilt. Her little defiance in going to the docks today would most likely cost Marcus his job. Mama would be very displeased if she was unable to attend the Lawrences' event because of a mishap she would surely blame on Marcus. There had to be a way to stop that from happening. Marcus was suffering enough because of her.

"Come along, Miss Margaret.'' Mrs. Marbury put her arm around Maggie's shoulder and tugged her in her wake as she moved toward the kitchen. "We'll clear the way for them, and then we'll make you presentable so you can make your excuses to your mother and the rector.''

Maggie glanced back over her shoulder just before they crossed the kitchen threshold. Gingerly, Devin Reilly was easing Marcus from the confines of the carriage, clearly straining from the older man's weight. Whatever words he spoke so softly to the coachman seemed to ease Marcus's embarrassment over his need for assistance. Her erstwhile hero had a way with people and horses that would stand him in good stead if he would accede to the plan she'd been formulating on the way home.

"Don't let Mr. Reilly leave once we have Marcus settled,'' she whispered to the housekeeper.

"What will your father say when he learns we've let an Irishman inside his house?'' Mrs. Marbury matched her low tone, as she frowned at the furniture that needed to be moved to accommodate Marcus.

"Leave Papa to me. You just see that Mr. Reilly stays put."

Pulling her hat off, Maggie headed through the kitchen as Mrs. Marbury hastily instructed Sally and Mrs. Smith, the cook, to clear away the tea preparations. "The least we can provide him for his trouble in all this is a decent meal."

He'd need it if she persuaded her parents to follow the solution she hoped to negotiate.

Chapter Three

From his vantage point across the spacious Brownley kitchen, Devin polished off his second apple tart while observing the doctor's deft wrapping of the splint on Marcus Watson's leg. The doctor, a capable looking fellow in his mid forties, had set right to his examination when he arrived. His firm and businesslike manner was tempered with compassion as he gently examined and treated Marcus.

White-faced, the coachman gripped the arms of his chair, his eyes closed tight and his lips set in a grim line as he tried not to make a sound while the physician did his work. Behind Marcus, his wife, Jenna, held fast to his shoulders and struggled to control the worry written on her gaunt features.

"Would you care for more tea, sir?" Bridget Smith, the cook, bustled over from the cluster of household staff gathered by the door awaiting the doctor's pronouncement.

''No. Thank you kindly, though. It is the finest meal I've had in many a week.'' Devin savored the warm spice smells of a real kitchen and smiled at the plump woman with her salt-and-pepper hair twisted in a knot at the top of her head.

In truth, it was probably the first whole meal he'd had since leaving home. His cursed seasickness had left him with little appetite for the swill that passed for food aboard the *Sweet Rose Marie*. Certainly the savory stew and sweet, cinnamon-laced pie tasted almost as good as any meal he'd ever eaten, save from his own mother's kitchen.

''It's the least owed you from this household for all you did to see our Miss Margaret safely home and then agreeing to stay on and help get Marcus settled.'' Bridget dusted her hands on her apron as she darted a glance over at the aging butler standing with his wife and the young maid, Sally. ''Marbury and young Timmy would never be able to get him up to his room between 'em, and that's the truth.''

Bridget had not only fed Devin a fine meal, she'd introduced him to the various members and duties of the household staff who served the Brownleys.

Brave words and common sense to the contrary, Devin was more reluctant to leave the warm brick and polished wood Brownley kitchen than he cared to admit. Striking out to find his destiny in this friendless land was a daunting prospect, indeed. Tempting as it was to see one of Quin's or Da's business associates here, something else tugged at his thoughts as well. Margaret Brownley had whisked from the room without so much as a backward glance, leaving him with a strange emptiness the excellent food didn't begin to touch.

Instead of angering him, he worried. There seemed more to the urgency of her departure than heedless ingratitude or self-centered concern over her social lapse in missing her appointment. In fact, the strain etched in the faces of all the small cluster of staff seemed all out of proportion to the extent of the coachman's injuries.

Dr. Raymond straightened as he finished his task. "You'll recover quite nicely, Watson, as long as you don't overdo things for the next few weeks. Absolutely no weight on the leg for at least a week."

"But I've my duties—"

The doctor waved away the protest. "You're to perform no duties, not even light ones, for at least a fortnight, man. The Brownleys will have to make other arrangements until well after then."

Marcus's rugged features blanched and his wife buried her face in her hands. A strangled sob escaped her as gasps and murmurs passed through the rest of the household staff. Devin marveled at their horrified reactions.

"They'll put us out on the street, they will. Just like they did poor Edith when she scalded her arm so bad two years ago." Jenna sat hard on the wood stool behind her.

Old Marbury nodded his head at the younger maid, Sally, and she slipped quietly across the brick floor and exited down the same passage Maggie had disappeared into nearly an hour earlier.

What kind of family did this girl he'd embroiled himself with come from? Devin shifted uncomfortably in his seat. Perhaps he'd misjudged her and she really had left the kitchen without any further thought than her tardiness with her guests and the tea awaiting her in the parlor.

What kind of people cared so little for those in their employ? His main concern in coming to this land and heading to the gold fields was to gain the means to keep the shipyard open for the good of not just his own family, but the people of Beannacht Island as well.

"Now don't fret, dear heart." Marcus attempted to shift around and comfort his wife. A grimace of pain stole his breath for a moment. ''We've been here since Miss Margaret were a nursling. She'll not let that happen to us, you'll see. She'll come up with something.''

Dr. Raymond patted Jenna on the shoulder. He quickly hid the faintest glimmer of dismay that had passed across his thin features. ''Would you like me to speak to your employers? Surely since your husband was injured performing his duties, they will understand the necessity.''

Hope lit Jenna Watson's slender face as she glanced first at her husband and then at the doctor. She dabbed at her tears with the corner of her apron, then straightened her shoulders. ''Perhaps a word from you would make a difference, sir. Thank you.''

''Very well.'' The physician tendered an encouraging smile. ''You men had better get Watson here settled into his quarters so he can set about getting the rest he needs to mend properly.''

He rummaged in his black case and produced a small brown bottle, which he handed to Jenna. ''Mix three drops of this laudanum in water for pain. Give him a dose every four hours or so whether he complains or no. He's got a nasty sprain.'' The bespectacled doctor snapped his leather bag shut. ''And don't let him tell you he feels fine or let him out of bed. Keep the leg elevated and warm until I return tomorrow.''

''Aye, sir.'' Jenna looked at the vial and nodded. ''He'll stay put if I have to tie him to the bed.''

Marbury motioned to Devin. ''If you don't mind, Reilly.''

The butler waved away the cook and Mrs. Marbury when they, too, would have advanced from their station by the door. ''Stand back and let us handle this, if you please,'' he instructed. ''You women will have your turn to fuss over the man once we're through.''

Devin crossed the room and bent to put one arm around

Marcus's chest and the other under his legs. "If Timmy here can manage the leg on his own and you lead the way, sir, I believe we can get this man safely to his bunk."

Marbury scooped up the lamp the doctor had used during his examination to supplement the afternoon light filtering through the kitchen windows. "Right this way." The balding butler indicated a narrow doorway near the hearth.

"I'll send up some broth as soon as you send Timmy back," Bridget called.

"And I'll fetch another set of linens and blankets for the morning," added Mrs. Marbury.

"Dr. Raymond! How serious is Marcus's injury? Is he still in such intense pain?" The questions preceded their owner into the kitchen.

Mo chroí, he'd called her on the docks. His own rebellious heart lurched now at the sound of her approach. Damnation. He never should have lingered for this meal.

Margaret Sylvia Worth Browning swished into the room looking far more orderly than the tousled young woman he'd rescued. Her tangle of curls had been sculpted back over her ears into a tight knot at the nape of her neck. Although she had not changed from her pale green gown, still bearing stains from the docks, gone were her leather bootlets, replaced by gold satin at-home slippers. The hand she held out to the physician was devoid of gloves, and her dainty fingers bespoke the young aristocrat.

After an assessing look and encouraging smile for Marcus Watson, she cast a quick glance filled with a mixture of appeal and alarm at Devin before turning her full attention back to Dr. Raymond. "Thank you so much for coming so promptly, Doctor."

"No trouble at all, my dear—though from the urgency of your message, I could have sworn it was one of the family who was injured."

"Marcus is family," Miss Brownley declared, slipping one arm around Jenna's waist. "So is Jenna. Please tell me everything."

"His knee is badly sprained, I'm afraid." Dr. Raymond went right to the point. "And he's severely bruised—"

"He's not to work for at least a fortnight, not even light duties, Miss. Whatever are we to do?" Jenna's worry burst from her lips just as a grimace passed over Marcus's. Devin felt the coachman's whole body tense as he fought a losing battle with the pain and exhaustion. A small groan escaped him.

"First, you must get this man to bed," Dr. Raymond interjected. "Then you can discuss what can be done to save his position. I do not wish him to contract a fever, given the shock to his system. He needs to be warm and resting."

The doctor nodded to Devin.

He slid his arm more completely around the coachman's chest. "On three, Timmy. Easy now, lad."

The lad nodded and mouthed the count.

"Please don't worry, Jenna. I have an idea that should work out for everyone, if Mr. Reilly is game for another rescue today."

Devin heard Miss Brownley's assurance to her maid, but couldn't stop to acknowledge or dispute her inclusion of him in her schemes as he grunted and hefted the older man. A loud groan escaped Marcus despite their best efforts to ease him from his seat. His head lolled over to rest on Devin's shoulder.

"You go on and get your husband settled, Jenna." Miss Brownley stepped out of their path, leaving a tantalizing hint of ginger and chamomile that appealed to Devin almost as powerfully as the concern in her tone. She might be a minx, but she was not heedless of the people in her employ. Not in the least.

"You concentrate on keeping Marcus as comfortable as possible. Everything will work out, you'll see. Miss Lenore and I will dress ourselves for the reception tonight. Let me know if there is anything you require to care for Marcus."

Margaret Brownley shooed her maid with forced cheer to follow the procession being led out of the kitchen by the butler, but Devin still caught the quiet thank you she breathed as they departed the room. Her gratitude shivered through him, carrying just a hint of distant thunder lurking behind the clouds hovering on their mutual horizons.

Only ye decide the course to joy or sorrow, The Blessing promised. But his course seemed to be steered here in America by a winsome lass with haunting amber eyes.

He shifted his burden slightly as they climbed gingerly up narrow stairs. Despite knowing the folly being snared by the spurious promise of a woman, Devin found himself anxious to return to the kitchen and see what she was hatching.

Maggie chewed her lip as the procession left the kitchen. *Please, God, let us work this out.* Her parents would be much more amenable to the arrangements if they were already in place—not that her mother was in the mood to be amenable toward much that involved her errant daughter. Maggie's ears still stung from being boxed soundly for appearing in the foyer not only late, but shamefully disheveled. It was clearly the latter that appalled her mother most, though she'd taken no time to hear of the accident that had created both problems.

"Oh, Miss Margaret, whatever will you do?" Mrs. Marbury collapsed into the chair only recently vacated by Marcus. "You know how agitated your mother is already over the doings at the Lawrences' this evening. She's likely to force poor Jenna and her Marcus out into the streets this very night when she learns of this mishap."

Bridget fixed her questioning eyes on Maggie. The knowledge that she'd gained her own position in the kitchen due to the previous cook's mishap on the eve of an important Brownley supper party glimmered unspoken in her gaze.

"Surely not." Shock showed clearly in Dr. Raymond's voice. He took a snowy handkerchief out of his waistcoat pocket and polished his glasses for a long moment.

"I'm certain Mama would only act so out of pique at missing the party." Maggie fought the waves of panic that swirled at the edges of her thoughts. She couldn't allow Marcus to lose his position just because she'd talked him into helping her. She just couldn't.

"If we can convince Mr. Reilly to take Marcus's place on a temporary basis, we could muddle through this without losing the Watsons," Maggie told Mrs. Marbury with far more confidence than she felt.

"I feel I should assure you, and your parents, Miss Brownley, that Mr. Watson's injuries will not have a permanent effect on his ability to serve your family once he has fully recovered. But to move him further or force him back to his duties before he is healed will prove extremely detrimental to his regaining full use of his knee."

"Thank you, Doctor. I do understand. Please give Mrs. Marbury your instructions so she can assist Jenna with whatever is needed. We will make certain Marcus rests, worry-free, for as long as it takes to regain his strength."

Brave words.

So much of her plan rested on the graces of a man she barely knew. Maggie laced her fingers in front of her to keep them from trembling.

Devin Reilly's insistence he'd done no more than any man should aside, he certainly seemed the stuff of heroes, given the events precipitating their meeting on the docks.

His daring rescue showed him to be quick-witted, coura-
geous, and in possession of a kind heart despite his scowl.
Add to that his way with horses and being absolutely
destitute, he seemed the ideal candidate for the position.
She tamped down her guilt over her part in creating the
latter circumstance. She'd deal with that after the immediate crisis was resolved.

She paced to the back windows overlooking the barn
and corral. Timmy had at least managed to unhitch the
team from the carriage. They grazed now in the back,
apparently unharmed from their misadventure. But the
carriage was still in the turnabout awaiting a wipe down.

She sighed. Papa would not be at all pleased if it was
still there when he returned.

She'd managed to talk privately with Tori for a few
minutes before they left to make further calls on All
Saint's parishioners. Her friend and most sensible of con-
fidants had agreed that asking Mr. Reilly to substitute for
Marcus should prove a solution for all concerned, at least
temporarily, bolstering Maggie's confidence. Meanwhile,
the Carltons could work on figuring out a way to get him
to his original destination. She owed him that. If only she
could make him understand.

Convincing the stern Irishman of the wisdom of her
plan was the next obstacle in her path, especially when
he learned of the particular discretion he would need if
this strategy for keeping the Watsons employed and a
roof over his own head was to work. Her parents would
be another matter, but she was used to dealing with them
and, given the awful outcome if she did not succeed, she
had little choice there, either.

Of course, she hadn't related all the events of his daring
rescue to Tori, nor would she until she'd digested the
nuances of the kiss they'd shared and the longings his
embrace had unleashed. *Mokree,* he'd said in a language

she'd never heard. She couldn't believe he meant mock-
ery, though that is what he'd made of all her previous
claims to modesty and self-control. She'd wanted more
and would gladly have given him the same if only he
hadn't broken their too-public embrace.

Was that why so much of her plan rested on Devin
Reilly? Was it an effort to keep him near for a little
longer? She hadn't the time to examine that.

Dr. Raymond interrupted Maggie's thoughts with a
polite cough. "That should be all until I see you in the
morning, Mrs. Marbury. It's the swelling I most want to
control at this point."

"You'll return tomorrow to check on Marcus, Doctor,
did you say earlier?" Maggie was grateful to turn away
from the temptations Devin Reilly had so freely shared
earlier and concentrate on the salvation he could bring
to the immediate future instead.

The doctor nodded before placing his bowler on his
head and picking up his case.

"Thank you so much for coming. Is there anything
else we need to look for until then?"

"I've explained everything to Mrs. Marbury, my dear."

Mrs. Marbury gave Maggie an efficient nod and headed
toward the back stairs, obviously bent on fulfilling whatever instructions the doctor had imparted.

Dr. Raymond peered at Maggie anxiously. "I understand you were actually in the carriage at the time of the
accident. Are you certain you did not sustain any injuries?
You had a severe shaking, if nothing else."

"I was in the coach's cushioned interior. Marcus was
thrown onto the street." She waved her hand in denial.
Whatever had been shaken loose in her occurred after the
accident, while she was in the arms of an Irishman with
the greenest eyes she'd ever seen.

The doctor took her hand in his and gave it a gentle

squeeze. "I offered to speak to your parents on Watson's behalf. Would you like me to stay?"

"Thank you, Dr. Raymond, but no. Mama is resting and my father is not at home. I'll explain everything to them."

"You're a remarkably strong young woman, Miss Brownley. Most girls would have been so overset they would need at least a day's bedrest with hartshorn and camphor compresses." His thin smile held approval.

Remarkably strong was anything but how Maggie felt when she heard her father returning home not five minutes after the doctor departed. They must have passed on the drive.

"Watson!" William Brownley Sr.'s bellow echoed through the house as he slammed the front door. "Why is the carriage out and still in such deplorable condition? And where is that rapscallion boy to take my mount round to the barn?"

Bridget scooped up the tray she'd been preparing for Marcus and retreated toward the back stairs with hasty steps. She cast a sympathetic glance at Maggie before disappearing from the room.

"Marbury!" Papa's roar reverberated from the foyer. "Why is it I was forced to open my own door just now? You'd best not be swilling tea when you should be attending your duties."

Papa's voice grew louder as he neared the kitchen. Maggie's stomach turned to stone and her throat felt dry as autumn leaves skittering over The Common. Her father's displeasure always affected her so, and Papa was often displeased.

She gripped her hands in front of her and fought for control. She would not let him intimidate her, no matter how angry he became. She would not. Marcus and Jenna were counting on her.

"Where the devil is everyone? Is today a holiday and the servants all gone to drunken revelry?" Papa scanned the empty kitchen and frowned as he stepped inside. His voice was quiet now, a sure warning of extreme agitation.

Maggie swallowed and stepped away from the windows to stand in front of her irate parent. "There was an accident in the city this morning, Papa. With our carriage."

At least her voice did not tremble. William Brownley Sr. halted by the stove. Displeasure added a gleam to his ice blue eyes. His lip raised in a sneer beneath the ends of his mustache.

"I've told that fool Watson he corners too sharply. If he's damaged either my horseflesh or equipage through carelessness, I'll take it from his pay." Papa's mustache fairly bristled with his indignation.

Not a word of concern over the driver or even his own child's welfare. Typical. Fighting to keep her tone calm, Maggie continued, "There was a brawl in the street that sent the horses off at a dash. Marcus struggled valiantly. There was no damage to your property."

"So having done no more than is his job, Watson now feels he can turn slackard toward the rest of his duties?" Papa squinted and looked once more about the kitchen. "Where is everyone? Gone to celebrate with him? Where's your mother? Can't a man leave his house for a few hours without returning to chaos?"

Papa peppered her with his questions without pausing to hear the answers.

Footsteps on the back stairs heralded the return of at least part of the staff. From the bounce of one set interlaced with a slower, heavier gait she recognized, and the sharp sound of leather boots, Timmy, Marbury, and Devin Reilly were headed into the storm brewing in the kitchen. If Papa was blowing angry now, he was about to bend the treetops.

"We got Mr. Marcus settled proper, Miss—" Timmy broke off his report as he saw who occupied the kitchen.

"You, boy, should know better than to interrupt your betters," Papa bristled. "Fetch my horse from around front and see he gets a good rubdown. At once."

Timmy didn't need to be told twice. He cast Maggie a wide-eyed look and skittered past his employer and out the door in a wink.

"Marbury." Papa faced the butler as he entered. "Perhaps you would be good enough to tell me why the devil I was forced to let myself into my own home and why I am forced to hunt down my entire staff. My daughter seems incapable of such a simple explanation."

While Marbury gave his summary to his employer, indignation burned a hole in Maggie's stomach. Papa treated all the women in his household as if they were half-wits. She detested the superiority he claimed in the name of the male species. If it were not for the fact that Marcus and Jenna's fate dangled so precariously in his hands, she'd override the accounting Marbury presented in her stead.

"I see." The color of her father's neck was an alarming red by the time Marbury was finished with Dr. Raymond's instructions, and his lips were pressed in a wrathful line.

Fixing his stare on Devin Reilly, who was standing behind the butler, Papa demanded, "Who are you? And what role did you play in this drama, sir, that allowed you free rein in my household?"

"Devin here is the gentleman who rescued Miss Margaret and saw she got home safely, Mr. Brownley."

Bless Marbury for speaking up before the younger man could open his mouth and prematurely betray his heritage. Although Mr. Reilly looked a bit flummoxed at not being allowed to speak for himself, he deferred to the old retainer. With no time to explain to him what she had in mind, Maggie prayed he would show the same discretion while she spoke to her father.

She took a deep breath. Best to get it over with.

"He not only saved my life, Papa, but prevented the carriage and horses from coming to great harm when Marcus was injured."

That drew her father's scrutiny back to her. She met his glare with a steady look. "In doing so, Papa, everything he owned was stolen. He drove us home and has been assisting with getting Marcus settled. He is bereft of his means for continuing to his original destination."

"How much of a reward does he demand?"

Maggie ignored the strangled snort from beside the hearth where Devin and Marbury stood. "He has refused all offers of reward or assistance."

Papa's eyebrows shot up, and he cast a suspicious glance at Devin. Maggie dared one, too. The red color staining the Irishman's cheeks had risen to an alarming shade. Thankfully, he continued to hold his peace despite his obvious struggle. She gave him what she hoped was a grateful look.

"The man has a way with horses, Papa, and he can handle our carriage quite well, if the trip home was any indication."

She could see the negative answer forming on her parent's lips, so she rushed on. "Mama will be devastated if we cannot attend the Lawrences' reception tonight, since Marcus's injuries will not allow him to drive us anywhere for weeks and it is too late to hire a public conveyance . . ."

Her father's jaw worked as he savored the nuances of all she had just imparted. Maggie knew he'd rather drive the carriage himself than miss the reception, but that would be too gauche for his plans to ally the Brownleys with the Lawrences through marriage. She was counting on those schemes to aid her own. Never before had she been grateful for her parents' social ambitions.

Fixing her with a hard stare, Papa turned back to the two men. "Very well. He's hired. Temporarily." He looked Devin up and down for a moment. "Marbury, tell Marcus I'm deducting the doctor's cost from his last pay. Since he is not working here for the time being, his room and board will come out of his wife's wages. I'm off to the library for a sherry."

"Very good, sir." Marbury nodded his head deferentially.

Devin still said nothing, though his fists were clenched at his side. Maggie moved her lips in a silent plea for his assent. *Reillys don't take charity,* he'd said. If anything, he must realize by now he would be giving the boon.

"I'll not pay you until we see how things work out." Papa addressed Devin directly. "I am not in the habit of engaging staff without references, but under the circumstances I seem forced to allow you this opportunity."

Hope drained out of Maggie like rain along a gutter. This man had saved her, and how did she repay him? By allowing her father to humiliate him.

"Mrs. Marbury will see you are loaned a decent livery." Papa had drawn himself up and was in full, imperious tirade. "You are not allowed anywhere in the house save the kitchen unless instructed otherwise. I expect you to be prompt. No spitting or cursing in public. No idle conversation with the family unless you are spoken to first. I hope I make myself quite clear."

"Perfectly." Devin nearly spit the word, although Papa did not appear to notice how his instructions were being taken by his new employee.

Maggie gripped the back of the chair she stood near, hoping the sturdy wood would impart some of its strength to her. He was going to refuse. How could he not? Papa was being insufferable, as always. Whatever would she do now to save Marcus and Jenna?

Instead of refusing outright, Devin flicked his gaze toward Maggie, centering his glance on her grip on the chair back. Returning his attention to his unwilling host, he nodded ever so slightly.

Gratitude flooded Maggie.

Papa returned the nod. "Very well. We shall manage. What is your name so I may tell my wife what to call you?"

"Reilly, sir." Though no warmth showed in the green sparkle of his eyes, a smile curved Devin's mouth and a distinctly Irish lilt thickened in his tone.

When he stuck out his hand, Maggie knew she was lost. "Devin Reilly."

Chapter Four

Devin fought the urge to rescue Margaret Brownley from her father's clutches as she was hustled unceremoniously from the kitchen. The cautioning hand old Marbury placed on his forearm added an extra deterrent to his own desire not to make things any worse for her.

Instead, he balled his hands into useless fists and planted his feet on the bricks to keep himself from escalating the scene beyond the disaster point it had already reached.

It was not his place, although he itched to make it so. William Brownley's broad face had blanched first, then turned an alarming red as he refused the hand Devin offered and dragged his daughter from the room without uttering another word.

In the distance a door slammed, underscoring her plight still further.

"Diabhal." Devin exhaled.

If only he hadn't taken such pleasure in revealing his

background, the guilty coils of dread winding through his gut at the moment might not pull quite so tight.

"Don't fret, Reilly," Marbury assured him. "Our Miss Margaret's held her own for nigh onto eighteen years. She'll find a way to make things right. She always does. Would you care for a cup of coffee or a small bracer while we wait for word?"

The silver-haired butler reached into a cupboard and pulled out a decanter and two tumblers.

"I'd best be on my way." Devin shook his head, amazed at the butler's aplomb in the face of *Miss Margaret's* undignified leave-taking. Despite the confidence that threaded the butler's reedy voice and the look of assurance the lass had shot him as she was pulled away, Devin doubted there could be an easy solution to the situation, given the hatred and revulsion he'd seen glistening in Brownley's eyes.

He walked to the table and retrieved his jacket. He should be on his way. Each time he helped her, he only served to thicken her predicament. But where would he go? The docks probably held the greatest chance of his finding work until the second ship departed for San Francisco. Poor seaman or not, he just might know more about ship maintenance and refurbishing than his family gave him credit for. He'd surely be able to convince one of the harbor masters or dock supervisors to take a chance on him, and perhaps he'd have a crack at tracking those two wastrels who'd stolen his belongings.

These plans provided little real hope for him. The proud defiance of his guarantee to Miss Brownley not withstanding—*Reillys are not partial to accepting charity*—he was not even sure he could find his way back to the docks at this point.

"Drink up, lad." Marbury handed him a glass. "My

brother in Philadelphia sends me a Christmas bottle each year. Brandy helps warm the spirit.''

At least the prejudices of the master did not seem to extend to the household. Devin accepted the tumbler, saluted the old man, and took a long swallow. The fiery liquor did little to ease the aching sense of failure haunting him from the reflection in Margaret Brownley's eyes as she was torn from his sight.

The knowin' is up to us, the doin's another part.

His questions over the thunder of The Blessing he'd found in her arms, the sizzle of lightning he'd discovered on her lips burned away for a moment. How could he leave without knowing the portent of what he'd experienced this day? Yet how could he stay?

''Blessing or no, I cannot linger in a place where my kind are so patently unwelcome.''

''If by 'your kind' you mean a ready friend and true gentleman, Devin Reilly, you'll have no trouble finding your welcome—if you look for it in the right places.'' Marbury smiled at him over the rim of his own glass before he tipped back the remainder of its contents. ''A man may rule his house without ever knowing what makes it a home.'' Marbury shuffled over to the cupboard and tucked the bottle back into its niche. ''You won't do wrong by waiting on Miss Margaret, Reilly. That's a fact.''

Puzzling through the butler's words, Devin shrugged into his jacket. The crackle of paper in the inner pocket reminded him that he still possessed his clipper ticket and the letter from his mother—a bit of the past and a hope for the future. Only his present needed clarifying.

What kind of man would let his present rest in such slender hands as Margaret Sylvia Worth Brownley's? Not Quintin Reilly, whose air of command made most men look to him for leadership whether on a deck or a dockside.

Not Bryan Reilly, whose legal acumen and negotiating skills made him one of Limerick's most sought after solicitors. And not Devin Reilly. Surely he had more pride than that.

"Mayhap you could go and check how young Timmy is making out with the horses," Marbury said.

"I'm sure the lad knows what he is about." Devin could delay the inevitable no more. He'd lost his berth to California, his belongings, and now his Blessing.

He shook Marbury's hand and turned to go.

"Wait!"

Hearing her soft cry from the other side of the kitchen, he nearly shivered with relief. He turned to face her.

Her eyes were wide, shimmering with a fine edge of tears she seemed to hold back by will alone as she walked a few feet forward into the room. The whisper of her slippers over the bricks echoed through him as he waited for her.

"My father has agreed you may stay, if you are still willing." Her words tumbled out, accompanied by a forlorn sigh that left him wondering just what price she had paid to be able to offer them. How far had she been willing to go to save these two members of her household?

She paused in the middle of the kitchen. The rays of the setting sun glinted through the windows to add an aura to her golden brown curls. She was deathly pale, and her hands trembled where she clutched her gown.

"Papa has several . . . requirements you may find difficult to accept, but if you will just look upon this as a temporary shelter . . ." She glanced away for a moment at the sound of Marbury shutting the back hall door and leaving them alone in the kitchen.

". . . I am sure you can muddle through and go on about your business without a backward glance. One day you may even laugh about this little side adventure." Her voice was strong, but the plea in her eyes spoke far more eloquently. She knew what she was asking him to accept.

She offered him a desolate grimace he supposed was an attempt at an encouraging grin and came to stand directly in front of him. The hint of ginger and chamomile and home reached out to him as surely as if she'd opened her arms to him.

She wanted him to save her friends. She was ready to discount her pride, to suffer any mistreatments, and more than willing to ask him to swallow her father's prejudice and his own pride in order to accept this dubious position she offered him. To put the needs of strangers before his own. Everything she thought glowed there in the depths of her smoked amber gaze, along with her belief that he would agree to her untenable proposal for the sake of the people she cared about.

Anger swamped him, accompanied by a good healthy dose of resentment. Only one thought came clear through the rest. If he opened his mouth now, all the indignation and umbrage he'd held at bay for her sake would come rushing out and raise the price for them both still further.

He held his lips firmly closed and nodded.

"Return for us in one half hour. We will remain within until we see you pull up. I detest being made to wait on the public walkway." Alberta Brownley's tone exuded utter contempt for those with whom she might be forced to share the thoroughfare.

Devin touched the brim of his hat and waited until the matron and her two daughters entered the milliner's shop before climbing onto the front seat of the carriage and directing the team back into the stream of traffic on Boston's busy Milk Street. He possessed neither the measure of will nor the proper humility of servitude to continue this charade much longer. What had he been thinking when he'd allowed himself to be levered into his current circumstances?

Thought had all too little to do with it, boy-o. He grimaced, hearing Quin's voice chiding him for what he all too certainly knew to be the truth without any input from his elder sibling.

The appeal of a pair of smoked amber eyes and the need of two innocent people with too few options, due in part to his own actions, had caused him to swallow a great deal more of his pride than he'd ever believed possible, even in the depths of the wretched voyage to this *land of opportunity*. Despite the discomfort of his position, he was still not prepared to abandon the Brownleys' dubious shelter or seek the assistance he was certain Quin's friends in Boston would offer him. Each time his exasperated thoughts dared to consider that option, the image of Maggie on the docks stopped him.

The too-tight collar of the shirt Mrs. Marbury had tried to let out for him choked him, and he tugged at it again as he steered the carriage to a halt around the corner on a quiet side street. The distant clang of a ship's bell and the slight tang of seawater and harbor told him they were near the docks and the beginnings of his misadventure.

His grandmother would have been pleased with his decision to swallow his pride and stay, to seek the meaning of his Blessing. His own mother would no doubt praise his self-sacrifice for taking on this role for the good of others. His father might see the wisdom in taking the shelter this job offered until he set himself to rights and could continue on his way.

But his brothers would laugh themselves helpless to see him playact the obedient servant's role, all because he'd been snared by a pair of pliant lips and the hope threatening to drown in a lass's tears.

So here he stood in borrowed livery, dancing attendance on a petulant Boston matron and her equally petulant daughters. No, that was hardly fair. The younger daughter, Maggie's sister Lenore, certainly seemed cut from the same righteous, haughty cloth as her mother. But somehow over the days since he'd begun piloting the Brownleys through their rounds of shopping and social engagements, Miss Margaret Sylvia Worth Brownley had been transformed into Maggie in his thoughts. Just Maggie.

Not that they'd exchanged more than the barest civilities as he'd delivered her to the various destinations charted for him by her faithful Marcus. He'd not seen her alone since that afternoon in the kitchen, and there could be little conversation between them under the disdainful eye of her mother.

"Just as well, I suppose." Despite his best attempts, he failed to convince himself of the honesty in that declaration. He might know better than to get any further embroiled with a lass such as Maggie, but the warmth with which all the servants spoke of her and the raft of *our Miss Margaret* stories they related had somehow added a glow that warmed him as well whenever she was near.

The burden of responsibility heaped on Miss Margaret's shoulders seemed too great for such a slender wisp. The servants looked to her for direction in dealing with their quarrelsome employers, and she seemed to advocate for the staff whenever the demands of her family grew too outrageous.

Feelings of false intimacy placed him no nearer to puzzling through the portent behind the sizzling thunder he'd experienced as he'd pulled Maggie into his arms on the docks. Blessing or lust? He shoved the thoughts of further intimacies aside. His vow at Seamus Dodd's unshriven grave prevented him from exploring those possibilities, no matter the restrictions and obstacles his position in her household placed between them.

Mayhap it was her father he'd been meant to find, to formulate a mutual business venture. Though from the disdainful sneers Brownley sent his way, that seemed more than a tad dubious.

More likely he hadn't really undergone The Blessing. Perhaps it was merely a reaction to all that had occurred on Boston's docks that morning—to disembarking from his roiling nightmare of a voyage and preparing to set off in search of a fortune, or maybe the effect of the rush down the docks, the thrill of the chase.

Anything but The Blessing here in this place so far from the Reilly legend's origins, especially for one who'd proved so foolhardy and unworthy. He cursed himself for the hundredth time in the past week for allowing those scurvies to rattle him into a confrontation.

He rubbed his thumb along his chin. None of this fruitless speculation got him any closer to California and reaping the gold his family needed to buy timber for masts and bulkheads. More like he'd fooled himself into thinking it was The Blessing and had been chasing his tail for naught.

Timmy Fletcher, the Brownley's stableboy, had brought word to Devin that the clipper he'd hoped to sail on was delayed in her launching for a week or more, since cracks were found in her mastings. More frustration.

Another carriage rounded the corner at a smart pace and nearly clipped the door as it rumbled past. The horses shied nervously and he pulled back on the reins to still their dancing until the other vehicle passed and turned the far corner.

Jumping down, he soothed the animals, stroking their jawlines and speaking to them quietly in the tongue of his ancestors, just as he'd been taught as a youngster.

They settled down and regarded him with a mellow gleam in their dark eyes.

"At least I've you to spend my days with, eh?" he whispered as he rubbed their noses. "We've all got fine beds of straw and good food in our bellies, thanks to the Brownleys. Mayhap that is simply all it's meant to be. Soon enough I'll be on my way. Marcus is gaining strength all the time. You'll have him back, and I'll find some means to work my way to California."

There it would no longer matter whether or not he secretly thought of Miss Margaret Sylvia Worth Brownley as Maggie.

The chiming in a bell tower claimed his attention. "Well, my dears, what say you? Shall we cease this malingering? It is time we went to fetch our charges and deliver them on to tea at the rectory." The bays regarded him for a solemn moment before tossing their heads as one.

A delivery cart blocked the street where the other carriage had turned minutes before, so he was forced further down the street toward the harbor before turning back. As he finally rounded the corner, he saw two shambling figures making their way into a dingy tavern—the two rough-cuts from the docks on the day of his arrival, the two who had started everything rolling and had most likely made off with his belongings.

The Eagle. Making note of the tavern's name, he vowed to return there as soon as possible and confront them. He was sure they'd already swilled away all his money, but there were several personal items he hoped to retrieve.

Although the street bustled with early afternoon shoppers, there was no sign of the Brownley women when he pulled the bays over in front of the milliner's. He dismounted from the carriage box and retrieved the crude map he and Marcus had fashioned using discarded newspaper and a scrap of pencil Marbury had provided.

"These are quite good." Maggie's voice pulled him from his study of the route from the shopping district to All Saint's rectory.

Dressed in russet taffeta, her small straw bonnet, edged with a deep brown pleat, matched the trim on her gown and offset her coloring perfectly, Margaret Brownley looked every inch the young lady her breeding and costume proclaimed. A twinge of regret for the rumpled hoyden he'd met his first day here flitted past his guard. He clamped those useless pangs tightly back under his control.

Clutched in her hand were several sheets of the paper he'd folded in with his map, sketches of some of the scenery he'd viewed so far here in Boston. They must have fallen out unnoticed.

"They're for my little sister, Meaghan." He held out his hand to retrieve them. "She sent me several sketches from the villa where she is staying in Italy. I thought she'd enjoy a look at the New World."

Good manners prevented Maggie from inquiring into the nature of his sister's sojourn in Italy, although he caught the glimmer of curiosity that lit her smoked amber eyes before they returned to the pages she still held.

"You've done a marvelous job of capturing our city. I like this one of Fanueil Hall, complete with the gleam of the grasshopper weathervane. And here, the people strolling past The Common look ever so lifelike. Even our own simple drive at home looks interesting."

The tantalizing hint of ginger and chamomile teased his senses. She handed the sketches to him, her smile brilliant. "I notice you include trees in each of your sketches. Do you have a fondness for nature?"

"The number of trees standing beside the cobblestones

everywhere impresses me. Nearly as many treetops as
rooftops grace Boston's skyline," he explained, inordi-
nately pleased that she'd notice the small motif he'd deliberately included. "A sight not often possible on our side
of the globe. It makes your city less formidable."

"Yes." She nodded. "I'm glad of the trees myself.
They add almost enough life to make the city tolerable,
though I prefer the wildness and freedom of the forests
around my Grandmother Worth's home to stilted trees
lining the streets like forlorn sentinels."

"There's something I'm anxious to see. Forests are
few and far between in Ireland. We must make do with
the occasional copse or isolated stand where the druids
held sway."

"Druids? How—"

"Oh, Mr. Lawrence. How fortuitous to run into you
like this." Mrs. Brownley's raised voice broke into the
conversation. Maggie's chin jerked up with a guilty start.
A hint of panic leaped in the amber depths of the gaze
she locked with his before she turned back to her mother
and sister.

Diabhal, Devin silently cursed. He'd completely forgotten his surroundings and his humble position. How must
it have looked for Brookline's Miss Brownley to be
engrossed in conversation with her driver over some
scraps of newsprint?

"Look who it is, Margaret darling. Jonathan Adams
Lawrence III. I'm sure you never expected to bump into
your swain on such a busy corner." Mrs. Brownley fixed
a reproving frown on Devin before bestowing a radiant
smile on the impeccably dressed gentleman who stood
next to her.

"You are an oasis in the churning sea, my dear Miss
Brownley." The pudgy man doffed his felt bowler and
sketched Maggie an elaborate bow before taking her hand.

Devin winced at the mangled metaphor. Lawrence held on to her fingers for a moment longer than was entirely proper while the fellow favored her with a proprietary smile, allowing his gaze to drift down her trim figure. His plump fingers clung to her slender ones with a possessiveness that made Devin itch to snatch them apart. Why did Maggie allow the fellow such liberties?

"Oh, you do have a way with words, sir, as I have so often told your dear mama," Mrs. Brownley trilled.

"It is always a pleasure to meet up with you, madam." He released Maggie's hand at last. "With or without your delightful daughters."

Was it Devin's imagination, or did Maggie appear to shrink back from the man, her expression set in a polite mask with none of the liveliness or spark of interest she'd shown just a moment before?

It was none of his affair, he reminded himself sternly, his internal voice sounding suspiciously like Quin's. She was his employer's daughter. Her suitors, her enthusiasm or lack thereof for those who desired her, meant nothing to him.

The tinkling of a shop bell and the sound of the door shutting drew the trio's attention.

"Well, here is our dear little Lenore at last." Mrs. Brownley pulled her younger daughter to her as she stepped from the shop. "We've just spent the most enjoyable hour outfitting this little minx. She is preparing to take her place in grown-up society."

Miss Lenore looked none too pleased at the description that made her sound more child than young lady. She collected herself quickly and favored Lawrence with a dazzling smile. "Do you attend the Andersons' soiree tomorrow evening, sir?"

"If you will be there, Miss Lenore," Larry of the damp hands—as Devin had decided to call him—answered the younger sister, but his gaze slid to the elder. "I will be certain to attend."

"Wonderful," breathed Mrs. Brownley. "You must claim Margaret for at least one of the waltzes."

"I would be delighted to claim Miss Brownley . . ."

A hint of alarm flickered in Maggie's eyes as he paused. She inhaled sharply and held her breath.

". . . for as many dances as she sees fit to favor me."

"Very well, then." Maggie took a deep breath and spoke for the first time. "Until tomorrow, Mr. Lawrence. I'm afraid we must take our leave. We are due at the rectory for tea."

"Ah yes." The man's smile did little to warm his expression as he hooked his walking cane over one arm. "I believe my sister is to attend, as well. Let me escort you to your carriage, Mrs. Brownley."

"Why, thank you, Mr. Lawrence. You are a true gentleman—as I have so often pointed out to my daughters." Mrs. Brownley's smile oozed approval.

Lawrence offered the matron one arm and Maggie the other. The party advanced across the walk with a petulant Lenore trailing behind. Devin opened the door.

"I'll help the ladies in, driver. You may go about your duties." Lawrence did not even flick his gaze at Devin as he addressed him. He assisted Mrs. Brownley and Lenore into the carriage, then drew Maggie's fingers up to his lips.

"Until tomorrow, my dear." He pressed a kiss to her fingers. Maggie merely nodded as she chewed her lip and practically jumped into the carriage's interior.

Larry of the smarmy charm jumped out of the way as Devin slammed the door shut behind her with enough force to make the horses peer back at him in surprise. He turned a reproving glare on Devin, the first time he'd actually looked directly at him.

"Beg pardon, sir. Don't wish my ladies to be late." Devin tugged on his cap with false humility and swung up onto the driver's box.

As he eased the carriage into the stream of traffic, he observed Lawrence striding down the street with a scowl on his features and his walking cane clutched in his meaty fist. Gone was the nicety of manners he'd just displayed as he elbowed his way past a young woman with two children and rounded the corner.

So much for Jonathan Adams Lawrence III being a true gentleman.

Chapter Five

The delicate clink of bone china and silver spoons tinkled through the parlor, undercutting the hum of voices as the Brookline Daughters of Grace concluded their official meeting and set about the *true* business of such gatherings—the exchange of vital information about anyone who was not present, or at least not within easy earshot.

Maggie grimaced as the usual monthly round of gossip and speculation began. This was not her idea of what they should concern themselves about. The Daughters of Grace had been formed to pursue charitable works, to provide food and shelter to those in need, not cucumber sandwiches and a chance to sharpen the talons of its members.

She'd deliberately sought the room's far corner to avoid being drawn in. There had been enough veiled hints and probing questions dropped her way over the past week for her to recognize that her ride home from the docks with the handsome stranger now employed as the family coachman had not gone as unremarked as she had hoped. Her forthcoming visit to Grandmother's would provide more than its usual relief.

"Don't fret so, Maggie." Tori handed her a cup of tea. "They mean no real harm, and they allow us the opportunity to do much more than we could as individuals."

"You speak of them as children." Maggie peered around her friend. Sure enough, a number of heads kept turning suspiciously in their direction. "They are the future mavens of society. How can they be content to dispense their largesse only as long as it causes them no hardship?"

Her friend joined her on the burgundy settee at the far end of the room, in front of the bay windows overlooking the street. A hint of sunlight through the lace curtains sparkled in Tori's auburn curls as she shook her head. "That they dispense anything at all is a victory for those who benefit from the mittens they knit or the blankets they donate. If the price is a small party or a few snippets of harmless gossip, who are we to censure?" Tori tempered her prim lecture with a wink as she rubbed her left leg, a gesture she almost never made in public unless she was very tired or overset.

"Spoken like a true minister's daughter." Maggie smiled at her friend. She could not bear to distress Tori further when she was obviously in pain. "Although I must say you are not dressed like one today. Where on earth did you find time to whip up this gorgeous blue? It matches the shade of your eyes to perfection."

Among her many accomplishments, besides running the rectory for her widowed father and assisting him with the raising of her twin brothers, Victoria Carlton was an expert seamstress.

A hint of color touched Tori's cheeks. "Actually, I cut

this down from one of Amelia Lawrence's cast-offs. Papa wished me to wear it today to show her how grateful I am for her bounty.''

The grimace that followed this revelation showed the true weight of her friend's gratitude. Maggie leaned over and squeezed her hand in sympathy for the position Tori's unknowing parent had put her in. ''I'm quite certain it looks lovelier on you than it ever did on her.''

''I decided this is a lesson in charity. Dignity is a requirement for both those who receive and those who give.'' Tori sighed. Then her eyes widened and she wiggled her eyebrows mischievously. Her ability to find the brightest side of situations was one of her most endearing traits. ''Pride is a difficult thing to swallow even in the direst of circumstances. We must have a care not to stuff our goodness down the throats of those who benefit from our work.''

''So true.'' Maggie agreed. She caught sight of Devin returning from watering the horses outside. He kept himself apart from the other coachmen wherever they went, most likely because of her father's stricture that he not reveal his origins, and also because the other drivers must sense he did not truly belong with them. They did not invite him to join in their conversations or games of chance while they waited.

Devin Reilly was alone and isolated in a strange land, all because of her. Guilt over the terrible position she had placed him in suffused her again.

Tori gestured to the windows. ''Speaking of being stuffed down the throat, now that we have a moment alone . . .''

She glanced conspiratorially at the rest of the chattering crowd, now intent on their various discussions of who was wearing what and who had fixed their interest on whom. She leaned close. ''How is your coachman recovering, and however did you convince your parents to employ your latest project in his stead?''

Maggie caught back a sigh. How could she tell her dearest friend she had bargained away her own future to secure the precarious present for the Watsons? Had practically forced a gentleman to play his role in her scheme by trading on the innate chivalry she'd discovered in him from the start of their brief acquaintance—a man who, because of her, had lost everything? And she still had no idea how she was going to repay him, to force him into accepting a new stake for his quest to reach California.

''Why, Miss Carlton, I was just remarking to Miss Lawrence how lovely you look today. The color of your gown quite compliments your eyes.'' Lenore's intrusion prevented Maggie from answering as her sibling and Jonathan Lawrence's sister, Amelia, joined them.

''The color is a shade too dark for my own liking.'' Amelia smiled coolly. ''But I knew you would be able to make some use of it.''

Color stained Tori's cheeks as she stood up. ''I should go and see if the tea tray needs replenishing.''

Maggie stood as well. She sent an appraising look at Lenore and Amelia, who both blinked in quiet innocence of the thinly veiled digs they'd inflicted.

''I'll help,'' she offered.

''Oh, pray stay a moment.'' Amelia placed a hand on her arm. ''I'm sure Miss Carlton won't mind. I've been desiring an opportunity to speak with you this past week.'' Amelia puckered her delicate lips into a little pout and then turned up the corners sweetly.

''Stay.'' Tori's eyes pleaded for the easy release an argument would be sure to delay. ''I'm sure I can manage to ring for more tea on my own.''

''Perhaps we'll have a chance to talk later.'' Maggie

squeezed her fingers. "Or you could come for a visit in the next day or two."

"We'll see." Tori looked doubtful. "Remember, I'm to leave for a brief stay with my aunt in Providence soon, and I've the whole household to organize first."

"Does that mean you will miss the dancing at the Andersons' tomorrow?" Lenore asked.

Tori flinched.

"Nora." Maggie shot a warning.

"Oh, beg pardon." Lenore had the grace to color over her faux pas, if that was what it was. "I'd quite forgotten you do not dance. I hope you have a safe trip and return to us soon, Miss Carlton."

"Thank you, Miss Lenore." Tori nodded. "Miss Lawrence. Miss Brownley, perhaps we'll speak again later."

She squared her shoulders and limped away with great dignity. Not for the first time, Maggie admired her friend's ability to withstand the scorn so often cast her way for an affliction that was none of her doing.

"Nora, how could you hurt her like that? She has been unfailingly sweet to you and to everyone else all her life, despite the pain her leg gives her daily."

"I begged her pardon, Margaret," he sister snapped. "And I'll thank you to remember I have not answered to Nora since I was ten."

Amelia ignored the exchange as she smoothed her dark hair in its plaited bun and took a seat. "I'm certain we all admire Miss Carlton for the bravery she displays. Would you be a dear, Miss Lenore, and fetch us some of the lemonade? I find I am quite parched."

Lenore looked ready to decline the request for a moment. Then she collected herself. Maggie knew Amelia Lawrence was everything her sister aspired to in life at the moment.

"Certainly," Nora told her idol and followed Tori across the room to where the refreshments were set up.

"Pray join me, Miss Brownley." Amelia patted the expanse of burgundy velvet next to her. "Or may I have leave to call you Margaret? I do so wish to know you as a sister."

Stunned by this revelation from the toast of Boston's society, Maggie sank to the spot indicated and merely nodded.

Things had progressed far further in her parents' campaign to ally themselves with the Lawrences than she'd allowed herself to fear if Amelia Lawrence wanted to know her as a sister. She fought both the churning nausea in her stomach and the unreasoning desire to run headlong out of the room and onto the streets.

"Thank you, Margaret. I am quite certain we shall be fast friends." Amelia favored her with a dazzling smile, one she no doubt used to charm her many admirers, but which she had never turned toward Maggie in all the years of their acquaintance.

She was very unlike her elder brother in outward appearance, being fair skinned, delicate-boned, and dark haired like her father. Jonathan more closely resembled his mother with his sandy colored hair and hardier build. Both, however, managed to keep hangers-on at bay with the mere raising of an eyebrow or an icy stare, a quality honed in their family over more than a century of leading Boston's elite. After all, they could trace their roots back to the *Mayflower* along many paths, as Maggie's mother took great relish in reminding her.

"And since we are to be such good friends"—Amelia drew back the lace curtain—"perhaps you will be good enough to enlighten me as to the particulars regarding your dashing new coachman."

Maggie found the avaricious gleam in the other girl's

pale blue gaze disconcerting. Devin sat sketching on the driver's box, and Amelia studied him as if he were a delicious confection she was about to devour.

"Your sister told me he rescued you on the streets last week and out of gratitude your papa rewarded him with his new position."

A smile of sorts curved Amelia's lips as she glanced over at Maggie with a speculative lift of her brow and then returned her regard to Devin. "He certainly does not have the air of the average man in service. Not only is he brave, but he is far easier on the eyes than that pale fellow who usually drives you. He has such an air of mystery. All of us are anxious to know more about him."

Guilt and anger warred in Maggie's breast. She was speechless. She had practically forced Devin to endure the humiliation of being made an unwanted servant in a hostile household, and now he was the object of idle speculation and gossip. Just wait until she was alone with Miss Lenore Brownley.

Amelia let the curtain drop and squeezed Maggie's hand. "You must tell me all about your adventure. Did you swoon when he took you in his arms and carried you from the carriage? Lenore says he is practically a mute, but who needs conversation with looks as fine as his? Perhaps you will indulge me in a ride around The Commons on Thursday so I may thank him firsthand for saving my dear friend."

Still stunned, Maggie had no time to formulate a reply before the pocket doors were drawn open and her mother swept into the room. "Margaret, Lenore, it is past time for us to be on our way."

She paused when she saw who sat next to Maggie. "Amelia, darling, how good to see you. I was just telling your dear mama how beautiful you have become. It's a good thing the town's most eligible bachelor is your own brother, or no one else would stand a chance with him.''

She tittered at her own sally and then waved to her girls to follow as she sailed back into the foyer in search of her wrap. Maggie bid a hasty farewell to Tori after halfheartedly agreeing to sit with Amelia for a time at the Andersons the following evening, and followed her mother—grateful, for once, the grand dame's imperious manner would allow no malingering.

Devin handed Maggie last into the carriage's spacious interior. She could not bring herself to meet his eyes as Amelia's words echoed in her thoughts. Despite her guilt, her pulse quickened as it always did when her hand touched his. There was something about his touch that left her unsettled, no matter how impersonally he appeared to perform his duties.

A hint of balsam, earthy musk, and the hidden freedoms of the wild called to her as she settled into her seat. *Not the air of the average man in service,* indeed.

''Well, young lady, I am most gratified you have finally become so amenable to all the plans your papa and I have worked so diligently to bring to fruition on your behalf these past six months.'' The smugness in her mother's voice barely penetrated Maggie's remorse.

''Mrs. Lawrence herself told me this very day how much she hoped you and Amelia would become friends. Your papa will be so pleased when I tell him of your efforts. Almost makes drinking tepid tea worthwhile for once.''

''Amelia said she'd always been a little put off by Margaret's intelligence. She practically begged me to ease her into a conversation this afternoon when we sought her out,'' Lenore interrupted.

''You should continue to address her as Miss Lawrence until the offer I am quite certain is in the making has actually been accepted by your papa. Your sister's future is very nearly secured.''

Offer? That snagged Maggie's attention. "Can we not discontinue any discussion regarding plans for my future until after my visit to Grandmother Worth's next month?''

"We do not believe it will be in your best interest to visit my mother this year, Margaret. There is some unfortunate speculation being cast your way due to that careless accident you had last week. It will be best for all concerned to seal the bargain before any scandal is brewed to spoil it.''

Maggie fought to keep her mouth from dropping open. She'd visited Grandmother every summer for years. Spending time in Maine had been the only bright spot she could picture when she had agreed to her father's terms to allow the Watsons and Devin to remain in their household.

"Grandmother counts on my visits. She is all alone up there.''

Mama drew herself up. "My mother chooses to live her life in the wilds. She did so for decades before you arrived. She will no doubt continue. You, on the other hand, will best be served spending the summer in preparation for your coming marriage.''

Mama settled back primly against the cushions as if that settled the matter, then sniffed. "Perhaps you may visit your grandmother in the company of your husband once the nuptials are over. You gave your papa your word, you will recall.''

"I agreed to consider Jonathan's suit should he propose. He's said nothing as yet, and Grandmother needs me.''

"I have every reason to believe Mr. Lawrence will come up to scratch in the very near future. This alliance is very important to us all.'' There was a glitter in Mama's eyes that hinted she would brook no argument on the matter. "As for Mother, we can always send dear Lenore to bear her company in your stead."

Lenore looked as if she would rather die a slow death, and Maggie felt a suffocating net was quickly closing over her.

"Hold still," Jenna warned in a stern voice. "I want to bind the poultice tight about your ribs to keep the swelling and bruising down."

Devin winced, but tried to comply as she tugged at the bindings around his chest. If they weren't broken before, his ribs might well be by the time Jenna Watson finished with him.

"Best mind her, Devin." Marcus chuckled from the bed set by the narrow room's small window. "She'll only do it again if she's not satisfied. You'll smell sweet enough as it is without a second dose."

Devin was used to the herbal smell. He'd passed quite a few hours in this room engaging the coachman in games of chess to help relieve the boredom of his inactivity, and he'd spent his nights sleeping in the barn loft.

"This mixture of comfrey and agrimony Dr. Raymond prescribed has done wonders for your own bruises, so you leave off teasing the man, Husband," Jenna clucked. "Any fool who walks brazenly into hell on his own can stand a little discomfort in his tending."

She stood back and admired her work with a practiced eye. Folding her arms in front of her, the maid cocked one eyebrow and scanned him from head to toe more thoroughly than he'd been looked at in many a month. Devin squirmed. His mother couldn't have offered a finer inspection, or a more sage summation of the lunacy that had landed him in this state.

"You'll do." Jenna nodded, though a frown continued

to crease her brow. "I'll fetch some of the powder Miss Lenore favors for covering her spots so you can hide the bruise on your chin. Gloves will take care of your knuckles. None will be the wiser of this foolish misadventure. The Brownleys would definitely not approve of someone in their household engaging in a tavern brawl."

With that warning, she bustled from the room with her basin and wrappings.

Foolish misadventure was one way to look at tonight's escapade, he supposed. Futile exercise was another.

"What were you thinking, man, confronting two dock rats in their lair?" Marcus probed as soon as his wife exited. "You're lucky the whole bar didn't turn on you, especially given the anti-Irish sentiments that run amongst that crowd."

"I don't believe these two particular rats are any more esteemed by the pack they run with." Devin stood up from the stool and cautiously took a deep breath. His side did feel better. "Besides, I didn't exactly walk into the pub and announce my intentions. I quietly ordered a pint and waited for them to stagger outside. Then I followed."

"Still, taking on two by yourself—"

Devin waved off the older coachman's concern. "I might have been the runt of the litter, but I did not grow up on a shipbuilder's island with two older brothers and not learn how to handle myself a little. Besides . . ." He shrugged, then winced. "They were hardly in any shape to do much damage."

He'd found little satisfaction in tonight's fruitless confrontation outside The Eagle. Tracking down the two besotted idiots who barely recognized him did nothing to relieve his situation or restore his property. After landing a lucky punch or two, Henry and his companion had subsided into a cringing heap that offered no information into the whereabouts of either his bag or his sketchbook.

"You know your money's long gone. What is it you hoped to recover?" Marcus's look glimmered with worry.

"Just a few mementos." Sentimental whimsies, really. "Sketches from my sister, a carving one of our ships' cooks made me years ago when I was ill, a map of Asia my brother brought home to me from one of his trips— pieces of home."

Not much to make such a fuss over, but they were all he'd brought with him on his hasty voyage. It was far better to believe his losses inspired tonight's debacle than dwelling on the rippling disquiet from the memory of that smarmy Lawrence and the avaricious gleam he'd turned toward Maggie earlier. Still, it was Jonathan Adams Lawrence III's pudgy image that had blazed most often into his thoughts during the height of the fight.

He raked a hand through his hair and returned the older man's rueful stare. "It would seem I've no more sense than the green lad Quin likened me to when he sent me packing from our da's office two months ago."

Quin's taunts echoed, hurtling over time and the ocean between them. *Only someone as green about the gills as you, Dev, would believe anything besides hard work by experienced hands will save Reilly Ship Works. The best way you can help, stripling, is to get back to Dublin and finish your term. Next you'll be telling me one of the Little Folk promised you his pot of gold.*

The words still stung. No matter how indulgently the elder of his brothers meant them, they'd unwittingly set him on his current course.

"But you're a college man. Educated. Why throw that all away?" Marcus picked up the theme of previous discussions they'd held regarding Devin's plans to continue on to California as soon as possible.

"My education's always been more Da's dream than my own. Quin was always after the sea. Bryan, too. But

Da determined Bryan needed to pursue the law. And once set to it, he's become a master.''

He staved off the guilt that always loomed when he thought of how Bryan had come to give up his quest for the sea and turned to the law. Compared to his brother's accomplishments, Devin had all too little to throw away. Devin paced over to the chessboard set on a table beside Marcus's bed. Perhaps that was why he mourned the loss of what little he'd brought with him.

"I landed in Limerick on my way back to Dublin with my ears properly pinned and my tail between my legs. Bryan nearly repeated Quin's direction word for word.'' He twirled a black pawn in his fingers, tracing the cool curves as he thought about the twist of fate that had delivered him to what he'd thought was his life's low point. Marcus held his peace.

"Sighting the *Sweet Rose Marie* just as I read my mother's latest letter was like an omen. She mentioned the number of Americans they'd met along the Mediterranean, Americans who'd made their fortunes in California.'' *Pot of gold.* "Inspiration collided with impulse underscored by a healthy dose of righteous chagrin.'' He put the pawn down with a small thud. "And here I am.''

"Can you not trade in your passage to California and still go back to your studies? Surely your mother did not mean for you to forsake everything you've ever known.''

Marcus's deep brown eyes bored into him, but it was a lighter pair of smoked amber Devin envisioned as he discarded the idea of returning home. He shook his head. "I cannot see myself as a man of letters, a teacher or professor. Da's idea was for Bryan to learn the law and me the culture so we could outsmart the English. But that will take years, and the shipyard's needs are more immediate. I can do them more good over here, I am certain of that.''

"I had no idea." Maggie's voice from the doorway caused him to turn.

Their gazes locked in the lamplight. She was dressed in a soft white nightgown with a deep green wrapper. Her hair tumbled loose to trail over her shoulders. For a heartbeat, his thoughts flashed back to the moment they'd met, and the desire to plunge his hands into the beckoning softness of her golden brown curls swept through him like thunder rolling in over the waves.

Her eyes moved to the bandages around his chest. "You're hurt." Concern rippled through her gasp.

He paced forward and reached for his shirt—as if another layer of cloth between them would provide enough barrier to stop the sizzling desire to gather her close that streaked up his spine.

"Perhaps you could come back in a few minutes, Miss Margaret," Marcus suggested. They both ignored him.

As he buttoned his shirt under her watchful scrutiny, Devin deliberately attributed the source of her frown to her concern over his ability to continue his role in their deal. There could be nothing more between them, no matter his wayward desires otherwise. "A small mishap. I'm fit for my duties. Don't fret, Miss Margaret. I'll get you to your dance tomorrow evening. We'd hate to disappoint your Larry."

"My Larry?" She seemed bewildered.

"Mr. Jonathan Adams Lawrence III. Larry of the damp hands." A hostile edge crept into his tone at the thought of the other man's proprietary air toward Maggie. He could not imagine her, dressed as she was at the moment, sharing intimacies with the pudgy snob. He would not.

The set of her shoulders stiffened. She might not understand the reason, but she surely recognized the insult.

The small room seemed to crackle with tension. None of this, not how she spent her present nor with whom she might share her future, was any of his business. He was bound for California. Maggie Brownley's destiny shouldn't matter. But it did.

"Devin," Marcus said, "Miss Margaret comes to read to me most nights. Me and Jenna. She's very clever at giving Mr. Shakespeare's characters life."

Now he noticed the red leather volume she clutched with whitened knuckles.

"*Midsummer Night's Dream*," she said.

"Beg pardon?"

"We're sharing *A Midsummer Night's Dream* right now." The admission seemed to gain her some confidence as she recalled her reason for being in the servant's wing. She stepped into the room. "We're almost to the second act."

"I'll leave you to it, then." He grabbed his jacket and moved past her to the door without looking directly at her. Her ginger and chamomile scent filled him with a sharp edge of regret.

"Please give Jenna my thanks, Marcus," he tossed over his shoulder as he made good his escape.

Chapter Six

"Hush now, *alainn*. It will seem much better once we've worked the knots out," Devin soothed the sorrel mare as he brushed her long white mane.

"Have a care, Tim," he cautioned as the lad moved by with the handcart. "This one's a beauty, but she has a tendency to sidestep when approached too quickly." It was a sure sign of a skittish temperament.

As if to prove his point, the mare lifted her dainty hoof a fraction. "There's an extra handful of oats for you, Missy, before you join the others, if you'll hold still a wee bit longer."

The hoof lowered. He spoke softly as he worked, just as he'd been taught by Siannon's grandfather so long ago. A tug of regret snagged his thoughts. He'd never made his intended call on the friend he'd spent so many childhood summer afternoons with before he departed Limerick. He couldn't help wondering how she and her young son were managing now that the early days of her widowhood had passed.

"Not that she's got money troubles, mind." He shared his thoughts with the mare. "But her father puts me in mind of Maggie's. I'd not put it past the old goat to marry Siannon off to one of his cronies again just to keep her under his thumb, though I'll wager she'd object a bit more strenuously than the last time. She's far stronger than her da gives her credit, and she has her lad to think of."

Devin shook his head, struggling to stave off the wave of homesickness that threatened.

The mare snorted and stamped her foot as if adding her own stubbornness to Siannon's.

"She'll manage." Devin assured the horse and himself as he finished his work with the mare and sent her out to the paddock for some exercise.

Rubbing the stiffness out of his shoulder, he took a breath of early morning air outside the Brownley barn and blessed Bridget Smith for the fine breakfast she'd fed them both an hour earlier. A rasher of bacon with eggs, topped off with fine, strong coffee had started the day on a high note, especially after the disaster of the night before—not the tavern brawl, nor the shredding of any hope for recovering his belongings. The true calamity had occurred in Marcus Watson's narrow room. He tried to turn his thoughts from the image of Maggie in soft white with her hair tumbling over her green shawl. And failed.

Again.

"*Diabhal.*" He exhaled slowly, but it did little to dislodge the image. She'd looked just as he'd imagined during too many sleepless hours since being marooned in Boston. Well, almost as he'd imagined. Most often he'd pictured her in closer proximity—in his arms smelling of ginger and chamomile and woman, gazing at him with the stars in her eyes and the moisture of his kiss still on her lips.

Such an embrace was never to be. Not last night under the watchful eye of her coachman chaperon—not ever, if he laid claim to any sense at all. Work would help him shed these unwanted desires. Hard physical labor.

Leading the black gelding to the barn's center, he set back to his grooming. This was his favorite part of the day, the quiet keeping of the animals while the family they served still slept. Timmy proved an able assistant, going about his tasks with a cheery smile and swiftly completing all that was asked of him. Marcus Watson had trained the lad well.

He stroked the gelding's back with the brush. There was no escaping the fact that he chafed to be gone from this place, this occupation. The urgency of the situation back home niggled at him even as the irritation of dealing with his present employers and their narrow-minded prejudice seared tight brands of anger around his gut. With a fair wind, he could be halfway to California by now, if not for the thunder of The Blessing and the siren call of a pair of amber eyes.

"What was I thinking, laddie?" He winced as he bent to the horse's legs. "I came to your land to collect fortune, not store up my gold in heaven by putting up with the likes of the Brownleys. I've more people depending on my success in California than Maggie Brownley can ever imagine. Even Quin cannot keep the shipyard running with empty tool bins and too little timber."

He was a fool for allowing mistaken feelings of summer rain and distant thunder to convince him he'd found The Blessing on Boston's docks. In Maggie's kiss.

"Yet here I stay with no money and no means of completing my journey." Timmy's news this morning that his ship would be under repair for another two weeks or more had done little to lighten his mood.

The black twitched his tail but remained statue-still while Devin moved to groom the other side of his smooth and glossy coat. Devin wished, not for the first time, that his purpose in life was as clear-cut as that of the horses he loved. "By the sweat of my brow and a little luck, I must help my family. I've no other choice."

"What sort of magic do you whisper to my horse to get him to stand so still?"

The hint of chamomile and ginger that overrode the barn's more noxious odors should have alerted him to Maggie's presence, but he'd been too busy wallowing in his past troubles to pay heed to the dangers of the present.

More than a fool.

She stood in the doorway for a moment, smiling at him, wearing the pale green dress that had haunted him since that first day on the docks. The day he'd met and kissed her and his life had spun out of control.

Her hair was tied back in a tight knot that inspired an irrational urge in him to pull it loose and reveal the bewitching siren of the night before.

She laughed then, a twinkle of sound that danced across his soul and sliced into his resolve to quit this farce and be off about his own business.

"You needn't look so guilty, Mr. Reilly. It's not as if I caught you in a seduction."

Seduction? Chagrin chafed at Maggie. Why had she blurted out such a telling remark, especially as the image of a very shirtless Devin standing in the lamplight the night before rose to taunt her?

Since her carriage had careened away on the docks, her whole world seemed tilted beyond her control. Fair or not, she laid the blame at a certain Irishman's feet— or, more accurately, in his hands.

She had stood at the barn's side door for a full five minutes or more, mesmerized by the play of Devin Reilly's hands on the gelding's sleek black coat. His long fingers, made for sketching or playing a musical instrument, stroked the animal with an intimacy that warmed her far more than it should.

She'd never planned on allowing a man to invade her life so thoroughly, never expected the flash of lightning or riotous clamor of a daring embrace to linger and intensify, never thought to be haunted by the lilt of a voice or the knowing sparkle in a green gaze.

Unsettling feelings at best, especially unwanted and unwelcome in the scheme of her life, no matter the tales of chivalrous knights, courtly romance, and tragic fates her grandmother had used to lull her to sleep on sultry summer nights.

Devin stopped his grooming and favored Maggie with a look that sent sparks shooting through her despite the frown that accompanied his regard. Annoyance flared at her own wayward reactions. "Seduction is one means of ensuring cooperation, Miss Brownley. A lesson many a young lass learns in the cradle, as I'm sure you know full well." He continued in the same quiet tone he'd used when speaking to the horse, but with an added twist of sarcasm.

The soft accusation flamed heat in her cheeks—or was it guilt that raised her irritation?

When she'd asked him to stay and help, to swallow the indignities foisted upon him by her father's prejudices, had she not been willing to use any means?

He returned to stroking the gelding's back with long, deliberate motions while his gaze remained locked with hers. Seduction in motion. Again the tug of the man's sensual appeal played havoc with her thoughts.

More times than she cared to admit since meeting him,

she'd found herself staring at his hands as he went about his work. Although it did little good, she told herself the diversion kept her from mooning over the curl of his black hair or the keenness of his green eyes, the way Nora did in the quiet seclusion of darkness when her sister still seemed the companion of their childhood and they shared whispered confessions. She prayed her tactic fooled others better than she fooled herself. In the cloister of Maggie's private thoughts, Devin Reilly dominated.

"Is there something I may do for you this morning, Miss Brownley? Your mother did not request the carriage be brought around until afternoon. Has her schedule changed?"

She shook head in wordless denial, pulling herself back to the original intent of her visit. She walked further into the barn. Her fingers tightened on the bundle she carried. She had come here with a purpose beyond the opportunity to gape at him.

"I brought you some drawing paper and supplies. I thought your sister might enjoy your renderings better if they were set on blank sheets rather than the distraction of newsprint."

Stepping around the black, he came to meet her. She caught a fresh whiff of balsam and earthy musk that rose over the staler barn smells as he took the gifts from her.

He weighed them in his hands and studied her face. "I thank you for the thought. But I told you before, Reillys are not partial to accepting charity." He dropped the pad and box of charcoals on a bale of hay next to them. "Is that all, Miss Brownley?"

He was refusing her gifts.

"Exactly what are Reillys partial to?" Annoyance flared, pushing the challenge from her. "Who are you, Devin Reilly? Why would you refuse such a simple ges-

ture when I'd thought merely to thank you for your help—
to ease some of the awkwardness of your position?''

"You know nothing of my position, lass.'' Bitter condemnation laced the truth behind Devin's taunt. Anger
flared in the depths of his gaze. He appeared ready to let
loose a fusillade, but held his peace for several long
breaths. The heat in his emerald eyes banked and he set
his lips in a thin line. "I arrived here and within the span
of an hour lost everything."

Guilt replaced Maggie's anger. The accident had happened to both of them, had overset both their lives and
plans, his more so than hers. He was alone and friendless,
while she remained in the dubious shelter of her home
and family. The cost to him was far greater than she could
ever repay. And now she had insulted his pride. She was
honor bound to make what she could up to him.

She placed a hand on his arm. "Tell me. Besides your
belongings, what did you lose on the docks last week? I
heard a little of what you told Marcus last night."

He winced, and for a moment she was certain he would
pull away and refuse to answer her—refuse her friendship,
along with her gift. His gaze flew to the pad and box on
the bale as if his thoughts mirrored hers.

He took a deep breath. "I am Reilly born and Reilly
bred."

There was a shift in his gaze with those words, as if
he scanned a horizon far away. "Though I am a poor
example, I must hold my own as best I can. Reillys are
men of the sea. For generations, my family has built and
sailed some of the finest vessels ever to ply the oceans.
Everyone on our island depends on Reilly Ship Works.
Viking raiders, English laws, even The Great Hunger did
not touch our people."

"You've been very blessed." She took an infinitesimal
step closer. He did not retreat.

"Blessed, aye—so some might say." A strange look of chagrin twisted his mouth for a moment. Then he fixed his gaze directly on her. "My destiny was never here, in this city. Our da's illness allowed unscrupulous curs to deplete the island's coffers. My brothers have their hands full trying to stem the losses. Quin was born to command, on a quarterdeck or a dry dock. Bryan has a facile mind for facts and the law. He'll buy Quin time."

He pulled away from her and picked up the pad of paper. "All I've ever been good for is sketching and grooming horses. They didn't need me underfoot. Reaping a fortune in California's gold was to be my part in bringing us back from ruin. My part in helping."

Guilt dripped from his voice, flowing into her. Self-loathing mingled with raw loneliness. He'd come ashore in a strange land to search for the means to reconcile his place in his family. She understood too well the feeling of never fitting in, of being different.

She stepped over to him and placed her hand on his cheek in wordless sympathy. For a timeless span, his gaze reflected the remorse with which he raked his soul. He searched her face and released a long breath. "Blessing or curse?"

With that inexplicable question, more condemnation than query, he brought his hands up to her shoulders and pulled her to him.

The realization that this was what she'd been longing for, that this was why she had sought him out in the barn, crackled through Maggie like lightning on a summer evening. Their kiss on the docks had opened a new and dangerous world of sensations for her, and she wanted more. Needed more.

His lips touched hers. He tasted of salt and rich coffee, a heady mix. Breathless, she slid her fingers into his hair and deepened the kiss, drinking in the sorrow and isolation that sluiced from him, trying to fill the void she sensed in him—the same void she knew existed in her.

She closed her eyes. Balsam and musk filled her senses, as if she'd been transported to her sanctuary in the heart of Maine's deep woods. Yet it was here, in Devin Reilly's arms, that she felt truly at home.

His lips probed hers and she returned the pressure. Tiny sparks whirled through her veins. His hands slid from her shoulders to cradle her back, and her breasts pressed against his chest. The layers of silk and cotton between them seemed to melt away from the heat.

She felt the tug of his fingers in her hair, releasing it. Releasing her.

His tongue teased the inner rim of her mouth and she opened to him on a sigh. Never had she imagined such excitement was possible from the gentle probing of a tongue as it sought and caressed her own. She floated in his arms, oblivious to all save the thundering of their hearts and the awakening demands of the fire that flamed through her from the touch of Devin's mouth on hers.

A low moan growled from the depths of his throat and he tore himself away from her, leaving her dazed and bereft.

"Cursed it is." He winced as he clenched his hands into fists and failed to meet her stunned gaze. "Pray keep your gratitude to yourself from now on, Miss Brownley. It will serve us all ill should anyone learn of the special benefits you offer for my post here."

Still feeling scattered and breathless, she panted, "I never . . . that . . . had nothing to do with gratitude."

A hollow knot of humiliation formed in her stomach. Was she really as certain as she protested?

Devin picked up the box she'd offered him earlier and weighed it in his hands again. "Will not your betrothed wonder at your giving such gifts to another man?

"Betrothed?" The knot in her stomach tightened with the certainty it was not art supplies he spoke of when he said "gifts."

He raised an eyebrow at her. "Jenna explained your parents' desires for your future happiness. Your Larry of the damp hands does not look to be the kind of man who shares his possessions with ease."

"Larry?" Anger flared. She wanted to slap the smugness from his voice. "Jonathan is not my—"

It was none of his business what Jonathan Lawrence was or was not to her. She stepped back from Devin and tried to control her conflicting emotions.

"As you said, my parents are the ones interested in obtaining Jonathan as a son-in-law." At least her tone was cool and her voice did not betray her inner trembling. She wove her fingers together in front of her. "I'll never willingly place myself in servitude to any man, or subjugate myself to the mercy of a husband—to a lifetime founded on manly whims."

His jaw worked as he met her stare for stare. "You'd best stick to well-lit paths and open company over stealing into quiet corners or secluded stables, then. Your parents will marry you off so quickly your head will spin if they get wind you're dallying with the lower classes."

Dallying? Anger choked her.

"I'll not play Seamus Dodd to your Clara." His declaration sliced through her reply.

Seamus Dodd? A figure from literature, perhaps? Her interest in the enigma of Devin's background shifted her attention. "Seamus—"

"My friend. He dared to love beyond himself and, in the end, despite all his Clara's sighs and pretty promises, she loved the comforts a rich man offered more. Seamus lost all, including his will to live."

"A bleak story."

Part of her wanted to slap him for the insults he heaped on her. Part of her longed to reach out and smooth the frown from his brow. But the very depth of his frown and the chasm that yawed between them forbade such a gesture.

The green in Devin's eyes dulled. "I cut him down from the church tower and swore an oath that night I'd never fall victim to a lass's merciless whims." He spread his arms and looked around the barn. "Yet here I am."

He fixed his gaze on her, and for a moment Maggie was quite certain she would drown in the bleak depths of his eyes.

The gelding whickered just then and pulled back on its tether. Maggie took the opportunity the interruption offered and picked up her skirts to flee the barn. She was not certain if Devin meant to frighten her or to save her from herself, but she burst through the open doorway with a speed that surprised her far more than the sound of a small box hitting the wall behind her.

The musicians picked up their instruments, signaling the beginning of the next set for dancing. Maggie took one look at Jonathan returning with a cup of punch for her and knew she could not face another turn on the dance floor with his sweating palms holding hers and his feet treading on her toes.

"I was certain this rose shade of taffeta was just the thing to highlight your coloring, Margaret. Mr. Lawrence can hardly stay away from you this night." Mama nearly purred her approval. "Straighten your shoulders, dear. Even across the room he practically devours you with his eyes."

"I am feeling a little unwell, Mama. Pray excuse me while I retire to refresh myself." Anything to escape for a few moments and hide from all the expectations that seemed to be weighing in on her.

"Nonsense. You excused yourself not more than an hour ago. You are just suffering from nerves, my girl, aggravated by the number of people in the room." Her mother placed a restraining hand on Maggie's arm as she made ready to rise.

Before she could protest further, Jonathan arrived to stand in front of them. Small beads of sweat glistened on his brow. With a sinking heart, Maggie accepted the punch he offered them both. She couldn't stand the thought of more meaningless small talk with the man, either. Perhaps another dance was the better alternative.

"Oh, Mr. Lawrence, you are so kind," her mother trilled. "It is ever so hot in here. I am wondering if I might impose a little further on you."

"You have but to name your desire." Jonathan looked directly at Maggie.

Mama took a sip from her cup and smiled like a cat over a saucer of cream. "Margaret is finding the crowds a bit oppressive. Would you be so kind as to escort her for a brief turn about the gardens for some air?"

No, no, no—not time alone with him. Maggie's breath hitched. Would this night never end?

A disconcerting glimmer sparked in Jonathan's ice blue eyes as he favored her mother with a small bow. "Anything for you, madam. I'd be more than delighted to offer my services to Miss Brownley. Shall we?" The corner of his mouth quirked up at an odd angle as he offered Maggie his arm.

To refuse would be insulting, to say the least, and would bring the full weight of her parents' wrath down not only on her, but on the Watsons. Yet could she stand a few minutes alone in the garden with the man and still avoid the proposal that seemed to dangle over her head?

What choice did she have?

She took his arm and they skirted their way around the dance floor toward the doors leading to the Andersons' much prized gardens, modeled after the family's estate in England a century before.

Amelia and Lenore, along with a small group from the Daughters of Grace, stared at them with knowing smiles as they passed. Maggie tried not to notice the number of other heads turned their way in speculation as they made their exit from the crowded ballroom. Did everyone in Boston know of her parents' ambitions?

"This is better now, isn't it?" Jonathan took a deep breath as they stepped outside at last. "It's quite dreadful bearing up under the weight of all those expectations in there."

Surprise rippled through Maggie. She'd never thought how Jonathan must be feeling as the object of her parents' pursuit, or that he might even feel much the same as she did.

He looked over at her, a disarming smile tugging at his lips. "There's a sprinkling of stars overhead and the fine scent of lilacs beckoning. What say we make good use of our little respite from the gossips and really enjoy the gardens?" He tugged her gently toward one of the torchlit paths.

This was the most appealing side of Jonathan Lawrence Maggie had ever seen. And he was right: They might as well enjoy this time away from the crowds while they could. Her feet felt a little lighter as they set off over the brick walkway lined with trimmed boxwood.

Jonathan guided her to a small bench set in an alcove near the far end of the garden. "Shall we sit for a few minutes and enjoy the night without prying eyes?"

"The torches do add a magical quality to the Andersons' grounds." She readily agreed to extend their respite and took the seat he indicated, her taffeta skirts whispering around her. "And the music sounds so beautiful carrying across the lawn like this."

"The music is nothing compared to your beauty, my dear Margaret." Jonathan clasped one hand over hers on her lap as he joined her on the bench.

He'd never used her given name before, never held her hand except in greeting. Her heart plummeted to the tips of her satin dancing slippers. Not now. Not when she'd thought herself safe, if only temporarily, from the marriage proposal she'd been dreading. He'd never approached her in anything but the politest of circumstances. This had to be it.

She attempted to extract herself from Jonathan's grasp, but he held her fingers firmly and edged closer. He smelled of stale sweat and spirits. His eyes glittered in the dim light with the same hardness she'd detected earlier. She shivered.

"Don't be alarmed. I only wish to sample the wares you so easily peddled on Boston's docks not so long ago." The whiskey on his breath was unmistakable at this distance.

"You've been drinking," she gasped and tried to stand.

His hands clamped down on her shoulders and held her fast. "Come now, my dear. Surely you did not expect such a juicy story to remained locked behind Milford's lips."

"Milford?" So the thin man whose horse Devin had borrowed had carried the tale after all, but not to Papa. Cold dread twisted her stomach.

"Do you think my family would allow any alliance to progress without a thorough investigation? Horace Milford was most helpful with his description of your dashing coachman's daring rescue and the reward you so freely gave him for his efforts."

Jonathan's fingers dug into her shoulders, and she looked at him in horror as he leaned closer.

"Mind, I've no objection to the woman who will share my bed and whelp my heirs having a little fire in her veins." His breath crawled across her cheeks. "Especially as I am fairly certain the brute's had no opportunity to despoil you."

With that, Jonathan pulled her to him and clamped his lips over hers. Maggie struggled for breath and pushed against his chest. This was not how a kiss was meant to feel—hard and harrowing, almost paralyzing in the dread it evoked. There were no whorls of sparks through her veins, no melting heat as he pressed his body against hers, no thundering of hearts or fire threatening to scorch away all reserves—just the merciless demands and wet thrust of a relentless mouth.

"Stop." She finally managed to tear herself away, gasping.

How much of a scene could she make and still escape the scandal? How much help could she expect when they were so isolated from the rest of the party?

Jonathan anchored a hand at the nape of her neck and locked her tight against his chest.

None. The dreadful certainty of her predicament thundered through her.

"You are a tasty morsel, Margaret Brownley. I cannot get enough of you." He breathed heavily in her ear and flicked his tongue along her lobe. Her outraged gasp afforded him the opportunity to claim her mouth once more. This time her lips were parted enough for him to thrust his tongue inside.

Maggie gagged, choking back bile from both the indignity and the taste of sour whiskey on Jonathan's tongue.

"Beg pardon, sir." A deep voice sounded from the path. "I've been sent to find Miss Brownley."

Devin. Relief raced through Maggie. She wrenched herself away from Jonathan to peer into the night.

"Can't you see we wish for some privacy, you dolt?" Jonathan shifted his weight, blocking her ability to rise. "Just say you cannot find her. I am in the process of seeking Miss Brownley's hand in marriage."

Devin stepped closer, looming over the bench. A dangerous light glittered in his eyes.

"There's an urgent message"—he focused his attention directly on her—"delivered within the hour from your grandmother, and another from her physician. Mr. Marbury thought you should know."

"Her physician?" Dread flooded Maggie and gave her added strength. She pushed past Jonathan and gained her feet. "Is Grandmother ill?"

"The Andersons' butler is gathering the rest of your family." Devin offered no relief from her worries.

Jonathan stood, as well. He pulled at his jacket to smooth out any wrinkles. "We're not finished, Margaret—"

"We most certainly are finished, Mr. Lawrence. Good night." Worry for her grandmother kept Maggie from truly enjoying her escape as she took Devin's arm and turned toward the path.

"We can go out the side gate, Maggie." Devin guided her over the grass.

He spoke in clipped, though gentle, tones. Distant. Impersonal. Did he believe she'd invited or welcomed the spectacle he'd just interrupted?

"Thank you for finding me. Things were not what they seemed back there . . ."

She fought the irrational need to explain herself and clamped her lips tight. Explanation would lead to delay, and right now she had more important matters to attend.

"I believe your Larry may be in need of an anatomy

esson if he truly were seeking your hand just now."
Devin's dry comment as he opened the wooden door in
he garden wall provided just enough whimsical humor
o ease the fine edge of tension building inside Maggie.
Grandmother must be in some drastic trouble or be dread-
fully ill if she had sent such an urgent message.

Chapter Seven

Moonlight drenched the stable yard in shades of silver, black, and deepest plum, which stretched into inky shadows as murky as Devin's thoughts.

With the horses bedded down for the night and the Brownley house dark and quiet, it was the image of peaceful serenity. Too peaceful. The intermittent chirping of crickets and the distant hooting of an owl mocked him to his depths.

"A night such as this is meant for strollin' with a pretty lass on yer arm," Daniel Mallory would say, winking, after a late night study session. But Daniel wasn't here and neither was the only lass Devin could picture himself sharing the night with.

"*Diabhal.*" He kicked at a stray clump of hay, releasing a dust cloud into a shaft of cold light. A far better match for his mood. What was it his old philosophy professor used to say? Something about a man's mood moving in ultimate harmony with his surroundings. Devin scrubbed a hand over the tight knots at the back of his neck as his lip curled. Though he couldn't remember old man Murphy's exact words on the subject, he'd be more than able to provide the professor with a debate bordering on hot denial at this point.

Maggie Brownley was only a couple of Boston's city blocks away, spending the night with her friend at All Saint's rectory, yet he was torn with frustration all out of proportion with the actual distance separating them. This did not bode well for his plans to put an entire continent and lifetime between them.

Nor did it help that her own future held imminent marriage to her parents' choice—Larry of the damp hands and smarmy manners.

Jonathan Adams Lawrence III, as Mrs. Brownley was so fond of saying in her most indulgent tone. What was it about these Bostonians that made them determined to bestow a person's full name on them at every opportunity? Like a litany of lineage.

Regardless of Larry's pedigree, Devin didn't like him. No, that was too watered down to describe how he felt about Maggie's suitor. The image of her struggling in Larry's arms the other night haunted Devin. He'd barely stopped himself from grabbing the fellow off her and smashing his fist into the man's condescending face. Only the urgency of his errand and the certain knowledge that any scene he created would cause delay had stopped him.

The sight of that man tasting her sweet lips, enjoying the soft tempting body Devin had already held against his own too many times for propriety's comfort, burned him like a hot brand. As her husband, Jonathan Lawrence would have every right to claim all that and more.

Devin shook his head, wishing he could force this whole train of thought from his mind. It only twisted the knot in his gut into tighter and tighter coils.

In the end, he might just as well have given Larry the thrashing he deserved for his ham-fisted and patently unwelcome embrace. The Brownleys had been furious at being summoned home by their butler and had refused to allow Maggie to leave immediately to visit her grandmother, who was indeed ill. She had argued in vain long into that night and all the next day, to no avail.

This visit to her friend had offered them all respite from the tension and recriminations. Maggie had left with a hollow and determined look that did not bode well for her return tomorrow.

"Hell." The soft-edged shadows swallowed his curse, mocking him still further. He'd no business standing in a barn door mooning over a lass he'd never have, no matter the circumstances. Maggie'd made it quite clear that, left to herself, she'd never marry—never place herself in servitude to any man, wasn't that how she'd phrased it?

"Well now, Miss Brownley, much as I'd love to prove you wrong," he mused, "I've other business I must attend."

The only hope he held of proving to his brothers—to himself—he could measure up to the rest of his family lay in gaining a fortune in the California gold fields. That was where he needed to concentrate his thoughts, his efforts.

Marcus Watson was recovering nicely. He had walked the upper halls of the house already. Tomorrow he was to try the stairs. Devin's role here was nearly through, and he had but a week to go until his ship was set to sail. He would leave Boston and all its troubles behind. Then he would succeed in rescuing the Ship Works.

He must.

From behind him in the shadowy recesses of the barn, shuffling noises crept into his thoughts. The barn cat in pursuit of a mouse? No, something larger—yet softer than the shuffle of horses in their stalls. A booted foot.

He turned soundlessly and narrowed his eyes to peer into the gloom. Definitely human footsteps. Every Irishman knew nothing good ever came on stealthy feet in the dark of night.

He crept forward, grateful for the chafing thoughts that had made sleep so impossible tonight. He never would have noticed the activity in the far stall had he been asleep in the loft—a fact this thief had no doubt counted on, if he even knew the Brownleys had an occupant in their barn. The paddock gate gaped open a fraction, marking the thief's entry.

Reaching the edge of the stall, Devin froze. The door latch was undone. He clearly recalled ramming it home after currying Maggie's mare earlier in the evening. Moonlight filtered through the opening in the back wall, casting eerie patches of light and shadow on the mounds of hay and the carriages stored on the other side. He inched forward to peer between the slats and size up his quarry.

The horse the thief was trying to saddle tossed its mane and stepped to the left, just enough to make the saddle slide to the floor with a muffled thud. A muttered curse reached his ears.

Cold amusement filtered through Devin, curling his lips. It would appear this rather inept thief was unable to saddle his prize quickly and retreat with it unnoticed. Devin relaxed some of the muscles that had bunched in anticipation of a fight.

His thief looked like a lad. No doubt hungry and in need of shelter, he must be acting out of desperation more than devilry.

''Ye'll not get far like that, boy-o.'' Devin deliberately rolled his brogue and had the satisfaction of seeing his thief stiffen in fear. The mare between them whickered softly as he stepped into the stall. ''Though at the moment I'm at a loss decidin' if it is the saddle ye wish ta steal or the horse.'' He started forward. ''Here, let's have a look at ye.''

''No.'' A mere gasp of a word. The thief twisted past him with desperate speed and took headlong flight across the barn toward the doors.

''Not yet, boy-o.'' Devin lunged for the lad, his fingers clasping air as they missed the thief's shirt. Far more nimble than Devin had suspected from his clumsy attempts at saddling the horse, the lad danced fleetly between the hay and tackle. It was probably his one claim to success in his nefarious occupation.

Pushing for more speed, Devin hurled himself forward and snagged the thief's collar, throwing him off balance long enough for the weight of Devin's body to carry them both down into the hay and a patch of moonlight.

The lad's breath whooshed out, mixing with a grunt of pain as Devin landed solidly atop him.

''Sorry, boy-o, but nobody steals on my watch.''

The lad squirmed beneath him, all taut indignant muscle. Trim, but solid even for a lad.

''Hold still.'' Devin held the lad's wrists with one of his hands and ran his other over the squirming boy's arms, shoulders, and back, searching for any concealed weapons. He moved downward in his search, finally gaining complete stillness from his captive as his hand ran down the boy's long, lithe legs—far too shapely for an average boy.

As his hand traveled over firm, rounded buttocks, slow and caressing, he realized his body already knew what his mind was just beginning to guess. This was no lad.

An indignant shriek, muffled by hay, rang his ears as

his hand confirmed the sex of his captive by tracing an intimate line against the softness between her thighs.

"Lass." He chuckled as the struggles beneath him renewed. "You'd have suffered a lesser indignity had you told me your gender to begin with."

A groan told him his point had struck home. "Release me at once." The tart command, accompanied by another wiggle, erased the smile from his lips.

"Maggie?" He pulled the cap from her head, releasing a fragrant cloud of curls. Ginger and chamomile surrounded him, only registering now as teasing him from the moment he'd touched her. He groaned.

"Yes."

He turned her in his arms, still pinning her amidst the hay with his body. A wash of moonlight highlighted the porcelain delicacy of her skin. How had he ever mistaken her for a lad? She was soft and yielding beneath him, even as her smoked amber eyes shot flames in his direction.

"What are you doing here, Maggie?" Fine young ladies from Boston's high society did not belong in a barn at this hour—or any hour, for that matter. Not dressed as a lad.

"I was saddling a horse before you interrupted." The tart heat in her voice amused him. "Why aren't you asleep, as you should be?"

He raised a brow at her and brushed stray curls from her face with gentle fingers. "My lady, you were not doing a very good job of saddling that horse. You would have made out much better had you simply asked me to do it for you."

She lifted her chin and tightened her lips—a mutinous gesture. "I was not planning on running into anyone, least of all you, Mr. Reilly."

"Indeed?" A chuckle escaped him. It was ridiculous really, for her to thrust a *Mr. Reilly* at him while she lay disheveled and lovely beneath him. A longing to kiss the stiffness from her soft full lips until they were pliant and clinging to his own surged within him.

Fine color swept over her cheeks.

"What exactly were you planning?"

"Not this." She squirmed again and he bit back a groan as her movements only heightened the desires sweeping through him in hot, hungry spirals.

"You did not plan to find yourself flat on your back?"

"No." More color washed her cheeks and spread over her neck, down into the open V of her shirt. "You can release me now, Devin. As you have discovered, I am not a thief."

"Saddling a horse in the dead of night—in disguise— could hardly be called an upright act."

He tightened his hold on her, shifting his weight just a bit so he could hold her still and yet free his arms. Tormenting her further to get to the truth seemed a good idea, until she shifted as well, lodging the painful pressure of his erection intimately between her thighs.

"Mayhap not the acts of a true villain," he ground out from between clenched teeth. He struggled to hold himself still as his intimate position against her threatened to steal every scrap of sanity he had ever laid claim to. "But most definitely an unrepentant thief."

She wriggled again and then gasped and stilled, glancing down at their scandalous proximity. Her teeth showed white against the rose-petal softness of her lips just inches from his own. Her wide-eyed gaze locked with his, caught between fear and appeal.

He took her lips with his then, unable to resist the seething calls of his body and the urgent needs she unleashed within him.

He caught her second gasp, tasting her breath as her lips parted beneath his. The raw power of his own desires overwhelmed him. Hot pictures of taking her here and now in the soft yielding hay tortured him, rolling through him in wave upon unforgiving wave.

Wild winds whipped his soul, tearing rational thought from him, rending whatever good intentions he harbored. She felt too good, tasted too good. He would never get enough. She made a little moan in the back of her throat as his tongue probed her mouth, sliding intimately against hers, making slow passionate love to her. And then her hands slipped over his shoulders and up into his hair, her fingers sliding against his scalp, urging him closer.

He slanted his face across hers, deepening the kiss still further, mindless to all but the heaven of having her in his arms, tasting each little whimper she made as she arched herself against him. Her breasts pressed against his chest, firm and deliciously rounded, teasing his senses to madness with images and desires he could not fulfill.

"Devin." She breathed his name as he tore his mouth from hers—a question, a plea he was only too tempted to oblige. This was no proper Boston miss pushing him away and demanding an apology for the liberties he took. But then Margaret Sylvia Worth Brownley was hardly an ordinary, proper miss at the best of times, let alone in the dead of night with her shapely figure clad in boy's clothing.

He broke away from her and rolled to his feet. His breath came ragged and harsh with wanting her and struggling to resist the sweet passion he found in her embrace—a passion neither of them could afford to indulge, though caution threatened to burn away when he looked at her still sprawled on the hay with a shaft of moonlight highlighting her kiss-dazed features.

What had forced her urgent need for a horse while all the world was sleeping? She was unlikely to reveal her plans. Still, he needed to know, if only to save her from herself. He'd shock her into telling him the truth if need be.

"If it is a wild bit of lovin' in the hay you came looking for, Maggie Brownley, I'll gladly oblige you. But somehow I doubt your soon-to-be betrothed will be too pleased to find you sullied."

He flung the words at her, not bothering to soften his tone, needing whatever blind space he could put between them as quickly and as completely as possible.

Anger snapped in the depths of her smoky eyes. Her lips tightened, dispelling the alluring image of a sultry siren and giving him his determined miss once more. Good.

"I don't care what Jonathan Lawrence thinks." She bit out the words.

He raised an eyebrow at her and reached for his belt buckle, releasing the clasp and watching her eyes widen as her gaze followed his movements.

"Then we'd best have to it, love. There's no telling when someone else might happen into the barn in search of a mount." Again crude words, anything to get her to leave and torture him no more. Anything to keep himself from pulling her back into his arms and worshipping every impudent inch of her lush body as he longed to do.

She scrabbled to her feet, her hair falling over her face and shoulders in a mass of wild curls. She swept them back with a gesture of impatience and faced him. Her lips were swollen and kiss bruised, her eyes unfathomable pools.

"I did not come here to be manhandled or seduced." She struggled for the type of haughty demeanor so well displayed by her mother and sister. The gaping front of her shirt dispelled the illusion, displaying the ripe swells of her breasts.

"Nay? Then you'd best put this to rights before I take

you up on the invitation." He flicked his fingers over her unwitting display, grazing her soft flesh with his knuckles.

She gasped at his touch. A shudder went through her as her gaze shot back to his. Vulnerability lurked in her wide amber eyes, mingling with an unspoken sensuality that made him groan. He doubted she had any notion what she did to his resolve with the simple honesty glowing in her gaze.

She clutched the shirt closed and, after several false starts, managed to conquer the buttons. He released a silent sigh of relief as he watched her.

"Is that better?" The tart edge was back in her tone. He couldn't help admiring her spirit. No matter the circumstances, she was always ready with an answer for him, even when he'd lost sight of the question.

"Aye, much." He nodded, folding his arms across his chest and leaning back against a stall. She bent to retrieve her cap from the hay behind her, demonstrating why her disguise would never work in daylight.

"Now as to the purpose of your late night visit in this"—he gestured the length of her as she straightened—"rather unconventional garb. I cannot think you believe your mother would approve."

She squared her shoulders, her expressive eyes mirroring an internal struggle, then focusing as she seemed to make a decision. She tossed her wild curls. "No, I'm sure she would not, but I am not here to please my parents."

"Indeed?"

She frowned at him, not missing the twist of sarcasm in his tone. "Yes. I intend to leave Boston. Tonight."

"And where might you be going?" He was certain he knew the answer.

"To Maine. To my grandmother's." She held up a

hand to forestall him, though he'd offered no protests. "I know my parents do not want me to go."

He smiled. "In truth, Maggie, they've forbidden it."

She frowned at him again and paced a few steps away. An interesting experiment in torture, truly, for the sway of her hips and the caress of her snug trousers against her sweet curves would bewitch and bewilder stronger men than he.

She twisted her hands together, a telling sign that despite her resolve she was conflicted in the course she'd chosen. Pacing back, she answered, "I cannot allow their social ambitions to stop me."

She halted in front of him and turned her face up to his. "My grandmother needs me, Devin. She would not have sent a message about being ill unless she was in dire need." Her voice dipped as pain and worry tugged at her expression.

Something twisted inside him in reply. He could all too easily sympathize with her. He would be doing the same thing if it were his grandmother. His memories of Granny might be hazy, but they were there just the same. Sometimes the faintest whiff of lavender could bring her to mind.

Maggie swallowed and then gestured with dismissive impatience toward the house. "Grandmother is a strong woman, the strongest I have ever known. To admit a need to anyone, but most especially to my parents, would be a tremendous weakness to her. She'd not have done that unless she saw no other course open to her."

She gripped his arms, and a sweet frisson of awareness shot through him. "I cannot let her down when she is counting on me. She needs me, Devin. I'm sure of it."

Her gaze held her soul deep within, bared for him to see just how much her grandmother meant to her.

"But you cannot go alone." He reached up and stroked

his fingers over her hot cheek. Her eyes closed at his touch, twisting desire through him like a knife. "You told me yourself that traveling to your grandmother's takes you through unsettled country. It would not be safe, Maggie. Handing your grandmother notice of your death or injury would surely do her more harm than good."

"I must." Her gaze locked with his again. "Marcus cannot travel with me, even though he is back on his feet a little. You know he is not well enough. Even if he were up to the journey, I could not ask him to abandon his post here and lose his position."

Her words tugged at Devin, further knotting his conflicted resolve. He should help her, he knew that on a gut-deep level, but he could not commit himself to her journey, nor to losing the tenuous security of this position himself, not when Reilly Ship Works was already so much in need. He resisted the lure, pulling away from her touch. His own loyalty to his family had to remain paramount. He'd need references if he was to secure another position when Marcus recovered. He needed to earn more funds for when he reached California.

"Surely your parents do not intend to ignore your grandmother."

"No. They want me to wait for Jonathan." Her lips twisted over the name. "I am to marry him in haste and allow him to handle all of my grandmother's problems for me."

Marry him in haste. Again the thought of Jonathan Lawrence's hands touching her, his lips claiming her, cut through Devin, leaving a trail of pain out of all proportion to his actual relationship with Margaret Brownley.

"When are you to wed?" he asked, his voice husky.

"Two weeks hence. But I shall not be here. I am leaving tonight." She stepped around him and proceeded to the stall she'd just fled.

"You cannot." He followed her as she moved forward to attempt her saddling maneuver with the horse again.

"I'm going."

"Maggie." He crossed to her in two quick strides and stopped her from grasping the saddle. He turned her in his arms, receiving a mutinous expression for his efforts. "Can you not listen? Be sensible. You cannot do this by yourself. It is too dangerous."

Ginger-laced chamomile edged through the noxious odors of the barn, warm and inviting. Even ramrod straight and layered in cloth beneath his fingers, the soft appeal of her body rippled through him as he held her at arm's length. "Perhaps it would be best for you to wait"—he swallowed and forced out the rest—"and marry."

Her gaze traced over his mouth in a caress he could almost feel. "I have no wish to marry."

Sadness and regret lingered in her tone, and she raised her gaze to meet his own. Doubts and questions hazed the glow in her eyes. Instead of pulling away, she stepped closer. He groaned and drew her to him, cupping her jaw with his palm and kissing her again. So soft, so pliant. The feel of her in his arms was heaven and hell in the same instant. She sighed against his lips, teasing their edges with her tongue.

He took a step back without losing the wonder of her embrace, leaning on the stall post so she melted against him. He slid his hand from her jaw to anchor in the curls at the back of her head, tilting her so he might taste the sweetness of her mouth more fully. Passion roared deep within him. She could not, would not, belong to Jonathan Lawrence. Not ever.

Her hands moved along his sides, sending spirals of heat through him. Their tongues met and mated in a primal dance that set his blood surging, pounding deep into his groin.

This woman was meant to be his. He stroked the small of her back and struggled to snag the last vestige of his common sense as it sailed away.

When he lifted his head, they were both breathless.

"Could you not take me, Devin?"

Her whispered plea sent a hot charge of pure animal desire through every part of his body.

"Take you?" She could not mean what it sounded like, though his body was more than ready to oblige. Right here. Right now. Over and over again.

"Please take me." The warmth of her breath shivered over his cheek.

He traced a path over her temple and cheek with his thumb, trying desperately to rein in his raging passions and the turbulent desires of his heart.

"I need you." Her words teased his lips as he tasted the corner of her mouth.

Not half so much as I need you. The thought shuddered through him, tearing at his pride, his goals, his very image of himself as a man. For he would surely love to answer all of her needs without questioning his motives or her virtue, or what would become of either of them when the deed was done.

"I can . . ." she offered, her voice breathless and husky, her lips parted and waiting, ". . . pay you."

Pay him? Shock at her proposal sluiced through him in a barrage of white-hot ice, followed quickly by a surge of anger.

"Pay me!" He released her so quickly she lost her balance and landed on her luscious rump, grunting in surprise.

"Yes." She frowned at him, rubbing her abused posterior in long slow circles. "Would that be so awful?"

"Aye." He stood over her with arms akimbo, trying

to restrain his indignation. "Lass, have you so little care for yourself? Or respect for me?"

"How is asking you to escort me to Maine showing you a lack of respect?" She struggled to her feet and faced him, her hands on her hips. "If anything, it should be a sign of respect. Even though you are new to America, I have every faith that you would see me to my grandmother's and offer me protection in the process."

"Escort you to Maine?" he asked stupidly, as her words at last began to cut through the unrestrained lust hazing his mind.

"Yes." Confusion knit her delicate brows together. "What did you think I meant?"

Devin threw his head back and laughed, really laughed, from way down deep inside him as her meaning came fully home. The sound boomed through the barn, echoing back with a slight mocking twist from the rafters.

Relief swept him like a soothing balm—relief tinged with a shade of regret. She was not proposing wild sex and indecent knowledge or offering the sweet boon of her virtue on the pyre of his manhood. So much for the exalted binding power of the Reilly Blessing. She merely wanted an escort. She was offering him a business proposition.

"What is so terribly amusing?" She arched a brow at him and tapped her booted foot in the hay. "You yourself said I needed an escort. Unlike Marcus, you have nothing to bind you here, and I can pay you as much as you need to get you to California."

"It would seem almost the perfect solution." He smiled at her, conflicted to the core that she was not offering herself to him, but pleased just the same. Perfect solution, indeed—if they could manage it.

He'd felt The Blessing when he'd taken her in his arms on the docks that first day, figuring he was meant to help this lass. As he'd played her servant these past weeks, he'd too often wondered if he'd chosen Curse over Blessing. Now she offered to provide the means for him to continue his quest, to earn his own way toward making the riches his family, his island, needed. And her obvious need to reach her grandmother was something he could not ignore in good conscience. How could he refuse?

"Then you'll do it?" Anticipation lit her eyes.

"Aye, Maggie. I'll do it—"

"Oh, thank you." She flung her arms around him and pressed her sweet body to his once again. He could almost feel Granny Reilly's nod of satisfaction.

With a pang of regret, he reached up and loosed Maggie's hold on his neck, forcing her arms gently to her sides.

"On one condition," he stated, trying to eye her with the same sternness Quin used on him to ensure compliance. He also tried to forget his own willful response to Quin's sternness.

I'll never willingly place myself in servitude to any man, her words echoed back.

We'll see.

She wilted slightly and offered him a glance filled with suspicion. "What condition?"

"That you, Miss Margaret Sylvia Worth Brownley, listen to my instructions, agree not to run off at the will and whim of your own desires and"—he held up a hand to forestall the objections he saw rising like a tide behind those beautiful amber eyes—"do not argue with me about any of the conditions I have set forth."

She closed her mouth with an audible snap and her mutinous expression was instantly back in place. She eyed him for a long moment in rebellious silence and then blew out a quick breath.

"Agreed, Mr. Reilly." Frost mantled her tone as she

held out her hand, but her agreement was what he sought, not her contentment. He took her hand briefly to seal their pact.

"You drive a hard bargain, Devin Reilly," she told him with a speculative lift of her chin. "I only hope the frustration is worth it."

"As do I." He didn't bother to hide his amusement at her less than gracious attitude. "First order of business, we saddle up and get out of here before we awaken anyone with the ruckus we've provided." He started toward one of the stalls and then glanced back at her. "Do you think you can manage to do that, lass?"

"Aye," she answered, mimicking his speech with a saucy toss of her curls. "I think I can manage one horse."

"Good. Then manage two, Miss Brownley," he said, deciding it was best to test her resolve to listen before they left the barn. "I've a few items to pack. After losing everything so recently, I'm not moved to leave behind what few possessions I have earned here."

Denial stiffened her shoulders and held her immobile for the space of several heartbeats. Then she blew out another quick breath and settled her hands against her hips once more.

"I can manage two horses," she said, without a hint of emotion behind her words. "Is there anything else you'd like?"

Ah, there was his tart miss.

"Aye." He nodded. "Be ready when I return, Miss Maggie. I've no wish to linger within earshot of your parents any longer than we have to."

He made for the loft, praying that for the time it took to get to her grandmother he hadn't damned himself to the fourth ring of hell—doomed to suffer endless temptations in the face and form of Maggie Brownley.

Chapter Eight

Saddle two then, Miss Brownley.

The sting of Devin Reilly's arrogance hung in the musty air after he disappeared into the darkened depths of the loft. Indeed, she could and would. Did he think her completely inept?

Her hands tightened into fists as she fought the urge to scream at him. Nothing would be served by waking the entire household just to satisfy the urge to lash one insignificant male with her tongue.

Heat burned her cheeks as images of what had just transpired between them rose to taunt her. She'd already quite literally lashed him with her tongue, and the act had nothing whatsoever to do with an exhibition of anger and frustration.

She smothered a groan and turned to the task before her. Thanks to her grandmother's determination that Maggie learn whatever she expressed an interest in, she'd more than enough experience to manage saddling a couple of horses. She'd show that Devin Reilly. The need for absolute silence had made her clumsy during her earlier attempt to flee with Missy.

First, she turned up the lamp to get a better look at what she was doing. Missy eyed her with a curious whicker as Maggie gripped the saddle and launched it onto the horse's back with far more agility than before.

"Take that, Mr. Reilly." She managed to cinch the saddle into place without losing her grip. The mare huffed, a noise that sounded suspiciously like a sigh of relief.

"Don't start with me, miss." Maggie shook a finger at the mare, then stroked her nose. "It's your fault I looked so foolish in the first place. Moving like that at the last minute—who were you trying to impress?"

The mare merely twitched her ears in response.

"Just you remember, it's due to my efforts that you are still here instead of out tilling some farmer's field. Although why I continue to favor you is beyond me."

She nudged the mare's flank to indicate she was done and watched as the horse sashayed out of the way with a impudent flick of her tail.

Biting back a sigh, Maggie coaxed her other favorite out of his stall with the lumps of sugar she'd put in her pocket to keep Missy quiet earlier. The black was magnificent, darker than pitch and shiny as ice. She knew Devin favored him, too. The least she could do was to provide a mount he would enjoy riding. The thought brought her up short as she reached for the gelding's saddle.

"Devin Reilly could walk, for all I care." She tightened her lips. "Accusing me of delaying him and leaving me to saddle the horses alone after he . . . after he . . ."

She couldn't seem to put voice to what he had done. Warmth pooled low in her belly as her thoughts brought the touch of Devin's lips, of his hands, into vivid life again.

Having the weight of him against her so intimately had sent wild yearning surging through her, untamable, overwhelming need—things she'd never thought to feel for any man. All she'd wanted in the midst of that mind-boggling insanity was to stay beneath him, cradling his hard length with her body, enjoying the heady touch of his strong fingers. The crazy need to twine her legs around his hips and hold him there was something she could not explain away.

Certainly Jonathan Adams Lawrence III had not evoked the palest imitation of the feelings Devin unleashed within her. Even without the distasteful scene the other night, Jonathan's ice blue eyes and sweaty hands left her cold. What was it about the green-eyed Irishman that caused his every smile to jumble her heartbeat and spiral heat through her stomach?

"Wouldn't Papa just love to know that?" She sighed and leaned her forehead against the black's side as she finished cinching the saddle.

"To know what?" Devin's soft brogue sounded from right behind her and she jumped, startling the black, who shied nervously at her unexpected movements.

"Whoa." Devin reached for the bridle, calming the big gelding with string of soft Gaelic.

Heat rushed into Maggie's cheeks. Again. He'd spoken some of those same words to her in the midst of their embrace, gentling her when fire had raced through her veins.

"You've a bit of a problem with horses." His state   t held just enough question to smart.

Maggie straightened. "No, I have no problem with horses at all. I have saddled *both* of them, just as you requested."

He nodded, ignoring her and proceeding to check the saddles and cinchings. His fingers moved thoroughly over saddle and harness, deftly checking for weak spots or looseness. She found her gaze riveted on his hands, his long fingers and the way they moved over the leather—touching, prodding, testing.

She bit back a sigh and forced her gaze away. Just watching his hands could drive her crazy. With an effort, she clung to her irritation, folding her arms beneath her breasts until he'd finished his insultingly thorough inspection.

"Satisfied?" The challenge escaped before she could draw it back. His gaze shot to hers with a speed that took her breath. Within those dark green confines brewed a variety of emotions. Satisfaction was not one of them.

"You did fine, lass." His gaze traveled her length again and he offered her a frown. "Do you not plan to change into something more suitable for travel?"

"No." She lifted her chin, waiting for him to tell her she was not appropriately dressed. She'd had more than enough of being appropriate her whole life long. What she chose to wear was her business. He was her escort, not her governess. "This outfit is far more comfortable for riding astride. It would take us twice as long if I were forced to go to Grandmother Worth's riding sidesaddle."

He quirked an eyebrow, but held his peace as his gaze slid to her breeches. Despite her determination to be daring and unconcerned with conventions, a blush burned across her cheeks at his speculative perusal.

"I do have other clothing in my pack," she relented enough to tell him. "I will change before we reach my grandmother's."

"What have you told your family?"

The question took her off guard. "About what?"

"Your leaving, lass." His tone held the exaggerated patience used with a small child. "We're heading to

Maine practically on the eve of your betrothal. It will surely be the first place they look for you.''

''Oh.'' She bit her lip, wishing for just a moment she could hold her explanation back on pure childish stubbornness. She blew out an impatient breath, feeling out of sorts and far too unsettled by his green Irish eyes.

''I've sent a message they'll receive first thing in the morning, telling them Tori's aunt in Rhode Island is ill. I have gone with her on visits before. Though Mama and Papa will be irritated with me, they will not publicly object, because Tori is the rector's daughter. The story will buy me enough time to reach Somerset. I'll send them a letter once I am there.''

Devin held her gaze for a long moment before finally offering a slow nod. He lifted a brow at her. ''Is Tori's aunt truly ill?''

''No.'' Maggie shook her head and forced herself to return his gaze without flinching. ''But Tori left on the afternoon train for a long overdue visit, so she will not be here and there will be no one to realize I am not with her until I am far enough away for it not to matter.''

''Oh, I'm certain it will matter.'' Devin offered the observation in a quiet tone she had to strain to hear. His dark green gaze held hers for a long moment.

Devin moved nearer until he stood but a breath away, close but not quite touching, as his gaze roved her face and wrought pure havoc in her stomach. ''It is not an easy journey you're contemplating. Not a ride in the park. You'll not have a comfortable carriage, but days bouncing on hard leather.''

In the shadowed glow of the lamp, his eyes looked far harder than weathered leather, as hard as the traveling he described. Her heart pounded as the realities of the journey, of a journey with this man, loomed.

''And we won't be able to risk staying in the cozy inns

you usually visit on the way,'' he continued, ''in case they tumble to your scheme before you anticipate. We will want to travel away from your expected route.''

Was he having second thoughts about escorting her and trying to scare her out of the trip? ''I am prepared for a rough journey. Didn't you tell me when you first arrived that if the goal was big enough, or the choices few enough, it was worth the risk of a little personal discomfort?''

''And what of afterward? A week or a month from now? Are you prepared for the discomfort or censure of all who know you? A lifetime of dealing with the scandal of running away?''

She knew all that she risked. All she had to lose. In the eyes of Boston society, in her parents' view, she would lose everything—her reputation, her opportunity to marry well, her chance at the life they coveted for her. But not the life she craved for herself.

''I am not running away from anything. I am running to the life of my choosing. My grandmother is worth everything to me.''

''You can fool many people in life, Margaret Brownley, but you should never try to fool yourself.'' He held her gaze for a moment that seemed to reach deep inside her and leave her raw with the honesty he demanded of her. That he wanted her to demand from herself.

Truth be told, she welcomed the opportunity to dash all the expectations, to remove herself from a place, from a life she had struggled to belong to, but had never fit. How was that for honesty? It was a relief to know she could never be Mrs. Jonathan Adams Lawrence III after this.

None of this was Devin's concern. All he need do was deliver her to Somerset and be on his own way to the life of his choosing. That thought left her feeling oddly cold and hollow. ''I am worried about Grandmother. She waited for weeks before writing, and her physician confirms she is not recovering to his liking.''

''We'd best get going, then.'' He turned away, leaving a gaping hole of anticipation in her middle. He placed a small satchel behind the black's saddle and doused the lamp before swinging up onto the gelding's back in one smooth movement.

Maggie hurried to snag her mare's reins and settle her own pack. She drew the horse to an upturned bucket, planning to use it as help in gaining the saddle. Never having ridden in trousers before, she feared she would not reach the horse's back with the same agility Devin had just displayed. And she wasn't about to tell him she'd never ridden any other way than sidesaddle.

''Now hold still.'' She begged the mare in a low whisper, before stepping up onto the bucket. She raised on her tiptoes and put one foot in the stirrup. Then the mare flicked her tail and did her little sashay sidestep, moving just enough to make Maggie lose her balance and land in an ignominious heap on the ground. A grunt of pain escaped her. She already felt pummeled and bruised. Riding at all was going to be an interesting experience, to say the least.

Devin Reilly's chuckle chafed her as embarrassment warred with fury over his nerve to laugh at her. A scuff from his boots notified her he'd dismounted.

''Here, lass.'' Devin slid his hands beneath her arms and scooped her easily to her feet.

Her breathing quickened as she stood before him, once again much too close. The rapid rhythm of her heart underscored her reaction. How could she feel these wild and wayward things for him when he aggravated her at every turn? And how could she have thought taking him with her as an escort would be a good idea—being alone, unchaperoned in the woods with a man who made her very skin burn and her thoughts churn with images no member of the Daughters of Grace should entertain?

She swallowed as his intent gaze brushed her lips and again stirred wild longing within her.

"Thank you, I can manage." Her voice came breathless and soft, far from the prim command she strove for.

"Are you sure?" A lazy half smile curved his mouth.

She realized with a bit of shock that he still held her. His hands rested beneath her arms, the pads of his thumbs almost grazing the undersides of her breasts through her jacket. Heat shot straight through her belly and lower still, making it difficult to breathe, let alone think. She had to put distance between them before she swooned right here in her father's stables or lost every shred of decency she possessed.

"Yes." She pulled away from him and struggled for control of her body's wayward responses. "I am quite sure. Thank you. Shall we go?"

"Aye, but let's see you properly seated first."

She turned from him, trying desperately to ignore his presence behind her as she corralled the reins once more. The mare shifted. "Honestly, Missy, have you no sense of decorum? You really must learn to behave more prettily."

Shades of a hundred such lectures Alberta Brownley had pealed over her wayward daughter's head.

Devin clucked his tongue. "Do you always speak to your horse like that?"

"Yes." She peered at him over her shoulder as she twisted her hair into a knot and jammed her hat down over the unruly mass.

"It is no wonder she reacts as she does." Devin brushed a gentle hand over the mare's nose. "There, lassie. I know she's a trial, but we've got to take care of her as best we can."

Maggie could have sworn the mare batted her eyes like the worst coquette.

Devin lifted a brow toward her. "Well?"

"I—" Maggie bit her lip. "I need the bucket."

"Nay, you don't. Hold still."

She complied.

"Good lass." He spoke softly, although she could not be sure if he complimented her or Missy. His breath warmed the back of Maggie's neck for a long moment, and then his hands gripped her waist. His long fingers slid over her stomach as he lifted her off the ground.

"There you go."

She grabbed for the pommel and positioned her foot in the stirrup. Heat burned pure fire in her cheeks as his hands slid downward with her movements, briefly cupping her buttocks, bracing her until she'd fully gained the saddle. She forced herself to look down at him, trying not to dwell on the way his hands felt against her and the way each finger seemed branded into the skin under her breeches.

"Thank you," she offered, securing her primmest tone with an effort.

"My pleasure." He expression was shuttered, though the warmth in his tone made her wonder if he knew all the strange and untoward feelings he let loose in her. With an effort, she ignored him as he turned away, mounted the black, and clicked his tongue.

Within moments they were outside in a night filled with moonlight and stars and cool summer air. As her mare fell into easy step behind the black, the tension and worry she'd been harboring since her grandmother's note arrived loosened just the tiniest bit. They rode slowly down the tree-lined drive and left her family's estate behind.

Maggie's loyalties twisted inside her, pulling guilt no

matter what her decision. Going so boldly against her parents' wishes could not be taken back.

She shuddered at the certainty that venturing off on a journey to Maine with the Irish coachman she'd brought into their household such a short time ago was something neither her mother nor her father would ever understand— or forgive. But she refused to give in to despair. Her parents might lose their hopes for her, but they would still have Nora. Lenore would be more than happy to step into Maggie's sullied shoes.

Sighing, Maggie focused her gaze on Devin's easy command of the black as she tried to turn her distracted thoughts forward, away from her worries and onto the mill and how she could best help her grandmother when she arrived.

Maggie's gaze seemed to burn a hole into Devin's back every step of the way down the Brownley's tree-lined drive. He found a small measure of satisfaction in her scarcely hidden frustration. Without hesitation, she had completely remapped his life for him from the moment he'd set foot on the docks in Boston Harbor. He couldn't help thinking back over the events of this last hour and wondering how he'd managed to go from temporary coachman to escort and guardian in such a small span of time.

Though he'd not been in America long, he knew enough of the geography to know this journey to Maine was in direct opposition to the course he needed to travel to California. Each mile would put more and more distance between him and the goals he had set for himself—goals he needed to meet, goals his family needed met as quickly as possible.

He knew in his bones he should not have capitulated to her wiles. Yet when he held her in his arms, wracked with the thundering of The Blessing and the desires she drew from him so easily, he could not have denied her request any more than he could have refused to draw his next breath. Why did his fate seem bound to Maggie's? Or was he allowing lust's rampage to fool him into believing his Granny's long-forgotten tales?

The horses' hooves clattered softly on the silent streets. The moon began its downward slide to dawn behind the buildings they passed. Each dark echo mocked the impulse that had prevented him from scooping her up and depositing her on her parents' doorstep.

Blessing indeed. Cursed by a woman's ruses as surely as poor Seamus, more like. Who was to know if he'd chosen the right course?

Reillys take heed and Reillys beware, for unto ye is delivered a great gift. A token of esteem, a promise, a fearsome gratitude. The ancient words spoke to him from across the ages and the whole ocean that separated him from his home. *Only ye can direct the course to joy or sorrow. Only ye decide if it is Blessing or Curse.*

His destiny was his own to make, like Cuchulainn and the Fians of old. Ancient battles clashed once more through his memories. The stories of great deeds and mighty struggles he'd loved to hear his granny tell dared him to match his pitiful concerns over being led by a lass's whims. She was but a means to an end, the destiny of his choosing. He'd take her to Maine and be on his way to California. That was all there'd be to it.

The choice, once made, cannot be undone.

He released a sigh that bordered on a groan and the black flicked his ears.

"Whoa." Devin blinked and shook his head, calling a halt as much to the horse beneath him as the thoughts running rampant through his head. With a slight sense of shock, he realized they had long since left Brookline behind. They now skirted the edges of the Charles River and would soon leave the city entirely.

"Amazing." He'd been so lost in his thoughts, he'd not noticed their route or the passing streets. Nothing had registered. Some escort. Any footpad or patrol could have waylaid them with him so unaware. It was a sobering realization.

"Yes, it is a lovely view." Maggie joined him, gazing back toward the lights of Charlestown and Boston proper beyond, a slight wistfulness in her tone. "Deceptive in its sleep."

Moonlight highlighted the curve of her cheek and the delicate line of her jaw, so stubborn and so soft all at once.

"Aye." His answer came low and seemed to pulse with the longings she unleashed inside him, longings he knew better than to indulge no matter how enticingly or freely offered. No woman's passing fancy was worth setting aside his life's goals and aspirations. He'd come to America for gold, nothing more and nothing less.

Maggie glanced at him, her eyes a glittering sheen in the waning moonlight.

Heat stung his cheeks and he bit back a curse, thankful the night hid the color burning his skin. He couldn't so much as have a conversation with the girl without losing his train of thought. Now he would be escorting her alone for days to come. What had he been thinking? How and why did he continue to embroil himself in her life and her troubles?

"Are you sure you want to do this?" he managed in an even tone. He'd tried to get her to face things more subtly in the barn. Now he might as well make her face things head-on before it was too late.

"Yes." No pause for thought. She had made her decision long before she ever reached the barn.

"Your future with Larry will be jeopardized, probably beyond repair."

He could almost feel her bristling.

"His name is Jonathan." She blew out a quick breath. "It doesn't really matter what I jeopardize. I never intended to marry, him or anyone. I've told you that before."

She was quiet and he waited, watching her as her gaze drifted over the tangled streets of Boston. He had never considered his sister spoiled, yet he could not picture his own parents ever treating Meaghan's wishes with such deliberate disregard as the Brownleys treated Maggie's.

"Although my interests seem of little consequence to my parents at the moment, I hope someday they are able to understand why I am doing what I am doing." She glanced back at him, her features shadowed and her tone touched with honest regret. "But I don't really expect them to. I'm as different from the rest of my family as milk from brandy." Loss echoed through her words. She sighed and closed her eyes. "Sometimes my mama and Nora say the same words at the same time in the same tone."

"Aye." Devin hid his smile. It was something he'd experienced on more than one occasion. "I've noticed that."

"Yet I am almost always at a loss as to why they want what they want." Her gaze focused on him once more. "Have you ever felt that way with your family?"

"Nay, lass." An easy denial hiding the truth about the distance he'd too often felt within his own family. He'd always understood his brothers' love of the sea. Quin was born to command a vessel and though Bryan was now a solicitor, Devin could still see the longing, the love that surged through his brother whenever he was aboard a ship.

He carried no such illusions himself. Pride in the ship-yard and the long history of success the Reillys enjoyed did not translate into the desire or the ability to race the wind. Doubts twisted inside him.

"I may not be a good seaman, but I'm Reilly born and Reilly bred, the same as Quin and Bryan. The shipyard has been in my family for generations." That sounded certain, but where was the honesty he'd demanded of her?

She frowned at him, her brows a thin tight line across her forehead. "But if you do not yearn for the sea and love ships, how can you possibly understand what drives them?"

"Perhaps I don't need to fully understand and experience their love and their longing in order to care." He clipped the words off, struggling against an unexpected surge of pain.

With her innocent questions and her struggle to understand herself, she rubbed raw all his own doubts. "Unless it is your plan to wait here on the hillside for your parents to discover us and drag you back home, I don't really think we've the luxury of time needed for discussing the finer points of life."

Her spine stiffened and her chin rose in surprise. He had, after all, invited the conversation, even encouraged it, if only to ascertain she knew her mind.

"Which way will lead us toward your grandmother's, Miss Brownley?"

"North." Clipped and precise.

He lifted a brow.

"Through the trees." She pointed off in the distant blackness.

He followed the line of her finger and frowned. "Perhaps it would be best for you to take the lead."

"Very well." She pulled out in front of him, coaxing a trot from her mount.

He and the black fell into step behind them. Watching the rhythmic bouncing of Maggie's enticing bottom against the saddle made his mouth go dry.

With a muffled groan Devin resolved to get her out of her boyish garb and into something more suitable as soon as possible. There was only so much torment and teasing a man could take. He was already more than familiar with the desires Maggie Brownley could let loose inside him at a moment's notice. He had no intention of spending days subjecting himself to further torture.

He nudged the black to a faster pace as Maggie leaned forward and the mare picked up speed. He gritted his teeth and blessed the clouds gathering in sky above them that scattered patches of darkness through what was left of the moonlight.

With any luck they would gain the shadows of the trees before the arch of Maggie's back and the impudent curves of her body could torment him in full daylight.

His groin tightened at the thought.

Blessing or Curse? He was quite sure he knew the answer.

Chapter Nine

"Stand back."

Maggie's words shot through the trees despite the distance still separating them. Devin couldn't see her, but she sounded deadly serious. He reigned in the gelding and slid from its back.

His hackles rose as a man's gruff tones replied to Maggie's threat.

Diabhal. What on earth was she involved in? He dropped the satchel of food he'd just purchased and advanced cautiously toward the spot where he'd left Maggie with strict orders to rest and keep out of sight.

"Believe me, I know how to use this." The very stalwartness of her challenge increased Devin's disquiet. He quickened his pace. He shouldn't have left her alone.

Swiftly and silently, he advanced through the rain-damp undergrowth, grateful the early morning's deluge kept the leaves from crackling beneath his steps and giving away his approach.

Pistol cocked and held in a tight grip, Maggie stood in the small clearing just ahead with the weapon leveled steadily at a surly ruffian. She certainly looked as if she knew full well how to use the gun she held in her white-knuckled grip.

Missy whickered nervously on one side of the small open space, and Maggie's pack had been taken off the mare's back. The items it contained were strewn across the ground. How had the scraggily bearded fellow had the opportunity to rifle Maggie's belongings so thoroughly and not find the pistol? Had she been harmed in the process?

Apparently not, he concluded after a cursory inspection. Her hair was loose around her shoulders and she had taken off her jacket, but her shirt and breeches did not bear evidence of a struggle. Praise God.

Afraid he would distract Maggie's aim and allow the blackguard to rush her if he entered the clearing from the wrong angle, Devin began a cautious circle through the underbrush. He kept his gaze fixed on the pair, only daring a few glances down to make certain his steps did not herald his arrival before he was ready.

"I was only lookin' fer a little fun," the scurvy snarled through his unkempt beard. "Any woman what fills breeches tight as you is bound ta be good sport."

The slightest of shudders shook Maggie's slim shoulders. "I'm not interested in your brand of sport," she declared, lifting her chin. She held the pistol an inch higher as the man moved a step closer.

The man narrowed his eyes. He appeared to think better of advancing and halted again.

"Ya never knows until ya gives it a try." The man offered a lecherous wink followed by a toothy grin. He sidled closer to Maggie, apparently having come to the conclusion that she wouldn't shoot him just for being *friendly*.

"I don't care to 'give it a try,' thank you." A tiny quiver of fear touched Maggie's voice. She leveled her weight and clutched the pistol in both hands, as though such a stance underlined her determination to use it. "Stand back, I say."

Her breeches drew much too snug across her rounded bottom. Devin's mouth went dry. He swallowed and forced his gaze away. It was little wonder the drifter thought Maggie fair game for his advances. At least the ruffian couldn't see her from this angle. She looked even more tempting in the light of day than Devin had feared when he had forbade her to accompany him to the small village they had skirted just after dawn. He'd known that outfit was more invitation than disguise and should have insisted she change. Another failure to lay at his feet. Quin's damning assessment of his readiness to be a leader struck home anew.

"Ya look far better'n anythin' I've seen in quite a while, Miss." The man practically drooled as he let his gaze sweep over Maggie. "I just couldn't pass ya by without a try once I spotted ya down by the stream."

Her knuckles grew tighter on the pistol grip. "I shot a man with this once. And I *liked* him. Don't think I won't shoot you."

While the drifter paused to evaluate the depth of Maggie's threat, Devin moved to a position behind him. He prepared to leap out should the man sidle any closer to his quarry and prayed his sudden appearance wouldn't spook Maggie into shooting her sworn protector instead of her attacker.

The combined fragrances of ginger and chamomile drifted toward Devin on a light breeze, overriding the scrawny drifter's ponderous aroma. No doubt she smelled far better than anything the other man had been close to in a while, but the scent stabbed clean through Devin as he tensed for action.

When the scurvy darted toward Maggie, Devin launched himself out of the bushes. He grabbed the man's shoulders, bringing them both down to the ground at her feet with a thud. Maggie screamed. Devin subdued the protesting drifter, holding the man's arms tight behind his back.

"Surely you don't intend to shoot us both, lass?" Devin lifted an eyebrow at her as he straightened atop his protesting captive and found himself eye to eye with the barrel of her gun.

Color washed out of her cheeks as she relaxed her wrist and turned the pistol downward. "Of course not. You surprised me."

"From the look of things, it would seem I'm not the only one. Did I not tell you stay put, darlin', just before I left?" Devin shot her a level glance and tightened his grip still further on the squirming man.

He didn't like the whiteness of her lips or the trembling of her fingers. A good healthy dose of anger would cure her immediate fright, at least long enough to get this situation under complete control. "If you cannot stick by your word—"

"I only went down to the stream to wash," she protested.

He examined her closely. Her shirt gaped open at the top button, showing the swelling of her breasts. The snug fit of her breeches would tempt most saints. Exactly the reason he'd insisted she could not accompany him into town to buy their day's food. The sooner he got her into long petticoats and circumspect skirts, the better. Still, the man did not appear to have laid a hand on her. She might be shaken by this encounter, but she was unharmed.

He pressed his point home. "Now you see the reason I told you to remain out of sight. If you cannot hold to your word to obey my orders, I'll escort you straight back to Brookline."

As he'd intended, anger seared away most of the fear in her eyes and straightened her shoulders. "I hardly think going a dozen paces to a stream violates our contract. I stayed put, just as you commanded."

The man he held firmly beneath him mumbled something into the grass. Devin increased the pressure of his grip and the man grew silent. "Not quite as I commanded, else you'd not have brought yourself to our friend's attention."

She gripped the pistol tighter and balled her other hand into a fist, but held her tongue. The argument she obviously longed to pursue sparkled in her gaze, completely replacing her fright.

"I'm pleased you at least remember the other portion of our bargain." He nodded and clamped his hand on the fellow's neck. "If this has taught you the wisdom of the first part, we may yet proceed with our journey once one or two petty details are dealt with."

"I placed myself in your care when we began. I believe I will not need a second demonstration." The quiet admission carried a hint of steel as she looked at the clothes-strewn clearing.

"Let us see if you have learned your lesson indeed, darlin'. I want you to pick up just one of those outfits right now and then go and find my horse." He nodded in the direction he'd first approached the clearing. "Take Missy with you and mind you tether them both tight. The black is on his own at the moment."

"What will we do with . . ." She looked down at her would-be swain, taking in his unkempt hair and dirty clothing. Her hand started to shake again.

"First things first, lass. You give me the pistol and go see to the horses."

The enormity of what had almost happened between her and this man shimmered in the gaze she locked with Devin's. He longed to pound the other man into the dust for what he'd intended to do. He yearned to gather her into his arms and let her cry out her fright. He could do neither at the moment.

"Now, Maggie." She needed him to be firm.

Handing him the gun, she turned on her boot heel. She bent down and hastily grabbed a swatch of green from the ground before untying her horse. She favored Devin with a look that cut through him, then chewed her lip and disappeared into the trees in the direction he'd indicated, leaving the two men to stare after her as her breeches displayed her firm bottom and the enticing sway of her hips.

"You'll turn your head, buck-o, or I'll twist it right off your neck," Devin growled, managing to restrain himself with an effort. "That lass is a lady born and bred. You're not fit for the likes of her, my friend." He leaned his elbow into the other man's back for emphasis, receiving obedience and a muffled grunt for his efforts.

"She don't look like no lady," the man grumbled into the dirt. He spit leaves and cursed when Devin didn't let up the pressure of his elbow. "All right, I won't look at 'er."

Devin waited until he was certain she was out of sight. "I should turn you over to the nearest constable, but I really haven't the time to deal with this properly."

After checking the man thoroughly for signs of a concealed weapon, he hauled the man up by his collar to a sitting position.

"On the run, are ya?" the scurvy cackled. "I imagine

her family thinks a sod like you's not fit fer the likes of her neither, her being a *lady* and all—''

''Perhaps I should just shoot you and be done with it,'' Devin threatened. There was more to this drifter than could be supposed from his appearance. The last thing they needed was to be embroiled in a situation with the local authorities. Too many questions, too many lies. Still, he had to do something with the fellow, at least until they were well on their way.

Maggie's scream and the squall of a frightened horse precluded any further consideration. Now what had she gotten herself into? As Devin turned toward the sound, the drifter gave a grunt of laughter and took off into the woods. For an instant Devin considered his chances of getting a clean shot off. Then he discarded the idea and raced through the trees toward Maggie.

He stopped when he reached the place he'd left the gelding. Maggie was there seeming whole, but with her back turned. She spun around to face him, tears streaking her cheeks. ''It was a rabbit. Just a rabbit.''

He held out his arms and she ran into them, burying her face in his shoulder. ''It jumped out of the bushes. Both horses ran away.''

She sobbed as he stroked her back and let her soak the front of his shirt. ''It is all right, lass. I see them both munching on a bit of sweet grass over yonder. There's nothing wrong that can't be set to rights.''

''I thought I could be strong, live up to my grandmother's expectations. Yet here I am crying over a rabbit.''

Devin smiled into her hair as she hiccuped. She was crying over far more than a wee rabbit, but now didn't seem the time to point that out to her. Slowly the shaking in her frame subsided and she took a long breath.

He pulled back enough to cup her face in his hands. ''You're overtired and you've had a fright. Two frights,

in fact. We'll go get the horses, then gather the rest of
your things. Once you've changed and eaten, we can
resume our travels.''

"What of that dreadful man?" Another shudder racked
her as she looked over his shoulder toward the clearing.

"Long gone and not likely to mention to anyone how
a mere slip of a girl got the drop on him," Devin smiled.
He could only hope that was true.

He dropped his hands to his sides as the scent of her,
skin-warmed ginger and chamomile, threatened to over-
whelm his other concerns. By all rights, he should escort
her home to her parents at once, before anything worse
happened. But he knew he could not.

Her shoulders relaxed as she mulled his statement over.
She turned her head to look at the horses, grazing side
by side. "Very well. I'm sure you're right."

She turned back to look at him. Her eyes flashed stubborn determination. "But I do not think it necessary for
me to change. I shall put my jacket on and wear my cap.
As long as we stick to the back roads, no one else should
notice me."

Devin's gaze shifted downward. The trousers she wore
caressed and highlighted each tender curve of her body—
her waist, her hips, her bottom, and the lithe line of her
legs. He could only too well remember the feel of her
against him in the stables last night.

"You're hardly a convincing man, Miss Brownley."

"Why not?"

She was serious.

He stepped back and deliberately ran his gaze over the
tempting picture she presented. It was the most exquisite
form of torture, to be sure. Desire leaped inside him. He
kept his perusal slow and thorough enough to be painful
to himself and embarrassing for her.

When his gaze at last met hers, whatever truth showed

on his face was enough to widen her eyes and bring another flush of color to her cheeks.

"I don't see any cause for you to be rude." She turned her back to him and strode toward the horses, presenting him again with that lovely view. "I was doing just fine taking care of myself before you arrived," she tossed over her shoulder.

Though relieved at the resurgence of her spirit, he could not let her statement go unchallenged. "You never released the firing pin." He raised his voice. "If I had not arrived when I did, you might even now be finding out exactly how much fun your friend really had in mind."

She turned back to face him. The shocked look on her face brought home to Devin the near shout he had ended his tirade on. Hell, he sounded like Da, or even Quin, on a tear. It was not in his nature to raise his voice to anyone. Devin took a deep breath and closed his eyes to try and gather the tattered shreds of his common sense.

"If you've decided your role in our journey together is to lecture me in place of my papa and mama, I can continue on by myself." Maggie's tart challenge forced his eyes open again. Her pale brows arched over her smoked amber gaze, questioning him with more than a touch of impatience.

"It was not my intention to rail at you as your parents are wont to do." Lord knew the way he thought of her could not remotely be confused with familial. He raked a hand through his hair, wishing he could bring a little order to the chaos she generated so easily inside him. The sight of her in danger had wrought all manner of havoc in his middle.

Her gaze narrowed and Devin forced himself onward, determined to deliver his decree before she could begin the inevitable argument.

"*I*"—he stressed the word with a wag of his finger—

"take my responsibilities and my oaths a bit more seriously than you do. I am not about to send one lone girl into the wilds alone."

She took a step toward him. "I am far more capable than you give me credit for."

"So you keep telling me." He met her step with one of his own, while lacing just enough sarcasm into his tone to arc a flush over her cheeks.

"And that is supposed to mean?" She lifted her chin and held his gaze.

"You've yet to prove your abilities, Miss Brownley."

Her color deepened still further. "How dare you speak to me like that?"

"I dare," he told her, forcing her to slowly retreat as he continued to close the distance between them, "because you *asked* for my help and brought me here this day. And it was helping you on the docks that caused the delay in my plans which allowed this whole drama to begin."

"I never intended to delay you—" She bit her lip, cutting her sentence short as she backed against a tree.

"Just as it was never my intention to stay." Everything in him burned at this close proximity to the one girl who could tear him away from his chosen course, make him do any manner of things against all reasonable expectations. The lass had torn him apart at first meeting while The Blessing echoed within him, undeniable and unshakable.

"Devin, I—"

"Nay." He put a finger over her lips. Their soft texture near undid him, and he gritted his teeth together to hold back a moan of desire. Ginger and chamomile, fresh and skin-warmed, teased him as he looked at her. "I dare because you placed yourself in my care. If we're to continue our bargain, you must change into more suitable apparel.''

"It is far easier to ride without the long skirts, and I will draw less attention." Her denial held breathless doubt for the first time.

"Nay, Miss Margaret Sylvia Worth Brownley. You will surely draw more of the same attention we just finished fending off." He cupped her chin, splaying his fingers over the soft warmth of her throat.

He covered her lips with his own, suddenly glad of the anchoring tree behind her as wild winds whipped through his soul and threatened to tear the moorings loose on his heart.

The Blessing.

No matter how hard he tried to convince himself otherwise, she was his. The thought surged through him in bolt after bolt of turbulent lightning. Tasting the sweet depths of her mouth as his tongue slid against hers only served to heighten and refine the yearning thundering through his blood.

Madness. Pure madness.

Now was not the time or place for this. Would there ever be a time? Certainty pulsed in opposite directions inside him. There had to be. There could never be.

He pulled away from her, watching in slow, tortured silence as her eyelids flickered open. Her shining gaze mirrored his own desires. Did she have any idea what she revealed or what that revelation did to him? He fisted his hands at his sides to keep from reaching for her again, and he struggled to find his voice.

"That, my dear Miss Brownley, should be clear evidence that your disguise does you no benefit and only serves to draw the very notice you seek to avoid."

Fine words, ruined only by the rough passion underlying

them. He bit back a groan, knowing it would further undermine his already depleted restraint.

Pink flowed over her cheeks as the glow in her eyes changed to a sparkle of indignation. Far easier on a man.

"Is that the only reason you—" She blew out a quick breath and closed her mouth with a snap, as though refusing to voice the rest of her question. The pink in her cheeks deepened still further.

"Nay, Maggie." He could have bitten his tongue off for answering her, but he didn't seem able to hold the information back. "I kissed you because I wanted to. I think you already know that."

The blaze of color in her cheeks was not lessened by his answer. She turned away from him, sweeping her curls over her shoulders. He fought the urge to draw her back into his arms and kiss her until she harbored no doubts about his reasons.

"Will you keep your end of our bargain, Maggie, and obey me in this?"

Devin's tone made Maggie grit her teeth together. How could she enjoy his touch so and remain so thoroughly aggravated by him at the same time?

"Yes."

She hated letting Devin know how right he'd been to question her attire from the outset of their travel. Despite herself, she might welcome the attentions Devin paid her, but the thought of garnering more leering regards from the type of man she'd caught rifling her bag earlier made her stomach churn. Wearing anything the dirty drifter had touched made her skin crawl.

She scooped up the riding outfit she'd rescued from the heap in the clearing and then dropped when the rabbit had surprised her. "Let's get the horses, then. And go back for my pack"—she spun back to face him—"oh, Devin—"

Concern laced his green gaze and he tensed, alert for trouble. "What is it?"

"My money pouch was still in my bag. What if that horrid man has found it?"

He swallowed hard. "If he has, he'll be long gone. If he's still lurking about, we'd best keep the horses and our wits about us."

He reached down and picked up a satchel from the ground. "If we're careful, this food can last us for two days. And I've a few coins left from my purchases, too. The loss of your money is a minor thing at this point."

Taking her by the elbow, Devin hurried to the horses and led them back to the clearing. Maggie berated herself for not having thought of her small store of money when she'd first discovered the man going through her bag. All she'd been grateful for was the impulse that had made her take the pistol with her when she'd gone down to the stream.

The least she could have done is remembered once Devin had the man subdued. Stupid, just plain stupid. Why had she ever thought she'd be capable of making this trip on her own?

Sure enough, they returned to the clearing to find the money missing, along with the rest of her clothing. What that filthy scavenger intended to do with those items she refused to contemplate.

"Change quickly, lass. Time is not our friend. There's no use fretting over what you've lost." The crooked smile Devin gave her with his advice revealed a small dimple in his cheek that sent lazy spirals of heat through her. "I learned that only recently myself."

After Devin checked to make sure the man was truly gone, she ducked behind a bush and hastily complied. "What do you mean, time is not our friend?" she asked as she slid her petticoat over her head after pulling off her breeches and boots.

"Your story of going to Providence with your friend will not serve you long. Your parents will know immediately where you have gone. Trust me. I've tried this before."

"Tried what?"

"Running away."

"Will you tell me about it?" She buttoned her riding skirt into place. The deep green of the serged wool reminded her of Devin's eyes.

"Aye. Once we are on our way."

She slipped on her jacket and tied her hair with a ribbon before stepping back into her boots.

"Devin."

"Aye?"

She stepped back into the clearing to face him. "I'm sorry about . . . the docks . . . about forcing you to stay and help protect Marcus." Heat crept over her cheeks.

His narrowed gaze roved her face in silence.

Then he cupped her face in his hands and stroked his fingers over her hot cheek. She couldn't hold back a shiver at his touch. Her breath caught in her throat as his hands slid upward. His fingers threaded through her hair and cupped the back of her scalp. Thrills shot through her from his fingertips and jangled along her nerve endings.

His lips were much too close to hers.

"I'm not. This is the path of my choosing," he said in a low growl, cut off by the hot, sweet melding of their mouths.

He arched her against him, deepening the kiss. Where before her blood had sparkled through her veins like summer sun shimmering across the waters in Boston harbor, now there was a melting wantonness throbbing through every part of her body, making her limbs heavy.

Abruptly he released her, taking her hands to steady her while she regained her breath. "We'd best get going if we're to accomplish anything this day."

The warmth was gone from Devin's tone, as though the fiery passion in his kiss had all been in her mind and not nearly so overwhelming to him as it was to her.

"Yes." She bit back a second apology that hovered behind her lips. What was she sorry for now? That he had kissed her? That she'd wanted him to?

If this break with her parents held true and she won her right to pursue the life she intended, she'd never again have the opportunity to experience the passion she'd discovered in Devin's arms, to enjoy a man's kisses without fear of stirring a deeper pot and placing herself, her heart, at risk. Devin was just passing through on his own journey. His path and hers would coincide for only a few days more. Then he would be off in search of his own destiny.

She gathered her skirts and tried not to pay attention to his hands as he helped her up onto Missy's saddle. No use. His fingers still seemed to burn into her flesh. She would savor this time—these feelings—while she could, unencumbered by thoughts of the future.

"Tell me your running away story," she reminded him as they crossed onto the road and headed northeast. She knew very little of his life before they met, and she very much wanted to know about him and his family.

"I was much younger than you. My brothers and I were playing Viking raiders." He chuckled, a rich sound that rumbled through her. "I got tired of being the lowly shepherd as they took turns playing the valiant Fian defenders—"

"You mentioned Fians before. What are they?"

"One tale at a time, lass. Warrior defenders of our land will do for now. In any event, while Quin and Bryan argued whose turn it was to defend my flock and me, I decided to show them I didn't need them and struck off on my own.''

He reached into their food satchel and brought out a roll, which he broke in half. He offered a piece to her. ''Eat this. We'd be best served to go as far as possible before dark.''

The bread was soft and fresh and tasted better than any she'd ever eaten before. Must be all the excitement combined with the fresh air.

She loved the rich timbre that threaded through Devin's voice as he spoke and the softness speaking of his home and brothers brought to his face. ''Please go on.''

''I got a little turned about and ended up farther from home than I realized, in a part of our island I was not familiar with. I could hear the boys calling to me, but couldn't see them. We circled the trees and hills for hours without finding one another.''

He must have been very frightened, lost and alone, but would most likely not appreciate her expressing concern for the boy he'd been at the time. Perhaps that helped explain his insistence she not travel alone—that and the honesty of his assessment that she was not ready to handle all travel problems on her own.

''How did you find your way home?''

''Finally I just got so tired I sat down under a tree and fell asleep.'' His eyes focused on the distance, obviously seeing another time, another place. ''When they found me, Quin refused to speak to me. He just picked me up and carried me home. Bryan berated me enough for the two of them, though. They'd almost missed me in the dark.''

A rueful smile touched his lips. ''He told me if it ever happened again, I was to find the highest spot I could and wait there.''

"Your parents must have been very worried." Her parents would have punished her for weeks.

"Aye." He nodded. "But the boys shouldered all the blame. They were very good at protecting me, especially from myself."

The twist in his tone spoke volumes, giving her insight into his drive to gain his fortune, to be the one to solve his family's business problems. They were both seeking independence.

"That is why you are so determined to succeed here, isn't it?" she asked, certain she was right. "Because you do not have them to protect you?"

"Aye." he nodded. He looked at her with a directness that stole her breath even as he exhaled slowly.

He quirked up one eyebrow. "I do believe it is your turn, Miss Brownley."

"My turn?"

"Did you not claim to have shot a man? I'd like to know if he was still standing or if he's breathed his last."

She laughed. It felt good, freeing, just thinking of the shock on her summer companion's face as the smoke cleared after the pistol had discharged while he'd been showing her how to load the weapon. "Standing is all poor Jake could manage for weeks. That or lying on his stomach."

Devin favored her with a puzzled look, and she watched as the realization regarding the true nature of the injury she'd inflicted registered on his face. "You cannot mean . . ."

"Oh, yes." She smiled as Devin's laughter rang through the trees. "I shot him in the rump."

Chapter Ten

Maggie bit her lip, determined to hold back any sign of her discomfort. She didn't have the heart to voice a complaint, not after yesterday's respite had brought about their current near-penniless state of affairs.

The cold rain dripping steadily down her back had been a constant companion all day. Adding in Devin's morose silence, her worries over Grandmother Worth's health, and the hunger pangs gnawing at her stomach, she had a monstrous headache. She longed for a hot bath, a warm fire, and some rest, not to mention a real meal, but they were several days away from any of those comforts. This journey had been her choice, and she'd just have to endure.

Shadowing the main road to Portsmouth as they were, they had little choice but to press on. Devin was surely right. Once her parents saw through her sham story of an impromptu trip to Providence with Tori, they would immediately know her destination. If she could make it to Grandmother's in Somerset before them, she had a fighting chance of staying. She was of age, after all, and Grandmother needed her.

Ambitious and overbearing as her parents might be, they would surely see the wisdom of her remaining outside Boston's social circle, where she clearly did not belong, especially if she were busy looking after the mill as well as Grandmother. Papa made no secret of coveting his mother-in-law's business success. He might think he needed a son-in-law to oversee his wife's eventual inheritance, but Maggie would prove him wrong.

Her gaze strayed to Devin, hunched atop the big black gelding as they made their way forward. They had set out from their encounter with the thief companionably enough, but had soon lapsed into exhausted silence.

At nightfall, Devin had traded an hour's chopping wood for permission to sleep in a farmer's barn. The sourness of his present mood had manifested itself just before dawn when he'd shaken her awake. They'd settled down separately to sleep in the farmer's spring sweet hay. During the night, the cold had drawn them together. She'd awakened warmed by the solid strength of his shoulder, dreaming of the balsam and musk depths of Maine's woods. The lingering trace of his breath on her temple, of his lips pressed to her hair were somehow mixed into the warmth of the dreams.

Devin had frowned his displeasure over their intimate proximity, but he held his peace. Why had he not blamed her for every bit of bad luck that had befallen them over the past two days? It was certainly her father's routine course of action, one she was long used to. She'd lost count over the years of the times Papa had railed at Mama, shoving the responsibility on his wife for things that most often no one could control or that were the direct result of his own mismanagement.

Even as a child, Maggie hated being a witness to the

injustice her father heaped on her mother's shoulders, and she'd hated the cowed manner in which her mother accepted such treatment.

All men behaved in such a way toward their wives and daughters, Grandmother Worth had offered by way of cold comfort when Maggie had questioned her mother's acceptance of such treatment. Fairness, Grandmother had explained, had nothing to do with a man's perception of a situation. If things did not go exactly as he envisioned, he needed someone to blame. In a man's eyes, the nearest woman was the surest object for censure.

This childhood insight, accompanied by the success Grandmother had made of her life following her own husband's death, fueled Maggie's determination never to place herself under a husband's rule. As much as Grandmother relied on Jake's father as the mill's foreman, it was clear Grandmother was in charge.

She shook her head, regretting it as the movement directed rain-slick tendrils of hair and a sluice of water from her cap into her eyes.

"There's a river up ahead." Devin's words whipped back to her on the wind.

"What?" She raised her voice and realized the wind and rain around them had grown steadily louder over the past few minutes.

He turned back toward her. The directness of his green eyes as he fully looked at her for the first time today stole her breath. "A river. We need to cross it. It looks as if there is a place to ford not far from here."

"All right." She caught his nod before he turned away. If Grandmother's summation of the nature of men was true, then why did Devin not castigate her for all the hardships they faced? Could it be that, based on her own disaster, Grandmother was as prejudiced against men as Papa was against the Irish? The implications of such heresy for Maggie's own life would bear closer examination.

She clucked to Missy and urged the mare to a faster pace. "A river. Just what we need—to get a little bit wetter before we call it a day."

She and Missy edged up to the bank just a little bit, then slipped and slid downward after the gelding as they approached the river. The churning water raced by closer and wider than she had expected. A frisson of fear shivered over her as she reached Devin's side. The thought of actually being in the middle of the surging waters in front of them made her shudder. She was more than thankful for Devin's presence beside her as she eyed the wild river water coursing before them. It seemed to be moving in more than one direction at once.

"Are you sure we need to do this here?"

Maggie's question only served to exacerbate the raging doubts inside Devin. Sure? Hell no, he wasn't at all sure. In fact, given the opportunity, he'd run so quickly the other way he'd leave a gale force wind in his wake.

The turbulent river waters before him made his stomach churn in long slow circles. He swallowed hard, wished for a cup of Granny's ginger tea, and glanced toward Maggie. The trust written on her features made his breath hitch in his throat. She'd no idea of the fear this churning river locked into his very bones, the memories it dredged from his soul. She believed he would get them across in one piece.

Retracing their path to join with the main road would cost them at least a half day and leave them vulnerable to the very discovery that Maggie also believed him capable of protecting her from.

For a moment, he indulged himself in the memory of waking to find her in his arms this morning, soft and warm, her curls tickling his nose and the innocent seduction of her ginger and chamomile scent stirring the slumbering passion in his very depths. He'd been so tempted to kiss her, to love her right there and then, but she'd looked at him with trusting eyes. She trusted him then; she trusted him now.

"Aye." He nodded, knowing they could not afford for him to be wrong. He looked away before she could read all the doubts sure to be unveiled in his own gaze. This was the spot the farmer had described. Cross here, or lose this day doubling back.

He forced himself to face the water as it passed them, writhing and twisting like a living thing. He couldn't hold back the memories of another time, another place— seawater instead of fresh, rocks, the sound of timber cracking, Bryan's voice, and the certain knowledge that he had failed. That failure had driven a wedge through the very heart of his family.

His fault. All his fault.

He shook his head and wiped the rain out of his eyes, determined to cross the river and put it all behind him. There was no use letting his memories get the best of him. What was done was done.

The knowin' is one thing, the doin' another.

His mother's letter seemed to burn in his pocket like a hot brand against his heart, searing him with the promise that the stain of guilt she'd never acknowledged could finally be undone. If only he could get on with his plan to seek riches in California and relieve her worries. Money might not fix all he'd innocently rent asunder, but it would help build a future they could all share.

The sooner he got Maggie Brownley to her grandmother's, the sooner he could be on his way, and the faster he could do what must be done to bring some solace to his family's financial woes.

"This way." He nudged the gelding, turning northwest

toward a slight thinning in the river. It would be easiest to ford the smallest crossing they could find. Easiest. Fastest. He was all for whatever would afford them the shortest time in the water.

In the water. He couldn't believe he was actually contemplating such action. He had not willingly gone into any large body of water since that terrible evening.

Maggie favored him with a wan smile, cinching his decision. He had to get her to shelter soon. Going back would keep her out in the rain far longer than any society miss, no matter how brave, could possibly stand. They'd ford the river and seek shelter on the other side. He'd beg a warm bed and supper for her this night if he had to.

He inched the gelding along, keeping an eye on the river and the water that seemed to beckon him with its siren song, luring him to come into the churning depths and release all his pain and worries. He shivered, remembering only too well the embracing arms of the sea as she welcomed him to her cold bosom when his struggling boy's arms could no longer hold him afloat.

Diabhal. He forced the intrusive hopelessness away and urged the gelding to a faster pace, guiding him toward what looked to be the shallowest point. The gelding's hooves clattered over water-smoothed stones at the river's edge as they reached their immediate goal.

He reined the horse to a stop.

"It doesn't look as bad right here, does it?" Maggie squinted up at him, her eyes half hidden by her cap. The hope in her tone, a mixture of fear and trust, tore at him.

Bryan had trusted him once to keep an eye out for the rocks ahead, trusted in the boyish eagerness of a young brother who had begged and wheedled to be taken along on their dangerous course.

"Aye, lass. It does not look as bad up close." Lightning

cracked in the distance, heralding the heightening of the
storm that had been threatening all day. Just what they
needed. But if he put off the crossing now, it would
only be worse when the storm had passed and the river's
courses were swollen and thick.

"We'd best hurry." His stomach swirled again with
the words, but Maggie only nodded her agreement, ready
to follow on his command. "Stay close behind me and
do not leave Missy's back."

He nudged the black forward even as everything within
him blazed in protest. With a few quick steps they were
in water as cold, dark, and virulent as the plague. He
shuddered and swallowed hard as it closed over his boots,
his ankles, and crept steadily up his calves, sinking him
closer and closer to an abyss he'd always shied away
from. Memories seized him in a talon-like grip, tearing
at the protective layers of forgetfulness he'd managed to
wrap around himself during the intervening years.

I'll watch out, Bryan, I will. His own voice. He'd been
twelve years old and so damned determined to prove
himself, vowing to be the lookout—a position of tremendous responsibility, especially considering what they were
about to do.

"No, Devi. I can't take you with me," Bryan had said,
his eyes serious and haunted by despair. Devin knew the
unfairness of Da's pronouncement had driven Bryan to
take Quin's boat. He could not allow his brother to face
his disappointment by himself.

"You can't take her alone, Bry. You'll sink her without
a lookout."

Even now the words pounded through his heart, threatening to rip him to shreds. "There's a storm coming."

Bryan had looked at him for a long moment, as though
measuring him against some invisible yardstick of matu-
rity and trust. Devin had held incredibly still, his heartbeat

drumming in his ears while he prayed he would measure up just this once in his brother's eyes.

"I don't know, Devi—"

"I'll do a good job, Bryan, I promise. You'll not be sorry you counted on me. We'll show them. We'll show Da and Ma and Quin what a good captain you are . . . together."

He had seen the moment in Bryan's eyes when his words had made the difference, when his brother had been swayed—partially by Devin's impassioned plea and partially by his own need to succeed at any cost.

He could feel Missy's breath on his arm as Maggie stayed beside him now. Higher and higher, the river water sucked hungrily at Devin's knees as his memories sucked the life and breath from his soul. He could hear again the wild creaking of Quin's new ship, protesting amidst the storm-tossed waters.

And he, so swelled with pride that Bryan had agreed to take him, was busy watching the crash and slap of the waves as the prow of Quin's ship split each crest with ease and power, demonstrating the kind of shipbuilding that had held the Reilly name in such respect for so long. Da was so proud of Quin, so certain that now they were ready to take their own place in Reilly history.

He wanted Da to be proud of him, too, and tonight he would be. Tonight he'd prove he could be a Reilly, too, that he bore the name for more reasons than just bone and sinew. He was born to the sea, just as his brothers were and—

Rocks.

They came out of nowhere. Too late, Devin spotted them.

No.

Bryan. He screamed for all he was worth, but it was not enough. Not near enough.

The ship tore into the rocks with the same enthusiasm she displayed toward each tremendous wave, ripping the prow open, splitting her hull, and spilling icy seawater into her pristine depths.

He lost sight of Bryan as he fell into the storm-tossed ocean, gulping down what felt like gallons of saltwater. He struggled in the dark, desperate to find the surface and some point of reference for his panic-stricken mind, all the while knowing down deep in his soul he had failed. He would never be a Reilly like the rest of them. He would never prove anything.

Even Bryan's finding him, tugging him to the surface, had failed to ease his torment. Bryan's words of guilt and apology had been lost in the torment of his own failure.

The gelding surged beneath him, calling Devin back from the murky depths of the sea. They were almost to the opposite side of the river. For a moment he chided himself for allowing his fears and his memories of what happened so long ago to govern him in the dangerous present. Even now the water had begun to swirl about his calves. He turned to check on Maggie.

She and Missy were right behind him. Safe.

A horrible cracking sound rent the air, so loud that for a moment he caught the echo of Quin's ship splintering against the rocks. It was no memory. Lightning split the sky in a fantastic display of spidered yellow and white light. Maggie's face was etched in stark relief as she sucked in a terrified gasp. Missy's eyes rolled in fear.

Horror clenched his middle with an iron fist.

"No!" He reached for the mare's bridle.

Thunder broke and rumbled like the sound of a thousand war-wagons descending into hell.

The mare reared. His fingers slid along her wet hide, finding no purchase.

Maggie's scream and the frightened mare's mingled in

an earsplitting shriek. As though time had slowed to an impossible crawl, he watched Maggie slide from the horse's back and disappear beneath the swirling currents of the river.

Pain knifed his heart.

No.

"Maggie!"

No!

He launched himself from the gelding's back and plunged into the grimy torment beneath the water. Sand and water rushed into his ears, his nose, his throat, and tossed him along as though he were naught but a leaf in the current. For a timeless moment, the old panic rose and gripped his heart, freezing him beneath the water. There was no hope, no rescue.

Maggie!

His mind screamed a reminder of the present danger. He lurched toward the surface in a series of awkward movements. It wasn't salt that filled his mouth and threatened to burst his lungs this time. It was the earthy grit of the river, thick and sludgy, rasping against his skin. This was not the ocean he fought.

He spat and scanned the riotous surface of the river. "Maggie!"

Rain poured around him as thunder rumbled again overhead. He would not fail her, could not chance failing as he had done before.

It was not mere timber and nails and rope he stood to lose this time, not the trust and confidence of his family. He stood to lose far more.

He spotted her not far from him, struggling amidst the surging water and the hampering confines of the riding skirt he'd insisted she don. Her hair clung to her as she gulped air. Surely the sodden petticoats and wool would suck her back down at any moment.

Refusing to give his fears any further space in his thoughts, let alone allow them to dominate, he focused on Maggie and fought his way forward. Gradually, old rhythms revived. An instinct as inbred as his very name seemed to take over. His body became less a floundering collection of arms and legs and more able to sustain him against the river's fierce, conflicting currents.

Bless Quin. Bless all those times his brother had forced him into the sea through accident or design. At least he was able to swim.

Devin pushed harder and reached Maggie as she went under again. He dived after her and sought her through touch, since the murky water offered him no point of reference. His fingers brushed her jacket and he kicked deeper. He scooped his arm beneath hers, locking it around her and dragging her to the surface.

She gulped in air, coughed, and clung to him.

"Devin?" Even choked with river water, the sound of her voice was pure heaven.

"Aye, Maggie darlin'." He shuddered and pulled her toward the riverbank. She could not make it alone in her gown's heavy confines. Trying to get her out of the damned thing now would be a waste of precious energy.

"Hold on to me." He strove for the bank, fighting the river's will with every ounce of strength he possessed.

Maggie hugged tight to his back and shoulders. The weight of her against him was a blessing in its own right. He dragged both of them up onto the muddy banks as a wave of giddiness crested and broke inside him.

Wild delight followed the sudden passage of fear. The storm still swelled around them. Jagged lightning split the sky, and rain spattered the ground in huge splotches. But to have them both safe was too great a joy to miss. And to have conquered his own worst fears left him feeling oddly off kilter, as though the world had somehow changed forever in the last few moments.

He pulled her to him because he needed her, because it seemed right, and because he couldn't not do so. He kissed her, mouth solidly to mouth, cold lips quivering against cold lips. Only the warmth within belied the cold as her lips parted to receive him and her tongue met his, fresh and incredibly sweet despite the river's gritty breath.

Then it was as though the storm around them was but a pale imitation of the feelings she unleashed inside him. A wild rush of power, of desire, a need so strong as to transcend anything that had come before awakened inside him and pushed to the surface, demanding satisfaction— demanding everything she had to give and more.

'Tis a sound once heard, always remembered, a feeling once felt and never forgot. You'll know, young Devin. Quin's voice and Granny Reilly's combined to roll through his memory with both promise and certainty.

Aye, he did know.

The knowin' is one thing, the doin' another.

Lightning frizzled the air around them, raising the hair on his arms and back of his neck. He could not keep her here at the river's edge and make love to her as his body demanded, not if he wanted them to live to see another day. Sanity prevailed as rain dripped over their faces. He needed to get her somewhere reasonably warm and dry.

He scrambled to his feet, pulling her along with him. "Come, darlin'."

She followed after him, slipping and sliding through the mud, twice almost losing her footing only to slide against him and giggle wildly. He began to wonder if they had both gone mad somewhere between the river's banks.

The horses had taken shelter beneath the great outspread branches of an oak tree well beyond the river's edge. He blessed them. Beneath the same oak stood a ramshackle collection of branches interlaced into a rough shelter or a graduated lean-to of sorts.

Whatever it was, it would have to do. Neither he nor Maggie were in any shape to continue their journey, especially with night swiftly approaching.

He motioned toward it, received her nod and picked up speed, reaching the lean-to as the very heavens above them seemed to open up. After several shoves, the door gave way. With just barely enough light to see, he could make out a small hearth and a pallet off to one side. No occupants. Good.

Maggie collapsed against the wall, drenched to the bone. Her riding habit clung to her, the green serge darkened to gray and brown. One sleeve was torn. Her hair was a sodden mass of curls. She was far from the upper crust Bostonian her parents wanted her to be. She looked more like a half-drowned kitten.

She looked beautiful.

"Stay here. I'll get the saddlebags." A quick dash back out into the driving rain should detain the direction his thoughts seemed determined to take.

Harder now, the water pelted him like stones. He gritted his teeth and tethered the horses, though he'd a pretty good idea they weren't going anywhere. After divesting them of saddles and bags, he scurried back to the relative security of the lean-to.

"We'll need a fire." Maggie greeted him with chattering teeth, but to her credit she'd made use of her time alone. She'd gathered kindling by the crude stone circle that served as a hearth and scrounged up a kettle.

"Good work, lass." He smiled at her, surprised to find his own teeth beginning to chatter as well.

"And we'll have to get out of these wet things."

He could only chuckle. "Aye. I suppose you're right.

But we've not much else to choose from." He bent to the hearth to put her kindling to good use with the one dry log he'd retrieved from the pile by the door. His mind provided all too vivid thoughts of Maggie once again clad in Marcus's trousers. He bit back a groan, not at all sure he was up to the challenge.

"These will have to do." Her voice came, a bit breathless and shaky, from behind him.

He turned to find her proffering a couple of thin blankets from the pallet in the corner. She eyed them with a shade of reluctance before holding one out to him. "You get this one."

The shorter of the two. Just as well.

Flames began to lick at his fingers and he jumped, pulling them away from the heat and mentally flaying himself for his inability to concentrate on anything beyond the image of Margaret Sylvia Worth Brownley clad in nothing but a thin blanket and clouds of wild golden brown curls.

Just the thought made his mouth go dry.

"Much as I'd like to see you get out of those wet clothes, I don't think *this*"—he hefted the blanket she'd thrown him—"is a good idea."

Despite her chattering teeth, she laughed. "Why not, Mr. Reilly? Are you afraid I shall peek at you?" She turned her back to him. Her skirts sloshed against the floor. "I promise not to."

"Peeking is not what I'm worried about." He pushed to his feet.

"Indeed?" She frowned at him over her shoulder.

He took a step toward her. "Aye."

"A-and just what might you be worried about?" She tipped her quivering chin to look up at him as he took another step.

I'm afraid I lost more than just my belongings that day

in Boston Harbor. How could any woman look half-drowned and so damned beautiful she stole his breath at one and the same time? How was any man to resist such a lure, especially when her every glance offered him passion and encapsulated The Blessing?

His Blessing.

Longing ached through him as he stretched his fingers out to touch her cheek. She was cold, too cold to stand there in dripping wet wool and soggy linen.

"Nothing I cannot handle." He forced the brazen words out, realizing she still awaited his answer. "You are entirely right, Miss Brownley. While I tend the fire, you get out of those wet things before you catch your death."

Chapter Eleven

"I am very cold, but you are just as wet as I am. You need to change, too."

Maggie's gaze held Devin mesmerized for several dangerous moments as she turned her cheek into his palm. So simple the movement, yet the wild longing she set loose in his gut held far too much risk for both of them. He wished he could reclaim the makeshift barriers of the supposed gulf separating their stations. At least that fiction of coachman and mistress had provided some distance, however small, between them.

As it was, he wanted to pull this woman to him, to touch each part of her body, to sear her image more deeply into his heart and soul, to hold her until neither of them could ever be cold again.

The direction of his thoughts sliced into him, and he struggled against this wild, uncontrollable yearning.

At what point had he completely lost control of his emotions? Of his desires? Was this how Seamus had felt with his Clara? Reality no longer mattered. Consequences did not matter. All that mattered was the moments spent with her? Madness.

"It is merely the shock and its aftermath." He released her cheek and turned away, as much from the sight of her as the dangerous needs she unleashed inside him. He felt too raw, too overwhelmed by all that had transpired within the last hour, to trust the emotions roiling through him now.

He'd conquered his deepest fear when he thrust himself into the river to save her, mastered what had held him apart from his family for the past fifteen years in the space of a few harrowing heartbeats. But his wild euphoria of the first few moments had drained away.

He felt a strange metamorphosis, a mix of renewal and certainty that he was still the same man he had been before they began the crossing. Yet everything inside him felt as though it had been completely torn apart and put back together, constant and yet forever altered.

Like the night his brother had held him up in the cold water, clinging to the wreckage of Quin's boat and Bryan's dreams, until at last Quin and one of Da's captains had found them. Everything in their lives changed that night, unmistakably for the worse. This change was different—lighter, and yet more ambivalent.

"You'd best get out of your wet things, Maggie." His voice came out as a gruff parody of himself.

"Devin?" Her hand brushed his shoulder and he bit back a groan as her touch shuddered through him. How could one simple gesture betray him so thoroughly? One contact leave him so undone?

"Just get changed," he repeated and moved away without further comment, shedding his own soaked shirt in the process.

He slapped his wet shirt to the floor near the fire,

exorcising only the tiniest portion of the demons feasting on his soul. Fisting his hands at his side, he strove to recall all the reasons why he should hold himself from her.

His own vow at Seamus's lonely funeral echoed through him: *No woman will ever drive me to forget my ambitions or deny my needs to satisfy her whims.*

What had become of that promise? Even recalling the pain and confusion of losing his friend was not enough to battle the feelings Maggie Brownley called forth inside him, not when he already stood on shaky ground.

He was tempted to curse The Blessing and the druids who had so long ago graced his family with what now felt more like a tremendous burden instead of a boon of gratitude.

The heavy slosh of fabric against wood sounded behind him. Maggie's gown, petticoats, and underpinnings. He closed his eyes and gritted his teeth, imagining her as she would be now.

Naked and beautiful.

Desire ripped into his belly with a vengeance. Perhaps this was his curse, then—to stand here knowing the woman he wanted stood behind him in nothing but her own glory and yet be unable to do anything about it, be unable to claim her as his body screamed he must.

Unable or unwilling?

Either created the perfect hell for him, a curse more complete than any demon could devise. At the moment it didn't matter which netherworld ring he traversed, it was a pain sweeter and sharper than any he could have anticipated.

He could all too easily picture Maggie in his arms, feel her against him as though that was where she had always belonged. The taste of her lips beneath his, the sighs she would make as he loved her all rose far too easily to his mind and burned in him with a power that threatened to consume him.

If he were to touch her now, they would both be lost. Surely this was his curse, indeed.

She sighed. The sound lanced him.

"Are you not planning to change, as well?"

So soft those words, and with just a hint of a tremor in them. Did she have any idea what she did to him with just the sound of her voice?

He didn't dare consider the possibilities if he were to shed the rest of his wet clothing. Indeed, his cold, wet trousers were probably the only thing saving her from the lust surging inside him at the moment.

"I think not." Good Lord, was that his voice? That strangled, need-ridden growl? He swallowed and tried again. "I can manage as I am."

She laughed, a breathless sound that threatened his sanity and her virtue.

He ground his teeth together, dreading her approach as she padded across the weathered floorboards.

"You can't stay in those . . . wet breeches." A reasonable tone, completely unreasonable in light of her own lack of clothing.

"I think it would be best if I did." What on earth had prompted him to start a fire? It was entirely too warm in here. He felt ready to burst into flames himself.

She sighed. "Men can be very stubborn at times. Papa has always been so. Stubborn, obstinate, and utterly unreasonable."

She would dare to compare him with her father? The very idea was like salt in an open wound. He turned toward her without thinking.

Her hair mantled her slender shoulders in soft, damp ringlets. She'd managed to drape the blanket over her in a mythic concoction reminiscent of his studies of ancient

Grecian gods and goddesses. A knot held the garment together at one shoulder, completely baring the other.

The dips and folds of weathered gray wool hinted at the tempting womanly charms she hid in its rough depths. A goddess, indeed—one ready to steal not only his mind, but his heart and soul as well.

Even wet trousers could not stem the floodtide of desire rising inside him. He groaned inwardly. He felt parched and completely incapable of telling her what danger she placed them in with her innocence. Her grace and her soft beauty words could neither deny nor describe.

She moved closer and reached out a hand to touch his arm. Her fingers seemed to etch themselves into his forearm. Destiny beckoned.

"Devin," she breathed, the flicker of the fire lighting her serious face and dancing on the sober edges of her eyes. "I want . . . I need . . ."

What, mo chroí—*my heart?* The endearment pulsed through him. Did she want him to kiss her breathless? Need him to show her the best way two people could combat the threatening cold together?

Anger needled him. Surely it was not his fate to stand here so tongue-tied he couldn't even tell her to keep her distance. Was she so completely innocent she had no inkling what could happen between them? Must he describe the dangers to her?

"You saved me. I know how difficult that was. The waters were so strong, but I knew from the moment I hit them you would not let me drown." A smile curved her lips and carved its way past the tension thrumming through him. "Thank you." She stood on the tips of her toes and leaned over to brush her lips against the rough stubble on his cheek.

"Maggie, you've no idea what you're tempting." He fought the need to shout at her and thereby release the terrible confusion building inside him in tandem with the storm still raging outside. Her thanks, her gratitude, were the last thing he wanted right now.

She lifted her chin, an unfortunate action that revealed the smooth white column of her neck. "I know enough to say you are being foolishly modest, Devin Reilly. If I can dress like this"—she gestured the length of her body—"surely you can manage as well. Wet breeches cannot be comfortable. You could take a chill."

Again the unreasoning anger stung, harder this time. Her concern was both impersonal and too personal. "You don't understand."

"Understand what?" She place her hands at her waist, tightening the blanket and emphasizing the soft curves of her hips and the fullness of her breasts. "Are you afraid?"

He lifted a brow at her. "Hardly."

"Then be sensible. You must be healthy if you are going to get me to Somerset and my grandmother in one piece." She nodded as though her argument were won. Her curls danced at her shoulders and swayed across her breasts. She swept them back with a careless movement. "I'll see what survived the dousing in the saddlebags. Maybe we can manage a small supper."

He watched her as she turned away from him and crossed to the saddlebags he'd left by the door. Her movements held a special grace at odds with the drab blanket that covered her. How could he explain to her that just being in this confined space with her was enough to drive him mad with wanting her, let alone adding the temptations of undressing himself?

A shiver wracked him, and the truth of her challenge clung to him tighter than his wet boots and pants. He could not afford to take a chill at this juncture in their journey.

There was only so much one man could take.

He shed the wet trousers as quickly as possible and looped the blanket around his waist, knotting it as best he could. Seaman's knots had not been his strong suit. Hell, anything to do with ships was not his strength. Still, he wished he had more expertise at this moment.

The blanket slid to his hips when he'd finished.

"There's enough here to start with—" Maggie's words died away as she turned toward him with what was left of a wheel of cheese in her hands.

Her gaze slid over him from his shoulders to his waist and lower, leaving a trail of heat like a caress. Every touch, every wayward kiss that had every happened between them seemed to hover in the humid air of the cabin, ghosts of what had been. Harbingers of what would be?

"Oh, my." Her cheeks colored. "Are ... are you hungry?"

"Aye." He groaned inwardly.

The smile she offered him held a tremulous quality. She was wary, he could see it in her luminous eyes. He reined in his passions with an effort. He should declare he would suffer the storm outside in order to protect her from the raw needs roiling through him like fire. He opened his mouth, wondering where to begin and just how much he could manage to tell her without losing control.

"Maggie, you are so beautiful." The words spilled from him of their own volition.

The glow in her eyes robbed him of breath as pink tinged her cheeks. His very skin ached for her. They were much too close. Ginger and chamomile filled his senses. Lightning stretched across the sky, followed too quickly by the crash of thunder.

"Devin." Only his name, yet the sound of it, whispered

from her lips with such awe, ripped at the slender threads of control he yet could claim.

As if from a distance he watched, unable to stop the impulse, as he lifted his hand to caress the smooth curve of her cheek, trace the delicate line of her jaw.

"Mo chroí." Again that husky tone in his voice shivered in the air, raw enough to bare his every impulse to her.

She leaned toward him, inviting all of the chaos inside him to take advantage of what she so innocently offered.

He was but a man.

He groaned and pulled her to him, clasping her shoulders tight. His mouth touched hers without any pause for gentleness, molding her lips beneath his, deepening the contact as her mouth opened to him and their tongues slid together. She tasted of wild summer berries and rich cream, of coming home. Lightning cracked in the distance, but the assault upon his soul had only just begun.

The Blessing soared through him, tearing at his last moorings to sanity and society, ripping the thin veneer of propriety from him—baring him to her in all the raw wonder of the passion she drew from him.

She arched against him as he kissed her, her breasts pressed against his chest, a soft resilience he ached to caress. She was sweeter than any fruit he had ever tasted. And she was his.

She was so soft and warm against him, the blanket but a thin and tempting veil over her body.

Vague warnings of the past crackled like wild lightning loose in the storm. But even the memory of Seamus's betrayal and death could not intrude on the palpable yearning that swirled in the air around them. Maggie was no weak-willed Clara.

She shuddered against him as he stroked his tongue along her own. Wildfire raged through his body, burning away any attempts to resist the passion ordained between them, passion that branded his body as hers, for her and of her.

Her hands slid over his shoulders, his chest, his back. Each touch left a trail of heat in its wake.

He lifted his head, breaking the wanton, sweet contact with her lips. She was so beautiful he had to swallow twice before he could speak around the lump that swelled in his throat.

Her eyes met his, warm and sparkling from the desire building between them. Gone was any sign of fright or hesitation. She traced the tips of her fingers along his jawline and offered him her soul with a smile that echoed within his own.

"Maggie, *mo chroí.*" Aye, she was his heart. How could he have doubted that?

His in ways that could never be defined by mere words—soul deep and overpowering, but more undeniable than each breath he needed to survive.

The thought rang an alarm along his nerve endings. He pulled away from her, shuddering at the warm sparkle of questions in her wide smoked-amber gaze.

"It is not a wise thing we do, Maggie." He set her from him with an effort. "Regardless of education or background, a man can only resist so much. You ask too much of me."

"What have I asked?"

He groaned and turned away, unable to think, let alone answer her, while hot blood surged in his veins and slammed into his groin like an angry fist. The storm outside shuddered the confines of their sanctuary, as though the very elements confirmed their oneness with the furor inside him.

"Have you no notion?" Did he really have to explain

it to her? Heaven help him, he didn't think he was up to the task.

"Tell me."

"Nay, lass. You play with more than fire here. This will not lead to a story of chivalrous make-believe to satisfy your bedtime imaginings."

"I seek no make-believe tale." Her hand touched his shoulder and traced a cool pathway over the back of his neck.

He groaned. She stepped nearer to him. He could feel the heat of her body, so close against his back.

"I want you, Maggie." He couldn't hold the words back, no matter his struggle. "I want you as completely as any man has ever wanted a woman."

Her hands stilled. He ground his teeth together in an agony of frustration. Now she would step back from him and vent all her maiden's offense that he would say such things to her. Such would be his test, then. Would he be able to let her turn away without reaching for her and drawing her back to him?

Maggie's heartbeat drummed in her ears as Devin's words quickened within her. His skin felt so smooth and so warm beneath her hands. She wanted to touch all of him, to be with him in ways no Brookline Daughter of Grace should entertain. Even though she stood in nothing but a thin blanket, she wanted to be so much nearer him, closer than she stood now or than she had been a only moment before when they kissed.

He wanted her. That knowledge, however incomplete and unsure in her mind, surged through her in powerful warm waves followed by incredibly sweet spirals, leaving her dizzy. She wanted him, too. Even confronted with the shakiness of their futures and the uncertainty of what would happen between them, she wanted him.

She stepped around him until he stood before her and

she could read the terrible conflict in his deep green eyes. His strain was evident in every line and angle of his face, in his tense shoulders, even in the slow steady drip of rainwater from his hair as he waited for her reply to his bald honesty.

If she shrank from him, from what was brewing between them, he would hold himself at bay for her sake alone. That was not what she wanted from this man. Not at all.

She realized, with something of a shock, that she loved him. Enough to follow her heart instead of her head. Enough to believe in the here and now and let tomorrow take care of itself. For the moment, that was enough.

She placed both of her hands on his bare chest, feeling the hard pounding of his heart beneath her palms.

Breath hissed in between his teeth.

"Maggie." Her name came out low, in a prayer, a threat, a promise. She had never heard anything more starkly beautiful than those two short syllables passing from his lips to shiver through her soul. The questions between them beat in the air.

"Devin." She gave his name and his answer back to him without trying to hide the strange mix of passion and fear he unleashed inside her.

His dark green gaze fixed on her face, tight and intent, making tiny tremors course over her skin.

"Lass, ye can't know what yer offerin'," he scolded, his musical brogue heavier than usual.

"I know I want you, Devin Reilly."

"Nay." He placed his fingers over her lips as though he needed to still her words before they could reach his ears. "Don't say—"

She kissed his fingertips, reveling in a purely female sense of power that surged inside her. So this is what Grandmother had meant when she said some things happened because they needed to happen.

"Aye." She mocked his Gaelic tones and then smiled at him as her heart filled near to bursting inside her. "Grandmother always says sometimes we cannot hide from what must be, even if we do not understand it all."

". . . from what must be," he repeated, soft and low. His brows drew together in a dark line above his eyes.

He gripped her shoulders and the soft light in his gaze grew fierce. "I would make love to you, Maggie. I would touch you in ways you have never even considered being touched. I would kiss each part of your body and love you until there is not strength enough in either one of us to move." His breath was warm against her cheeks and his fingers tightened on her skin. "Understand that much, at least when you stand before a man and tell him you want him."

She swallowed as his gaze bored into hers, branding her. And she knew in the deepest part of herself that this was what she wanted, what must be. In this moment, in this hour, she would be his as completely as he wanted her to be. Tomorrow would have to take care of itself.

"I understand."

"Then God help us both." He bent his head to hers as he covered her mouth with his own. The taste of him, raw and storm-tossed as the sea his family loved, shivered through her all the way to her toes and rippled wild gooseflesh along her skin.

He pulled her back against him, and she shuddered as the warm solid wall of his chest met her breasts. She twined her arms around his neck, needing each small contact, needing to be closer to him, closer than she could possibly imagine.

"Maggie. *Mo chroí.*" His words caressed her, shivering over her skin as he kissed her cheek, her brow, and the sensitive flesh behind her ear.

"Devin." She could only clutch his shoulders as his

lips trailed along the side her neck, nibbling and licking. Each hot touch of his tongue against her flesh sent sparks spiraling through her middle. Her knees felt weak and warm as he pressed his mouth to her shoulder, tracing the line of her collarbone, nipping her shoulder with his teeth.

"It's more than mere wanting I feel for ye, Maggie, *mo chroí*. I need you." He rasped the words, his breath raising the fine hairs along her arms.

"Yes." The word sighed out of her as his hand boldly cupped her breast through the rough wool of the blanket. He groaned and claimed her lips again as he caressed her, weighing and teasing her, drawing his hand across the tightened peak. Every touch seemed to tense some invisible cord within her and pool liquid heat low in her belly.

"Not enough. Not near enough." He growled the words as he scooped her into his arms and bore her through the darkened cabin to the small pallet in the corner.

Firelight flickered over his face, highlighting his dark brows and those deep green eyes that seemed able to see into her soul. He released one arm, holding her against him as her legs slid down over his body, hard and so warm. She wanted to twine her legs around him and pull him against that part of her that ached for him.

"You are mine, *mo chroí*." Harsh lines twisted his brow. "Understand that now as you have nothing else. Mine unto death and darkness."

"Yes." She understood him, perhaps more now than she had at any other time—this strange chivalrous man, who had put aside his own life to help her from the moment they met. She wanted to be his, in any way she could—in every way she could.

"Make love to me, Devin." The words came from her

in a voice she barely recognized, husky with longing and breathless with urgency.

"Aye." He kissed her then, molding her lips to his, bending her to his will as his tongue laved her own. His strokes shivered through her, promising the deeper invasion of his body and a rapture that would be theirs alone.

His hands swept her back, arching her against his chest, his torso, the hard heat of the desire he held for her. She clung to him, granting him access to her heart, her soul, and her body.

His fingers made short work of the knotted ends of worn blanket on her shoulder. The blanket hung for a moment as though suspended by invisible cords, then whispered to the floor.

The sharp intake of his breath was the only sound save the patter of the rain outside.

"*Mo chroí*, you are more beautiful than I imagined." His words came soft and low, reverent.

She felt beautiful, standing before him in nothing but her own skin. She had never felt beautiful before. Such was the realm of Amelia and Lenore and Tori. But here and now, she felt every inch a beauty in his eyes. She straightened her shoulders, standing proud even when her breasts thrust forward beneath his gaze.

"Aye." More groan than word as he stood ever so slightly back from her and allowed his dark green gaze to travel over her in slow sweet torment.

Devin's mouth went dry at the sight of Maggie shimmering in the firelight, her shoulders back, her breasts high and rounded, her nipples tight and pink, begging for his mouth. Her waist nipped in, tiny enough to span with his hands above the flare of her hips and the long lithe line of her legs. He reached out and traced his hands over her back, her shoulders, her arms. She shuddered beneath his touch. Then, more boldly, he moved his hands over her soft, full breasts, enjoying the swift intake of her breath as he paused to caress her. His fingers moved lower, over the sleek plane of her belly to the thatch of curls at the apex of her legs.

He pulled her to him and kissed her, holding himself back with an effort, making the caress soft and slow as he eased his fingers between her silken thighs. Damp heat greeted him, almost unmanning him where he stood as she gasped into his mouth.

Her hands sought his shoulders, clinging to him as he deepened the kiss, laving her tongue in long slow strokes that echoed the movement of his fingers against her slick velvet folds.

She groaned as he released her swollen lips. A flush rode her cheekbones and passion glazed her eyes as he watched her. He stroked her, slow and steady, teasing her with his fingers, ready to burst with wanting her.

"Devin." Urgently, she panted his name.

"Aye, my heart." He kissed her very gently and then dipped his head to her breasts, claiming one sweet nipple.

She gasped as he suckled the tip of her breast, grazing her with his teeth as he continued the rhythmic stroking of his fingers below.

He parted her slick folds and transferred his attentions to her other breast, feasting on the taut bud as he eased his fingers inside her tight sheath. She stiffened against him as he reached the shield of her maidenhead.

For a moment sanity threatened. What the hell was he doing?

But the urges driving him now were too primitive and too powerful to be denied. Her fingers laced through the hair at the nape of his neck, urging him onward.

She gasped again as he breached her with his fingers, opening her to a deeper invasion. He raised his head and kissed her, long and slow and sweet, tasting the heady mix of sudden fear and wild passion on her lips.

Gradually she relaxed against him. When she did, he couldn't hold back a growl of pure male domination. She was his, so completely his.

With his fingers hugged deeply inside her body, he teased the engorged nubbin nested within her small curls, stroking and rubbing as he kissed her.

Her breathing quickened and she clung to him as he coaxed her to release her all to him.

"Oh, Devin." A breathless pant. He could feel the throbbing begin deep within her body.

"Aye, *mo chroí*. Let go."

She shuddered then, over and over, contractions rippling deep within her, tensing around his fingers as she cried out, at the mercy of the climax he triumphantly drew from her.

Chapter Twelve

"Maggie, *mo chroí.*" Devin bore her naked form down onto the pallet with him, overcome with the strange mixture of tenderness and passion that swelled his heart.

He kissed her, tasting her release on her lips. Desire so strong it nearly overwhelmed him washed through him.

"I had no idea." Her tremulous awe forced a rough chuckle from him.

"Indeed." He'd never quite realized the wonder such shared passion could bring even as his own physical needs cried out for surcease.

His own blanket had come undone somewhere between her climax and the pallet. She glanced down at him, his engorged phallus a bold endorsement of the passions she drew from him.

She swallowed and reached out to touch him, her hand cool and soft against him.

He groaned. "Maggie."

Her gaze flew back to his face, though she did not

release him from the intimate torture of her touch. Her eyes seemed like molten pools in the flicker of the firelight.

"Are you in pain, Devin?" She chewed the edge of her lip.

"Only from wanting you, lass." He forced the words out through clenched teeth as her fingers tightened around him.

"But what we ... what you just did ..." Her voice trailed away as rosy color bloomed over her features.

"Mo chroí, what we just did was only a beginning."

He groaned again as her fingers tested his length, stroking slowly over his engorged flesh, teasing him to madness. If he did not stop her, he would unman himself against her palm.

He grasped her wrist. "Cease, lass."

Her gaze went back and forth between his face and the heated length she gripped. "Why?"

"Because you trifle with more than fire." Strain cracked through the words.

"Mayhap it is a fire I wish to trifle with," she purred with husky feminine satisfaction.

He groaned as her fingers twitched against him.

"Nay." He tensed, able to do naught but clutch her wrist and shudder beneath her touch.

She leaned toward him, resting the sweet pressure of her breasts against his chest as her lips feathered over his in a mere breath of a kiss.

"You said it was a beginning." Again her fingers teased him, tightening until he sucked in a harsh breath.

"Aye." More moan than answer.

"Then show me, Devin Reilly. Show me everything."

"As you wish, *mo chroí."* He pulled her to him, anchoring his arm around her waist and claiming her soft lips with a hot kiss.

"Oh," escaped her as he let her feel all the passion

driving him, pounding through his blood in a red hot haze that blotted out reason and accountability, leaving nothing but his need for her.

He caressed the soft flesh of her buttocks, drawing her to him, so that the soft thatch of curls at the apex of her thighs cradled the hard need of his erection. He pressed her to him, kneading her buttocks with both hands as he kissed her deeply, tangling his tongue with hers.

As he massaged her soft flesh, her legs parted, sliding down over his hips. He could feel the moist heat of her against him, a haven he was all too ready to seek.

He groaned her name against her lips, sliding his hands along her torso to cup the full resilience of her breasts. Her nipples were taut peaks against his palms as he rubbed and stroked her. Relentlessly he stoked the fire so recently quenched. He wanted her to enjoy him as fully as he intended to enjoy her, to gasp with pleasure when he finally breached her body and made himself part of her.

Her hands clutched his shoulders as she returned his ardor with equal measure, sucking his lips and breathing out soft cries of encouragement that rippled through him.

He grasped her beneath the full swells of her breasts and lifted her slightly, arching her so that her breasts thrust toward him. And then he tasted her, both taut buds in turn, teasing them in slow circles, sucking, nipping, grazing her with his teeth until she began to moan and arch her hips atop him.

He slid his fingers down between them, testing her velvety heat. She was so wet, so incredibly ready for him. He could wait no longer.

He guided her down toward his aching span of flesh, groaning in half pain, half pleasure as her body parted to take the tip of him inside her.

She shuddered. "Devin."

"Aye, Maggie-mine." He struggled to hold himself

still against the raging desire to pound himself deep inside her, to surrender all to primitive rhythms older than time itself. "I've a need to be inside you."

"Yes." She slid herself down over his hard length in one swift stroke. He shuddered.

Completion.

Communion.

Twin gasps mingled in the air.

Pleasure so thorough it was blinding thundered through his veins, battering reality through him with the power of gale force winds.

She was truly his now, his in ways that could never be undone. He tightened his hold on her silken limbs. So be it.

Her eyes were wide. Surprise and pleasure warred with pain in their smoked amber depths. He gritted his teeth, afraid to move, to so much as breathe now that she had sheathed him so deeply inside her. The heat, the primal satisfaction was so intense he would go mad from it, but he dared not move for fear he would cause her further pain. She was so tight, so wonderfully tight and soft.

"You are inside me," she gasped, her breathing harsh and quick, "as if we were one."

After several moments of mingled ecstasy and torture, she wriggled atop him, experimentally, and closed her eyes. "Mmmm."

Heaven help him, she was smiling.

"Maggie."

"Is there more?" Her gaze met his and he saw the deep passion rising within her, sending his own blood on a white hot rush through his body.

"Aye, lass. There is." He groaned and grasped her hips, meeting her gaze as he guided her slowly up and down over his hard length, biting his lip at the incredibly sweet pain of loving her. Pleasure rippled through him in wave upon unbearable wave.

"Ohhhhh," she moaned, her eyelids drifting closed as she accepted the rhythm he had begun. Her breasts glistened in the firelight, shimmering with the dance of passion.

Sweeter still.

In, out. In. Out.

Honeyed friction built the pressure within to impossible heights.

The sight of her riding him, accepting each thrust into her body and waiting for more, twisted inside him, boring through the layers of denial he'd wrapped around his heart. He slid his hands up over her silky skin, testing her belly, her breasts, watching his hands cup and fondle her as firelight flickered against her, caressing her even as he did.

How long could he prolong this wondrous torment when already he wanted her so badly it was a ripe and painful ache?

"Oh, Devin." She leaned her head back, arching her breasts into his palms, brushing his thighs with her soft springy curls, clutching him with her hands as desire spiraled between them.

"Aye, love, aye." And then it was not enough. The slow torment could not satisfy the demands his body could no longer hold back.

He threaded his fingers through her hair, cupping her scalp and drawing her down to him for a kiss that became a wild mating of tongues and mouths and souls.

"I cannot get enough of you." He rasped the words against her lips.

"Yes. No. Never enough." Her answers came in breathless pants as he turned her beneath him. Her hands clasped his neck and drew him down into a searing kiss.

Her hips cradled him and he sank even deeper inside
her as she wrapped her legs around him.

"Maggie." He groaned her name and thrust into her
with all the lust and longing trapped inside him.

"Devin," she cried out. She hugged him tighter,
accepting kiss after wild kiss while he moved deep within
her, arching her hips toward him as her body shuddered
beneath his demands and urged fathomless passion from
him with her sweet abandon.

This was where he belonged, where he had always
belonged. There was no denying the connection between
them. He was hers just as surely as she was his. Nothing
would separate them, not heaven, not hell.

Harder, faster, his body took control, driving into her
over and over. He could not stop himself, could not shield
her from the rough longings demanding satisfaction. With
each sweet invasion, he sought surcease, exacting a precious toll from each of them. She did not shrink from
him, but welcomed each thrust, her body clutching him
tight as the convulsions he'd wrung from her with his
fingers began anew, spasming over his flesh.

"Devin." She cried his name in a breathless gasp that
echoed through him, shattering forever the illusion that
he could ever leave her behind.

"Aye, *mo chroí, muirneach.*" The ancient words of
love rippled out without conscious thought, born of a
deep need to say them as ageless pleasure ripped through
him in soul-splintering release.

Maggie awoke slowly. Her head lay cradled against
something warm and much harder than her usual pillow.
She turned. A deep sensual ache sluiced through her lower
body, and then it all came back to her—the storm, the

river, the wonder of Devin's body against hers. Inside hers.

Heat rushed through her, inside and out. Even now they lay in an intimate tangle of limbs upon the pallet. The rain outside had ceased long ago and sunlight glimmered through the rough-hewn walls of their sanctuary. Her gaze drifted over the ragged slats that formed the wall and ceiling. She couldn't help wondering just what Mama would have to say if she discovered her daughter's current scandalous state.

She caught back a sigh, somewhere between satisfaction and guilt.

Regret. Wasn't that what she should be feeling? Regret, embarrassment. She should be wailing her heart out, tearing at her hair, and demanding Devin Reilly do right by her. At the very least, she should have her nearest male relative shoot him dead on the spot. Yet just as she had never fit in with the other societal norms of her family, those reactions did not conform to what lay inside her.

Loving Devin Reilly seemed more natural to her than anything she had ever done in her life, more right than any strictures could prevent. From the instant on the wharf in Boston when her carriage careened out of control, from the moment he'd pulled her from the vehicle's overturned depths, from the first time he'd kissed her for all the world to see, she had been his and he hers.

Loving him, taking him as her lover, was a sweet inevitability she could never regret. Her only sorrow was the knowledge that what they shared was a fragile, short-lived dream.

Devin had a mission to complete for his family, a goal she had no right to further prevent him from achieving. And she had the independent life she hoped to create once they reached Somerset and her grandmother.

She turned her head to find him watching her, his dark

green gaze unfathomable in the dim light. Did he regret the intimacies they'd shared?

"Hello." Her cheeks burned beneath his regard.

"Hello, Maggie-mine." His husky tone, so intimate given their present position, only heightened the wanton chaos churning through her.

He traced a finger along her brow. "What were you thinking just now?"

"I—" What could she give him as an answer? *I was justifying our lovemaking to myself and wondering if my grandmother would approve* did not seem appropriate.

His fingers brushed her cheek and across her lips. She could too well remember the feel of those strong fingers playing expertly over her body. "It was a serious look you had, Margaret Sylvia Worth Brownley."

The sound of her full name coming from his lips made the whole situation seem off kilter, as though they parried casual conversation at a supper party. The feel of his warm skin and solid muscle lying intimately against her made her cheeks flame anew.

She looked away from him, unable to frame any answer while gazing into those deep green eyes.

"Maggie?" He caught her chin and turned her gently back to face him.

Why did she now feel all shivery and weak, so incredibly feminine at the simple touch of his fingers and the deep timbre of his voice? Tears sparked at the backs of her eyes and she had no answer, not for him or herself. She held her tears back with an effort.

"I was thinking about Grandmother," she managed, her voice high and thin despite herself.

He stroked her cheek. "Are you sure?"

She shrugged her shoulders, an agitated movement that only served to rub his arm over her breasts. She stiffened. "Yes."

"Mo chroí, I cannot apologize for what happened between us. I'll only regret what we shared if you have regrets."

The flames scorching her cheeks could not possibly get any hotter. He saw straight through her with far too much ease. How could he speak so casually about something she couldn't even find the words to describe?

She reached a tentative finger up to trace along his jawline. The roughness of his stubble pricked her conscience. His gaze dared her to bare her soul.

How awkward! She didn't want an apology. She wished she were up and dressed. She wished they had already reached Maine and he was on his way to California. She wished he would make love to her again and again until he'd blotted everything else from her world.

"Devin . . ." Nothing more than his name came from her lips. Everything in her squirmed. So much for the fabulous sophistication her mama had been so determined to drill into her. But then there was nothing in the rules of polite society to prepare a girl for how to react the morning after a man made love to her.

Her gaze fled his.

He propped himself up on his elbow and leaned over her, drawing her gaze back to him with the movement. He seemed so strong, so virile, leaning over her, his broad shoulders bare and kissed by a ray of early sun streaking through a crack in the wall. Those green eyes refused to allow her to evade the issue.

She lifted her chin.

"I haven't asked for an apology." Her primmest tone, but at least it didn't sound shivery and weak.

"Nay, you have not, lass." He nodded, his gaze holding all the intimate knowledge of what had passed between them. "Still, I thought you should know one would probably not be forthcoming."

"Oh. Why not?" The question popped out without prior thought and then surged through her in a blaze of heat.

He smiled at her and leaned down as though he needed to whisper his answer. Then she felt his lips against her ear and the hot invasion of his tongue swirling over her earlobe.

She shuddered and closed her eyes on a sigh she couldn't hold back. The feel of his lips on her, his breath against her skin was all too right.

"That's why." His words came on a rough chuckle.

"Mmmm?" Her eyelids drifted open and she looked into his humor-filled gaze.

"Your answer, *mo chroí.*"

"My answer?" She blinked. Confusion warred with the lingering heat he evoked. "Oh. Yes. I . . . what kind of an answer was that?"

"This kind." He leaned down again and repeated his ministrations to her ear, nipping the lobe and swirling his tongue over the pulse beating just below.

She struggled to think. "But . . . that is not an answer."

"Nay?" He asked the word against her throat and then kissed her shoulder.

"Nay . . ." Delicious pleasure rippled through her. "I mean no."

"Then mayhap this is the answer you seek." He claimed her lips with his. Soft, warm, welcome—the intimate touch of her lover. Heat suffused her from head to foot as she parted her lips and his tongue slid against hers, slow and thorough and sensual.

As her breathing quickened and wildfire spiraled in her belly, he lifted his head, breaking the contact and leaving her wanting more. Dark heat swirled in his gaze.

She licked her lips and struggled to bring her senses back under her own control. Maybe if she didn't face him. She turned her back to him and took a calming breath. "No regrets," she whispered.

"Ah, Maggie." His hand swept the bared length of her spine from her shoulders down to the small of her back and lower still over the curves of her buttocks. She couldn't hold back a shiver. Those long fingers would yet be her undoing.

"Devin." What she'd meant as complaint somehow came out sounding husky and filled with need.

He squeezed and stroked her buttocks with a slow precision that took her breath.

"Maggie, there is more between us than one simple question can answer." His words tickled the back of her neck as he kissed her there.

"Mmmm?" *Question?* Her thoughts had begun to spiral beneath the touch of those exquisite hands. *What question?*

She struggled to think as he slid one hand over her hip and across her belly, tracing her navel in lazy circles. Her skin felt so sensitive. Each contact from the brush of his fingers to the feel of his lips to the heat radiating from his body seemed to reverberate through her.

"Aye, *mo chroí.*" His hand drifted up over her ribs, a slow, tantalizing caress. "I want to make love to you again."

"Oh, yes." She couldn't hold back her breathless agreement as his hand splayed over her breast, claiming her. She knew she had questions for him and herself, important thoughts to think, but she could concentrate on nothing beyond the touch of his fingers against her flesh.

Her eyes closed in anticipation, overcome with the sensations he drew from her and the need to feel him inside her.

He slipped his arm beneath her and pulled her against him. She couldn't hold back the moan that seemed to well from her very depths. He was so warm, and the hard length of him pressed intimately against her.

She could feel her body flowering open to accommodate him. She moved against him, drawing his harsh breath against her ear.

"Mo chroí." A groan, part warning, part plea, pushed from him as his hands fondled her breasts, teasing her nipples.

"Devin." She moved again, feeling the hard length of his arousal pressing against her buttocks. "Make love to me."

Maggie's words shuddered through Devin.

"You would drive a man mad." He nipped her shoulder in a series of hungry kisses, tasting the silken warmth of her flesh. Hunger burned low in his belly, threatening to escalate what he'd meant as a slow, leisurely loving into the white-hot, demanding passion he'd shown her last night.

He still couldn't believe she hadn't shrank from him when he'd finally lost control of the rough needs roiling through him when he joined with her, couldn't believe that even now she responded to his caresses with welcoming tremors and seemed scorched by the same fire burning in him.

Each time she innocently arched that delectable little bottom of hers against him, she strained whatever control he was able to claim. She arched again as he fondled one breast and splayed his other fingers down over her soft belly and into the nest of curls below, seeking and finding the pathways to her pleasure.

He groaned and bit his lip against the lust surging through him, even as he slid his fingers down between her warm thighs and tested the moist yielding flesh he found there.

"Mo chroí." He trailed hot kisses along her neck and

shoulder as her soft curls tickled his nose and chest with delectable sweetness.

"Oh, yes." She moved yet again, rubbing her tantalizing curves against him as he stroked her. Back and forth, back and forth she rocked until he was quite certain he would not survive the mindless pleasure she was giving him. Yet he dared not stop her as she sought her own pleasure at the touch of his fingers. Only when she was shuddering against him, broken whispers of release falling from her lips, did he stop.

The air in the cabin echoed with their harsh breathing.

"I don't know how you do that." A breathless chuckle shook her in his arms.

"Do what?" he asked, smiling against her shoulder even as the painful pressure building inside him begged for release.

"Make me feel the way you do."

"It is a blessing," he said, intending to toss the comment off lightly, but as the words left his lips he felt the truth resound through him.

"Indeed," she agreed, and then peered back at him. "Would you like me to turn around?"

"Nay, *mo chroí.*" He smiled again, knowing she sought to accommodate him and hopefully repeat her own pleasure. His fingers rubbed the nipple of the breast he still cradled.

"But—" Her breath caught as the bud tightened with his teasing caress.

"Hush." He brushed his thumb over her lips. "There is much you do not yet know."

He slid his hands down and cupped her sweet bottom, arching her just a little and parting her legs to find her softness with his engorged length.

She gasped as he pushed forward, parting her silken

heat and sliding fully into her until he was nestled tight against her silken rump.

"Oh."

"Aye." He held her still for a long, torturous moment, feeling her so tight and hot around him. Then he began to move, sliding in and out of her as slowly as he could force himself to go.

She shivered against each thrust, releasing little cries that tore at his control. Her hand reached back to clutch him to her, digging into his flesh and urging him closer, faster. He suckled the side of her neck, tasting her sweetness and reveling in her little breaths of pleasure as his teeth grazed her and claimed her.

When he could stand it no longer, could hold out against the sweet pleasure-pain no more, he surrendered to the raging passions churning through him and drove into her, releasing all the hunger within.

"Oh, yes." She accepted him, catching his wild rhythm and moving her body in time to his. "Oh, yes."

Her words, her actions intensified the incredible pressure and built it to a height he could not withstand.

He pulled her tight against him and shuddered as his release came, pounding through them both with no mercy, draining every ounce of sanity and self-preservation as he gave her everything he had to give.

Her body shivered, clutching him tighter as she followed him over the edge, her cries of pleasure echoing in the small confines of their shelter.

For long dazed moments, he could do nothing but listen to the labored cadence of their breathing and watch sunlight glisten in the light sheen of moisture along her flesh.

His entire body lay awash in satisfaction and a rich pleasure he had never known before. Such was the difference between enjoying the favors of a tavern wench and truly making love to a woman.

Whatever his intentions when he had first carried her to the safety of their ramshackle cabin, it had not been to steal her virginity and enjoy her over and over again.

What now?

"Maggie—"

"No." Her tone was low and gentle, but very serious. "Please don't try to apologize again."

Guilt washed over him. What had begun as a clumsy attempt to explain his feelings earlier had hardly become the apology he surely owed her for his intimate invasion of her body. Hell, he was supposed to protect her, not seduce her.

"I—"

"No." Louder this time, but still just as gentle. She pulled away slightly, disengaging their intimate link, and turned to face him.

"Devin, I enjoyed what just passed between us as much as you did." High color rode her cheeks and determination glowed in the depth of her beautiful amber eyes. "What we did was as much my decision as yours, as much my choice as yours. You do not owe me anything more."

She smiled and tossed the mass of her curls over her shoulders. "Other than the escort to Maine you originally promised."

He traced his fingers over her cheek. What manner of woman had he stumbled upon the day he disembarked from the *Sweet Rose Marie?*

"Very well, *mo chroí*. What we've shared was as much your decision as mine."

Tension he hadn't realized was there eased out of her shoulders. She leaned forward and pressed her lips very briefly to his.

"We still have a ways to go before we reach my grandmother's." She pushed away from him and gained her feet in one graceful movement, her hair cascading over her breasts in a wild tangle.

He could only watch her in wordless wonder. The sight of her standing so proud and unashamedly beautiful before him made his throat tighten.

She gathered her clothes from their place before the crude hearth and its long dead fire. Turning to peer at him over her shoulder, she shot him a direct look. "Don't you think you'd better get dressed?"

"Aye." He struggled to his feet and retrieved his own clothing, which had mercifully dried through the night. "I'll get the horses."

She nodded agreement as she shook out the layers of clothing she had peeled off the night before and began to dress. He pushed out into the sunlight feeling shaken.

She might no longer be a maiden, but she was still the same Maggie, the same maddening mix of intelligence and compassion and vibrancy that had stolen his heart and put his feet firmly on the path he now trod. Yet within himself there was a difference he could not explain. And that was scarier still.

After pulling on his trousers and boots and shrugging into his shirt and jacket, Devin took a deep breath of the rain-freshened air. The world seemed a brighter place this morning, its colors scrubbed clean and ready to be enjoyed. Random drops of water from the oak boughs overhead fell with the soft breeze that caressed him. He looked back at the rough lean-to that had provided them more than shelter from the storm. In the light of day, it seemed hardly able to withstand the terrible downpour of the previous night, but it looked like heaven to him for the events it had sheltered and the treasure it still harbored.

"Maggie-mine." He could say the words for the duration of their journey together, at least. Only a day or two more.

He corralled the reins for both horses, then checked and saddled them both as his mind trailed over what had happened since yesterday morning. He needed to put all the changes aside and set his life and his goals back where they should be—firmly on California and the gold fields, instead of focused so intently on a beauty with smoked amber eyes and an independent spirit to match his own.

"Are we ready?" Maggie closed the door to the cabin behind her. The sound had a finality about it that unsettled him.

"Aye, lass, but Missy is not. She's thrown a shoe and will not be able to carry you. She'll need to be shod before we go on. You'll have to ride with me."

"Oh." Maggie nibbled her lip as she glanced toward the black and then back to him. "We'll need to find a blacksmith to attend her."

"Aye." He swung up into the saddle and leaned down to offer his arm.

Her dark gaze locked with his for a moment. She was so close. The scent of ginger and chamomile went through him like a caress. He wanted to jump down from the horse's back, carry her back into the cabin, and never leave. He bit back the urge to tell her just that and waited in silence until she took his hand and allowed him to hoist her up in front of him.

She settled against him. So soft. Even through her riding habit, the dips and curves of her body tempted him anew. No matter how close the nearest town might be, this was going to be a long ride.

Chapter Thirteen

Maggie sighed against Devin's collar. The soft sound glided through him, adding to the torture of holding her so intimately against his chest as they rode toward a future destined to tear them apart.

Breathing the muted scents of ginger and chamomile rising from her hair as she napped in his arms further heightened the conflict raging in his thoughts. Never again would he be able to sip Granny Reilly's special ginger tea without remembering Maggie Brownley's cloud of golden brown curls nestled against him and a simple woodland shelter transformed into heaven by her embrace.

Each step they took north was another step closer to losing her. Each mile marker they passed put him another mile closer to leaving her and continuing on his own journey. Alone. Alone as he had never been before. Alone as he would always be without her beside him, in his arms and in his bed.

He glanced back at Missy, walking gamely along behind

the gelding despite her missing shoe. So far this morning they had passed several farms and small hamlets, but none with a smithy. If they did not get her taken care of soon, they'd have to consider trading her for a mount fit to take them the rest of the way to Maine.

"Maggie." He shook her gently. "Maggie. We've reached the fork in the road the men at the crossroads described. I've got to climb down now."

"Have we gone two miles already?" Maggie's voice sounded thick and husky with sleep, an instant reminder of their lovemaking. The memory sent a bolt of desire straight through his gut.

"Aye, *mo chroí.* There's the sign sayin' Pattee."

Two old codgers playing chess on the porch of a small crossroads store had told them the nearest smith could be found just outside the town of North Salem. As they'd started to ride away, one of them had yelled that there was a celebration at the Pattee property today and they'd most likely find the town's inhabitants there.

Maggie inched forward and arched her back in a waking stretch that tightened her blouse across the swell of her breasts. A flash of temptation seared him with images of peeling her jacket and blouse from her slender shoulders, of helping her shed every bit of her clothing until she was gloriously naked and ready for lovemaking.

If they stopped to indulge every time such thoughts invaded, he scolded himself, they'd be lucky to reach Maggie's grandmother by deep winter.

"Hold on tight." He slipped the reins into her hand and swung down from the gelding.

The faint sounds of a fiddle echoed through the trees along the lane they entered.

"Perhaps I should walk, too," Maggie offered from atop the horse as Devin tugged at Missy's tether. "Stretching my legs would probably do me good."

One glance at the dark circles under her eyes betrayed how tired she felt. And why not? She'd nearly drowned, and instead of insisting she get a good night's sleep, he'd twice made physical demands of her she'd never dealt with before. Then today she'd been forced to share a ride cramped onto a saddle meant for one.

Some protector he had become.

"I think it best you save your strength, *mo chroí.*" He smiled at her, and her answering grin sent a sizzle of heat streaking straight through him, confirming his need to put this extra distance between them. "For the journey ahead, lass."

He almost laughed at the look of disappointment that flitted over her features. Instead, he took a deep breath and launched into the subject that had plagued his thoughts since morning.

"While I heartily dislike dissemblance, Miss Brownley, I believe we will have to consider how to explain our sudden appearance in this community in a way that will cause the least notice or scandal."

After their dousing and the days of roughing it on the road, he doubted anyone would believe Maggie needed a servant, and he was fairly certain the intimacies they had built between them last night could no longer be hidden.

"Why not tell them the truth, that my grandmother is ill and you are escorting me to Maine?"

"Which will lead to immediate speculation regarding the nature of our relationship."

The nature of our relationship. Maggie's thoughts froze. Devin was right to broach the subject. She could hardly come riding into a party seeking help and introduce him—let alone treat him—as her servant.

What then? Her husband? Everything she'd ever considered true about herself balked at that deception. If she was not willing to consider such a connection in reality, she would hardly be able to play the part of a dutiful wife, even for an afternoon.

"Could you not say you are my brother and we are both going to Grandmother's?" Perhaps that would work for a cursory explanation to strangers—though the way Devin made her feel whenever he touched her had nothing to do with brotherly or sisterly love.

"That will surely work, being we look so very much alike, is that it?" Sunlight glinted in Devin's dark hair as he raised a skeptical brow at her. The mischievous dimple she loved appeared on his cheek as he favored her with a lopsided smile. How dare he seek a serious remedy that required her to think and then cause her stomach to flip with a teasing look that prevented all rational thought?

Sounds of applause and laughter rang from close by as the music stopped. Whatever they were going to say they'd better decide quickly.

"Cousins, then?"

Devin nodded. "I could believe that, especially given the disapproval written all over your face when you frown down on me like that. Only family members or . . . well, only someone close could look so—"

"Catch him, Harvey!" a young voice piped from the bushes. "Quick, he's getting away."

A spotted puppy bounded out of the underbrush, followed by young two boys. All three skidded to a halt on the dirt as Maggie tightened the reins to keep the gelding from shying.

"That's a mighty fine horse, ma'am." The older of the boys, a towheaded angel with huge blue eyes, spoke with awe. It occurred to Maggie that she had never been called ma'am before. She tried to swallow her move into the ranks of the elderly while the first boy looked the black over with an expert eye and the younger one stooped to scoop the puppy into his arms.

"What's wrong with the brown horse?" the boy with the puppy asked. He smiled shyly at Devin, revealing a missing front tooth. His struggles to hold on to the puppy squirming in his embrace made Maggie want to laugh.

"She's lost her shoe." Devin knelt on one knee and tickled the puppy's throat. "We've come in search of the blacksmith. Would either of you happen to know if he's nearby?"

"Our papa is the smith. He's sampling some of Mrs. Pattee's rhubarb pie over at the party." The smaller boy pointed through the trees, then giggled as the puppy enthusiastically licked his chin.

The towhead wrinkled his nose. "Papa don't much like rhubarb. He's jest bein' polite."

"Do you think he would mind us interrupting the fun and asking him to look after our horse?" Maggie asked.

"No, ma'am." The boy's wide-gapped grin made her forgive his including her with the older set. "Papa told Mama this morning he didn't see much sense in losing a whole day's work just to look over the Pattees' fancy new house."

"He said if the Pattees wanted to warm up their house, they should wait and set it on fire like everyone else come winter," the smaller boy added while the puppy chewed on his collar.

"It's a house-*warming* party, Harry. Papa didn't mean they should set it on fire." The older boy, obviously the Harvey they'd heard Harry calling to earlier, kicked a stone off the road.

Amusement twinkled in Devin's eyes as he sought Maggie's gaze for a moment. He raised an amused brow. She wondered if he was thinking of similar exchanges shared with his own brothers.

"Would you fine lads mind showing us the way?" Devin addressed the boys as equals, and Maggie could almost see them swell with importance. "We hate to intrude, but we must get back on the road to Maine as quickly as possible."

"You talk funny, mister. Where are ya from?" Harry scrunched up his face as he examined Devin.

"That ain't polite, Harry. Mama says ya can't ask people personal stuff like that. Ya gotta wait for them to tell you themselves."

Devin laughed. "Although your mother is quite correct, it's all right. I am from far away from here, from the other side of the ocean. I live in a land filled with ancient legends and magic. I'll tell you about the island I'm from while we find your father."

Their eyes rounded in amazement, the boys nodded their agreement.

Devin stood then and reached up to help Maggie off the gelding. As she slid into his embrace, she wished with all her heart that they were back in the little shelter under the oak, and that she could stay there with this man who smelled of balsam and earth and home forever. But that could not be. They both had their destinies waiting for them at the end of that road to Maine. Devin's family needed him, just as Grandmother needed her.

The short walk proved quite interesting, between being peppered with questions about their travels and trying to absorb information shared from the boys' lives. They learned that the Paulson family consisted of Harvey, age eight; Harry, six; and their twin sisters, Hannah and Hope, just learning to walk. The black and white puppy, appropriately named Spots, was a present from their uncle.

They reached the edge of a clearing with a wide yard that angled uphill to a newly constructed home sitting at the top and surrounded by strange granite structures.

"This place is called Mystery Hill," Harvey informed them in a low tone.

"They say it's haunted by witches," Harry whispered.

"Ghosts do the haunting, you dolt," Harvey scolded. "Witches make human sacrifices."

"They remind me of the dolmans the Celts erected back home," Devin said after studying the rock formations. "I doubt there are any ghosts or witches here. Places like this are considered to hold only good magic where I come from."

"Really?" both boys breathed, their eyes round with curiosity. "There's other places like this?"

"Yes, and from what my Granny told us, these are holy places filled with kindness and protection. The Pattees are fortunate to have a home here."

The fiddle started up again, echoing down the hill. "But where is everyone?" Maggie asked.

"Oh, the party's out back behind the house where the walls and all are. Would ya like to see?"

"Do you think you could ask your father to come speak to us instead?"

Devin's answer would at least preclude them from having to lie to a large number of people. Still, Maggie was disappointed. Something about this place was timeless and enticing—a mystery indeed—and it called to her. She'd love an excuse for a closer look.

"Wait right here." The boys nodded and took off across the hill, Spots nipping at their heels.

The fiddle's tempo softened, sounding solemn and eerie as it floated down to them.

"Dance with me, Maggie-mine." Devin held out his hands to her and smiled. A strange glow lit the depths of his green eyes. "Just this once, *mo chroí.*"

She put one hand in his and the other on his shoulder. *Just this once.*

Bittersweet warmth flowed through her like the plaintive notes from beyond the house. The rough layers of jacket and shirt separating her fingers from Devin's skin seemed to burn away while they twirled in a slow circle at the edge of the trees. She could feel his muscles as she had last night, bunched and yet silky beneath her, surrounding her.

She glanced up, but the intensity of the gaze he fixed on her proved too unnerving and she looked quickly away. When he stared at her with his fathomless green eyes, she could not seem to muster a coherent thought—not that she wanted to think. She wanted to give herself up to the bewitching magic of being in his arms, of dancing with him to a distant melody on a sun-dappled forest edge as if nothing in the world were more important to either one of them.

She looked instead at their two hands, joined together. His long fingers cradled hers. She loved to watch his hands at work—grooming the horses, holding the reins, sketching—but all she could think of now was the incredible sensations those fingers had drawn from her depths and wrought intimately within her.

"What does *mo-kree* mean?" She thought she might already know, but suddenly she quite fiercely wanted to hear the meaning behind his soft endearment for herself, a treasure she could store up for the lonely times when he was long gone to California.

"It is the Gaelic way of saying *my heart,* Maggie-mine. It is all I have to offer you. All I have to leave you . . ."

The music had stopped some time before. They slowly came to a halt. Maggie's breath hitched as they stood looking deep into one another's eyes—saying nothing and everything.

"Over this way, Papa. There they are."

"Wait 'til you see the big horse, Mama. He's wonderful!"

The enthusiastic piping of young voices heralded the return of the Paulson boys and their parents. Devin dropped his hand from her waist as they turned to face the family approaching down the hill. His fingers lingered for a moment, locked with hers for an extra heartbeat, and then he released her.

The two boys had tied a red ribbon around Spots and were busy leading him and a handsome couple, each carrying a little girl, toward them.

The woman looked hardly older than Amelia Lawrence. Could she possibly be the mother of four children? Her blond hair was pulled back in a chignon and net and the soft blue of her gown complimented the fairness of her skin.

Striding ahead of her was a pleasant-looking fellow with massive shoulders and sandy-brown hair which thinned at the temples. The baby he carried sprawled sleeping against his neck, her wispy blond curls blowing over her cheeks and his chest.

Spots stopped to investigate a clump of blue wildflowers, halting the boys' progress, but their parents soon joined Devin and Maggie at the edge of the clearing.

"Are you the travelers my boys say need my help?" The smith's voice, a deep baritone, sliced across the remaining distance between them.

"Aye." Devin nodded and gestured toward Missy. "The mare threw a shoe fording a river yesterday. We're trying to get to Maine to our grandmother. It's urgent, too, else we'd not think to ask you to leave the party."

"Is your grandmother ill?" The woman gave Maggie a sympathetic smile.

"Yes," Maggie affirmed. "Her doctor sent word. We're trying to get to her as quickly as possible."

The man shook his head at Devin. "Don't fret over this party. I've had about all the polite conversation and useless consultation over the weather I can take for one day. I'm Bernard Paulson, town selectman and black-smith. This is my wife, Abigail."

"I'm Devin." He glanced at Maggie and the dimple appeared in his cheek to wreak havoc on her thoughts. "And this is Maggie—my cousin."

"I'd like to have a look at the horse." Bernard Paulson looked over at Missy, then glanced down at the babe sleeping in his arms.

"Could I take her?" Maggie looked to the child's mother for approval.

After Abigail Paulson's nod, Maggie accepted the small bundle from the blacksmith and settled her against her own shoulder. The babe felt soft and yielding and smelled of warm milk and sweet grass. For that moment, Maggie felt as if her world were complete.

Devin and Bernard walked over to the mare; the two boys and their puppy tagged along behind.

"There's nothing like holding a baby, is there?" Abigail moved closer and tucked a stray wisp of curl behind the ear of the sleeping child she cuddled.

"They look so alike. Our rector's boys are twins, but look nothing like one another," Maggie said. She and Tori had long ago dubbed the Carlton brothers the *Dreaded Duo* based on their mischievous behavior. "Still, they share a closeness that's hard to describe."

Abigail nodded. "It is as if they have a language all their own. It makes no sense to us, but they are happy as they play. I'll wager those two lead their parents a merry dance, though. My own brother's a minister, and his children create as much havoc as the rest of the children put together—without having a special bond."

Maggie chuckled her agreement as the child in her arms sighed against her neck and burrowed against her collar.

"I keep a fire banked in my smithy most days for just this sort of occasion. We'll have this little lady fixed up in no time." Bernard Paulson's assurance turned their attention back to the men.

"There is the matter of payment. We haven't much left in the way of money." Devin's reminder stabbed Maggie. What were they going to do? A man with four children could hardly afford to give his labors away.

"Have you any thing to barter? A skill we might exchange?" Bernard Paulson asked after giving his wife a quizzical look and receiving her nod.

"Devin is a skilled artist. He could sketch your family," Maggie offered.

"A picture of my family . . ." Bernard's gaze followed Harry and Harvey as they tumbled with Spots on the grass for a moment. He looked at his wife and smiled as her own gaze flew to her boys. "Are you any good?"

Devin reached into his saddlebag and drew out the sketchbook she'd given him. He handed it to the smith. "Judge for yourself."

The blacksmith opened the book and studied its contents wordlessly, one page at a time. He moved to the other side of his wife and showed her one or two. Both of them glanced at Maggie, shifted to Devin, then back to her.

"They're lovely," Abigail exclaimed. "He's captured you perfectly, no matter the setting. It will make a wonderful exchange."

Her husband smiled and handed the book back to Devin. "You heard the boss. We'd best set off for our place so we can get you back on the road with as little delay as possible."

With a gentleness surprising for a man of his size, the smith reached for his daughter, still snuggled fast asleep in Maggie's arms. They traded the book for the babe, and for a second Maggie's arms felt oddly empty. Unexpected regret over her decision never to marry and have children tugged at her. She clutched the sketchbook as the Paulson family turned to troop down a wide path through the woods.

"Do you mind if I look, too?" she asked Devin.

After a moment's hesitation, he nodded his assent, though a frown furrowed his brow. He walked by her to go and fetch the horses. Maggie opened the sketchbook, anticipating more of the detailed scenes of Boston he'd drawn on the newsprint. Instead she discovered a collection of sketches featuring herself.

In one, she was standing on the front steps of her parents' Federalist mansion; in another, entering a simple saltbox home to deliver a basket from the Daughters of Grace to an elderly parishioner. Next she was surrounded by stacks of books in the Boston Public Library. Then she and Nora were pouting before mirrors as they tried on elaborately feathered confections in a milliner's shop.

She turned the next page and laughed to see a likeness of Jonathan gripping her hand, to her obvious horror, while a huge puddle of water formed on the street as it dripped from his hand. *Larry of the damp hands,* isn't that what Devin had called him?

There was a picture of her sitting on an elaborate Empire chair sipping from a delicate teacup and looking bored. Ah, he'd captured her feelings about the Daughters of Grace tea perfectly. Despite being consigned to wait with the horses, he'd so neatly depicted her in each scene, it was eerie.

The final sketch was of her dancing under the stars with a man whose face was turned so she could not make out his features. She recognized him instantly as Devin.

It warmed her straight through to find herself the object of such an intense study.

"Thank you," was all she could think to say to him when Devin walked back to stand beside her, leading the two horses. He reached for the book. She hoped her smile told him how wonderful she thought his sketches were.

"You don't mind, do you?" His smile held too much sadness to add any sparkle to his eyes. "I wanted to take these memories with me when I left."

The reminder that he would soon be gone from her life stole the warmth right out of her. Her throat constricted, and tears stung the corners of her eyes. She fought to hold them back, for his sake as well as hers. As dearly as she wished for her own freedom, she knew she needed to allow him to leave her with dignity and as little regret as possible.

"I don't mind." Her voice choked despite her efforts. "Perhaps you will make me a copy of the last one, though, so I might remember, too."

His gaze locked and held hers for a timeless moment that carried all the could-be's and never-would-be's between them.

"Papa says we're to take our time. He's got to warm the forge for a bit before he can take care of things for your mare." Harvey's message drew them back to the matter at hand.

"Can I ride your horse on the way?" Harry asked, his toothless grin wide and hopeful.

"Me, too?" His older brother favored them with a equally eager smile.

"Certainly," Devin laughed. "You may take turns playing tour guide and point out the highlights of our route to your home."

He swung Harry up onto the gelding's saddle and then

gripped the horse by his bridle to guide him. "You must hold tight and I will walk right here beside you."

Harry nodded while Harvey raced ahead, tugging Spots on his red ribbon leader. Maggie accepted Missy's reins from Devin after tucking the sketchbook she'd never surrendered under her arm, and they set off.

"The boss says you're to take these with you." Bernie Paulson handed Devin a satchel. They stood outside the smithy door readying their farewells now that Missy was shod and saddled once more.

"It's not much." The smith's apology when he had already been so generous with his help pinched Devin's conscience. "But these supplies should last you the two days you have left on your journey."

Devin appreciated the offer. "We can't pay—"

Bernie waved away his protest. "It's a small boon for the lasting pleasure you've given us. Abby's already gone to show her mother the sketch, she's so delighted with it. Besides, you must take it for your cousin's sake, if not for your own."

Devin looked across the smithy yard to where Maggie and the two Paulson boys were throwing small sticks for Spots to fetch. Most of the time the puppy raced for the stick and then trotted out of reach with his trophy in his mouth. The ones doing the fetching were Harry and Harvey.

Giggles flitted over the grass as the three of them took turns tussling with the pet. *Reillys are not partial to accepting charity.* Harsh words in the generous light of friendship this man offered. And Devin had promised to keep her safe. Eating regularly surely counted in that promise.

"Thank you," seemed the only response he could make

as he accepted the bag and tied it onto Missy's saddle. "We'll put it to good use."

"Mind, it's no business of ours. But you both seem like such nice folks. If there's anything else we can do for you . . ." Bernie fixed him with a stare that seemed to see right through the deception of Maggie and Devin posing as relatives.

Devin could almost picture Quin speaking instead of Bernie as the smith continued, "If there is some other assistance we can offer or you need a place to stay for a spell, I'm certain you'll have a number of customers for your family sketches."

Devin shook his head. His worries and the weight of his responsibilities nearly spilled out under the keen, knowing eyes of Bernie Paulson. Here was a fellow any man would be proud to call friend.

"Thank you, but we must push on," he answered, truthfully enough.

"Very well. You can get back to the road you need much faster if you cut behind my father-in-law's hostelry and take the right fork when you get to it." Bernie untied his leather apron and hung it on a peg. "You'll still pass by the Mystery Hill property, but you'll come to the road faster."

"Thank you again." Devin shook Bernie's hand and led the horses over to Maggie. She was sitting on the grass, pulling on a stick with the dog.

"Is it time for you to leave?" Harvey's laughter disappeared.

"We was havin' fun." Harry looked equally unhappy.

"My . . . our grandmother is ill and needs us to get there right away." The joy seeped from Maggie's eyes, too.

"Will ya come back sometime and play again?" Harry asked.

"If we can, lad." Devin tousled the boy's hair. "If we can."

He helped Maggie mount her horse, then swung up on the gelding.

"If you see him, tell my uncle at the crossroads I'll be down Sunday afternoon for our chess match," Bernie called.

With a final wave, they set off at a slow trot. There were only a few hours of daylight left to them and Devin wanted to be as far along their journey as he could by nightfall. Still, he didn't argue when Maggie stopped at the little bridge crossing the stream behind the inn for a last look.

He followed her gaze as it swept across the little settlement—Paulson's smithy and cottage, a snug inn belonging to his in-laws, three other homes belonging to relatives, and a small church run by one of his brothers-in-law. A cozy haven.

"I thought my grandmother's home was close to heaven, but this place . . . this family . . ." She took a deep breath and looked up at him with a curious mixture of sadness and loneliness etched in the amber depths of her gaze.

"Aye," he nodded, feeling much the same. The Paulsons made the idea of marriage and sharing a life seem so natural, so desirable.

"Come on, lass, we can't afford to linger." *In more ways than one.* The temptations of a home and hearth shared with Maggie beckoned.

They journeyed through the trees, making slow progress as they rode, picking their way over roots. This path might be more direct, but it was also less traveled. Impatience rippled through him. "We might be safer if we walk the horses through here," he said at last.

"Look, Devin." Maggie gestured through the trees

when he went to help her down. "There's some kind of writing on those stones. Harvey says there's all sorts of strange pilings and inscriptions scattered throughout these woods."

"Reminds me of the way to my gran's cottage on our island." He looked in the direction she pointed. "There were many such ancient structures and markings. But we've no time to investigate them right now."

She reached down to him and slid into his embrace. The temptation to kiss her dangled in the air between them.

"Harvey says the best parts are on Mystery Hill itself, behind the house. He and his cousins play here quite a bit. There are even underground sections. Was your grandmother's house built on such? Was it haunted?" Her teasing smile sent sparks shooting through him.

"My gran's cottage was uninhabited. By the time I was born, she'd moved up to the house with us, though it was always kept ready against the day she could return. We used it as a fortress." He smiled as he pictured the simple stone cottage with its thatched roof, haunted only by three boys. Maggie looked disappointed.

"But there were caves and strange druid mounds we loved to explore as often as possible," he added. "Seeing these reminds me of home. It makes me feel connected."

The satisfaction in her smile was nearly his undoing, but they were already stopped, and he had to speak plainly with her before things got out of hand between them later this night. He'd been mulling this over since she'd cradled one of the Paulson twins in the clearing.

She seemed to sparkle from playing with the boys and the time she'd spent rocking the babies in the kitchen. Abby had fixed them a small meal after he was finished sketching the family. Surprisingly for a girl raised with servants, Maggie had pitched right in. If she'd let herself, she would make someone a fine wife one day.

"Maggie, we must speak openly about a subject you may find a wee bit embarrassing." He stepped back and took her hands in his.

She looked at him, solemn and listening. He couldn't find the words to begin. "You know I must go on . . . that when we reach your grandmother's I cannot stay . . . my family . . ."

"I understand you still plan to continue your quest for gold in California, Devin. Why would I think you would change your mind just because—" Her eyes widened. "Oh."

"Oh, indeed. What we did . . . what I did was thoughtless and reckless. Even now my seed may have taken root within you, lass. How am I to leave you when that may be the case?"

She tugged at her lip with her teeth. "What are you saying?"

"I'll take you with me, if you'll come, though the journey will be far rougher than this." He was making a mess of what he wanted to say. He could tell from the death grip she had on his hands. "Still, it would be better than facing the scorn of all society for carrying my bastard."

She shook her head in denial as a blush crept across her cheeks. She did not meet his gaze as she answered him. "It is unlikely I carry your child, Devin. My mother never deemed it necessary to speak of such things, but from talking to Jenna I do not think it likely. The time is not right."

"Still—"

She raised her chin, strength glistening in the depths of her amber gaze. "My grandmother needs me just as your family needs you. Perhaps someday you will return, but I will build my life for myself with no regrets if you cannot.''

Worry still chafed him. ''We cannot risk any further chance of a lasting bond,'' he said softly. Their gazes locked until at last she nodded.

Chapter Fourteen

"We're almost there." Maggie's voice echoed with fresh enthusiasm as the forest thickened, stretching higher and more magnificent than Devin had ever imagined.

He couldn't blame her for her excitement. He, too, felt something indefinable amid the towering pine and ancient oaks—stirrings of secret protections, welcoming whispers. The horses had noticed the shift some time ago, as well. Since crossing the last finger of the Piscataqua River and officially entering the state of Maine, the gelding had begun tossing his mane and Missy was back to practicing her prancing little sidesteps. Maggie's stern scolding brought the mare up short with a huff of disappointment more than once.

The atmosphere was substantially different here, and it wasn't just his inexperience with heavily wooded areas. A tangible feeling surrounded them. The smell of balsam and pine carried into him with each crisp breath and changed the very air to something altogether new and intoxicating. His fingers itched to sketch the scenes filtering through his mind and add them to the small store he had collected to carry with him to California.

He inhaled slowly and caught Maggie watching him with an appreciative smile.

"You feel it, too, don't you?" Her smoked amber eyes sparkled as she looked at him. He had not seen her look so alive since their lovemaking after the river dousing three days earlier.

"It?" He paused for a moment as his gaze held hers, but she was not fooled.

"Yes." She laughed then, a clear, free sound that lifted into the trees to mix with the rustle of leaves and boughs high overhead. "Not everyone seems so aware. There's a special essence you feel only here amidst the trees. Don't try to tell me you didn't notice, because the wonder is clearly written on your face."

She spread her hands wide and closed her eyes, breathing deeply and holding so still she could have been a portrait on living canvas. His breath hitched. God, how he wanted this woman. Too many times to number over this last leg of their travels he'd looked at her and been instantly ready to carry her back to the small pallet they'd shared and taste again her wonders. Holding himself back had become agony these past days—and nights.

But to make love to her with the wild abandon his heart and body cried out for would be cruelly unfair to them both. Her surprising assurance, gleaned from girlhood conversations with Jenna Watson, that it was not the time in her cycle to worry about his child growing within her did little to assuage the guilt he felt for creating the possibility when his own commitments called him far away.

Reillys take heed and Reillys beware. The evergreens

seemed to whisper a warning from Granny's tale. His imagination ran rampant.

If only there were some other way, some other path he could find to bring the financing his family needed. He knew with a lonely certainty, already mourning his loss, that Maggie Brownley was his Blessing and that he must abandon her all too soon.

"Oh, Devin. This is home." She opened her eyes and fixed her gaze on him once again. "This is where I truly belong."

Aye, he couldn't argue that certainty. She glowed. The longing to sweep her from the mare's back and savor the happiness on her lips trailed through him, leaving an ache he was becoming more and more familiar with. "I can see that."

The joy of yer heart, the wish of yer soul, the direction of yer life, the path of yer choosing.

The tall oaks creaked a reminder of The Blessing's promise. Too late for him. His path was already set, and Maggie had made it clear she had no intention of altering her own destiny. She'd left Boston to help her grandmother run the mill and to create an independent life for herself. He could not ask her to subjugate her own dreams and needs to his.

Color heightened Maggie's cheeks, and she turned Missy back toward the trail they had been following. "The rest of the world always ceases to matter once I reach the heart of this forest, as though I've crossed some invisible barrier."

He understood what she meant. It was her family she strove to block from her mind and heart when she crossed into this forest's shadowed core. Her father's domineering demands, her mother's social expectations, overwhelmed her soul. Still, Maine's trees, no matter how spiritually sheltering, could hardly offer her the protection she sought.

By now her parents must have realized Maggie had not gone to Providence with Tori. Somehow he doubted anything would keep the Brownleys from attempting to reclaim their daughter and turn her back toward their own objectives for her life. A cold lump settled in his stomach. If the Brownleys appeared, would she return to Boston with them? Would she end up marrying Larry of the damp hands despite all she had been through? The thought burned a trail like acid through him.

Could he truly leave her to such a fate?

The choice, once made, cannot be undone. The finality of The Blessing mocked him. He would be too far away to be any help to her after this day.

The trail brightened ahead of them and Maggie urged the mare to a faster pace. The gelding picked up speed without any encouragement, and they rode into a clearing.

"Oh." Maggie's voice broke over the sound and Devin realized it was not really a clearing. The trees had abruptly ended and before them spread a meadow, deep green and dotted with wildflowers. Beyond that, a low rise arched out of the ground. Perched atop this natural pedestal stood a house, rough-hewn and stalwart, born of the same massive trees they had just passed through.

"Grandmother's, I presume." He reached Maggie's side.

"Yes, it's my grandmother's cottage." She spoke the words in a reverent tone and then met his gaze with a dazzling smile. "The first sight of it is always the most glorious."

Devin looked over the structure which, despite its rugged appearance, put him more in mind of a mansion. "Cottage hardly does it justice."

Maggie laughed. "Don't let Grandmother hear you say

that. This is what she wanted from the time she was very small—a cottage built on that rise overlooking the ocean. She built it after my grandfather died and she has run Worth Lumber from here ever since.''

She kicked Missy into a canter and headed toward the house.

Ocean? Only as she said the word did Devin realize the scent of salt and sea graced the air around them almost as fully as the forest perfumes. The distant cry of gulls carried toward them on a light breeze. A pang of homesickness struck and brought him back to the questions he'd been struggling with only a few moments before.

What now? The gelding easily caught the mare as they crossed the meadow.

"Hey, Maggie! Hello!" Distinctly male shouts hailed them from the broad porch of Grandmother Worth's cottage.

A man waved and then started down the steps toward them.

"Oh, it's Jake!" Maggie tossed the explanation over her shoulder. She slid from Missy's back without even glancing toward Devin and ran forward, meeting Jake halfway up the hill.

The man caught her in his arms and twirled her about, accompanied by her delighted laughter. He was a big man, Devin noted, as he gathered Missy's fallen reins and followed in Maggie's wake. Tall and broad shouldered. Someone she obviously cared about and who had held her far too close for far too long already.

"I'm so happy to see you." Again delight rang in her voice. She clearly could not get enough of this Jake. She stood back from him and gave him a thorough examination with her eyes, her hands still locked with his. Too long, indeed.

"I've not seen you since last summer. I finished at

Harvard earlier this spring. You look different. Grown-up, almost.'' Jake twirled her around again and kissed her soundly, catching the corner of her mouth with his own.

Devin did a slow burn, though he tried to remind himself that regardless of what had passed between them, he had no claim on her. Soon he would leave, and what she did with her life was her own affair. Somehow, the reminders did not cool his anger.

''So you are truly *Doctor* Warren now? I wasn't sure when you wrote to my mother.''

''Yup. I have the beginnings of a flourishing practice in Kittery.''

Maggie gave a joyful cry and hugged him again. ''Jake, that's wonderful. I always knew you could do it. Your father must be so proud.''

''Yes.'' Jake slid his hands over her back. ''He is.''

The man seemed to notice Devin for the first time as his hands found Maggie's trim waist. The urge to knock him flat tightened Devin's fist at his side.

''Hello.'' Jake nodded toward Devin. ''Mags, who's your friend?''

''Oh.'' She pulled away from Jake with a start and glanced over her shoulder at Devin. ''I'm so sorry. Jake, this is Devin Reilly. He was kind enough to offer me escort when our coachman was injured. Devin, this is Jake Warren.''

''Thank you for taking care of her, Reilly. She can be a handful at times, but she's one of the best people I know.'' Jake Warren extended his hand.

Devin took it. Picturing which handfuls Jake Warren might be referring to twisted the hot knife of jealousy in Devin's stomach. He couldn't escape the notion he was being thoroughly judged in return as the doctor pumped his hand.

Maggie turned to Devin. "Jake is an old and dear friend. We used to spend our summers together here when we were children."

She turned a twinkling gaze back toward the other man.

"Like I said, you've grown up a bit since then," Jake Warren observed—with an all too appreciative eye, in Devin's opinion.

"So have you," she replied in a pert tone before linking her arm with his. "But tell me, how is Grandmother?"

Jake sighed as they began the walk up toward the house—the cottage, Devin corrected himself—leaving him to tug the horses along behind them.

"She's better than she was a few weeks ago," Jake said in a careful tone.

"What does that mean?" Worry was back in Maggie's voice, erasing the buoyant pleasure that had marked her since they reached the forest. Despite Jake Warren's presence, Devin wished he could put the easier tone back for her.

"You did receive my letter?" Jake Warren frowned down at her. "I thought—"

"Yes." She interrupted, stopping in her tracks to put her hands on Jake's for emphasis. "We received yours and a note from her as well. But they did not describe what the problem was or truly how serious. She only asked that I come at once and be prepared to stay for longer than usual. You know how I feel about her, about this place. I'd have come without any extra urging."

"I knew you would." Jake nodded approval, having no idea what the journey had cost her so far or what further price might yet be exacted.

"I didn't intend to send for you at first. Her illness didn't seem to be that grave. But then she *asked* me to send for you. You know how independent she has always been. The fact that it was her request made me send the message posthaste.''

Devin looped the horses' reins to a hitching post by the porch as Jake and Maggie climbed the steps. The hollow sounds of their footsteps echoed with the childish thought that now that Maggie had her Jake, she seemed not to notice his own presence at all.

''Thank you for your speed.'' Maggie squeezed Jake's hands before reaching for the front door. ''I felt the same way. It's so unlike Grandmother to ask for any kind of help. When she did, I knew I needed to come immediately.''

Maggie took a deep breath, all the worry she had kept banked on the road leaping into her gaze. ''But, Jake, you haven't answered me. What is wrong with her? I've been imagining all kinds of things.''

''I'm sorry, Mags.'' Jake patted her shoulder. ''She's had a bout of pneumonia.''

Maggie gasped. ''Oh, no.''

''Yes, but it's not life threatening. I truly thought she was recovering quite nicely. Then she seemed to have some kind of a setback. There is nothing I can consider as the true source of the problem, except perhaps her own determination to work. She is too determined for her own good. What she needs most is rest, Mags, a good solid month or more of no worry. And that is, of course, the hardest thing anyone has ever been able to make her do. Even my father cannot get through to her, and you know she usually listens to him when push comes to shove.''

''Where is she now''

''In the front parlor.'' Jake nodded in what Devin presumed was the direction of the room.

''The parlor?''

''Yes.'' Jake smiled. ''Today she would not tolerate being sent to bed.'' He chuckled. ''I've been dismissed.

She told me she'd seen enough of me for at least the next week.''

Grandmother Worth sounded wiser all the time to Devin.

"Very well." Maggie nodded as though she had expected as much and reached for the front door before turning her gaze back to Devin's. "You'll come with me?"

As calmly as she appeared to take Jake's information, concern etched deep lines across her brow. It tied his stomach in a knot to see her face her worry so stoically in front of her friend and yet still feel free enough to share her fears with him.

Devin needed to start putting distance between them, as much for Maggie's sake as his own. Before too long there would be an entire continent separating them, not just the span of a few steps. But the entreaty in her gaze could not be ignored.

"Aye. I'll come." He reached for the doorknob, his fingers brushing hers as she relinquished it.

"Thank you," she whispered. The words rasped over his heart as she turned and disappeared into the darkened confines of her grandmother's cottage.

What now? He thought again and followed her.

She looks almost normal. Despite all her imaginings and Jake's preparations, that was the first impression that flew through Maggie's mind as they reached her grandmother's front room. She crossed the vast confines her mother would have called a grand receiving room, picking up speed as she went, overcome with relief.

"Margaret? Is that you finally?" Grandmother smiled, looking almost as pleased as Maggie felt.

Maggie knelt next to her grandmother's chair and put her arms around the woman who had always been far closer to her than her own mother.

"Grandmother. I came as soon as I could." Her throat

tightened as her grandmother's hands came up to stroke her hair.

"Yes, child." Grandmother coughed as she spoke, and the slight rattle afterward underscored what Jake had already told Maggie.

"How do you feel?"

"Not as bad as some people would have you think." Her tart reply was accompanied by a disapproving glance toward Jake, who lounged in the entryway, obviously deciding to brave her grandmother's censure.

"But—"

"Now, now, dear." Grandmother patted her cheek. "I'm not feeling quite up to snuff, but I'm not so ill I won't survive. In truth, I'm very happy to have you here earlier than usual. Perhaps we'll be able to extend this stay for a while, as well."

Grandmother's wide hazel eyes twinkled with a mischief that comforted Maggie. She knew how much Maggie's parents disliked these annual visits.

A pang of worry shot through Maggie even as she returned her grandmother's smile. What would happen if Mama and Papa turned up on Grandmother's doorstep, demanding she come back to Boston with them and marry Jonathan as they planned?

In truth, she'd been gambling they would not come after her. They had not been north in almost five years. Her very defiance of them should shock them into immobility long enough for her to help her grandmother get well.

She was of age. She could go where she wanted, not marry if she did not choose to, or marry whomever she chose without their consent, but she didn't want the fuss to land on Grandmother's doorstep and create additional stress until she was stronger. Then perhaps together they could put into place all the plans they had dreamed of

and make Maggie's visit permanent. At this point, she
could not imagine ever going back to Boston willingly.

"Margaret." Grandmother's voice pulled her back to
the parlor. "Who is the young gentleman you have
brought with you?"

Gentleman. Maggie smiled. It didn't matter that Devin
was dressed in clothes that had seen the worst of a river
and a storm or days on the road. Grandmother always
could judge down to the soul of a person and see him
for what he was.

"This is Devin Reilly. His family owns a shipyard in
Ireland—Reilly Ship Works. He has come to America to
seek his fortune in the California gold fields. When our
coachman was injured, Devin stepped in and escorted me
here."

"Reilly?" Grandmother's eyes narrowed as her gaze
traveled his length. "I've heard the name before." There
was approval in her tone.

"Thank you, madam." Devin bowed his head ever so
slightly.

"Jake."

"Yes?" Jake straightened from his pose in the doorway.

"Take young Reilly here to get cleaned up for supper,
and tell Kate to set some more plates. Then be off with
you. I thought I told you to make yourself scarce a half
hour ago."

Maggie hid a smile as Grandmother ordered Jake about
with the same imperious tones she had always used and
with total disregard for his new title and position. To his
credit, Jake didn't bat an eye.

"Come along with me, Reilly." Jake laughed and
clapped Devin on the shoulder. "Nobody dares ignore
Sylvia Worth when she gives a direct command."

"Impertinent imp." But Grandmother smiled indulgently as Jake moved to do her bidding.

Devin had little choice but to accept. "Thank you, Mrs. Worth, for your hospitality."

Grandmother nodded with the dignity she wore as easily as the silk shawl draped around her shoulders.

When the men had left, Grandmother's shrewd gaze focused on Maggie once more. "What is between you and that young man, Margaret?"

No preamble—but Maggie hadn't expected any.

Maggie took a breath. "Grandmother—"

"Don't think to prevaricate, my dear, for it is plain to me there is more than polite acquaintance between the two of you. Your eyes give you both away. His linger on you. Yours fly to his when you are feeling uncertain."

How could she describe what she felt for Devin? Her grandmother was such a strong woman, a woman who did not place her life's happiness in a man's hands. A woman Maggie had wanted to be like all her life.

"Margaret, I'm waiting for an answer."

Maggie sat back on her heels and smiled. "You're not even giving me a chance."

"I'll give you as many chances as you need. You mean more to me than anyone else in the world." Grandmother reached for Maggie's hand. Tears stung Maggie's eyes and she blinked them away, determined to match her grandmother's strength.

"I know that." She took a deep breath and blew it out slowly. "There is more to Devin than his escorting me to Maine."

Far more than she felt ready to share openly with anyone, even her grandmother. Far more than she wanted to admit to herself in the face of his impending exit from her life, if not from her heart.

"Beyond that there is little I can tell you. Devin has goals of his own. His family means everything to him. They have had some setbacks and he is determined to help save the shipyard any way he can. He must go to California as much, or more, for the family he loves as for himself.''

''Oh, dear.'' Grandmother sounded dismayed. She looked away from Maggie, her gaze distant and sad.

''What is it?'' Maggie straightened and leaned forward, searching the older woman's face for signs of pain or discomfort.

''You love him.''

Maggie's breath caught. Her grandmother always had been able to see through her as easily as she did a pane of glass.

''Yes.'' A strange mix of anguish and euphoria swirled in Maggie's stomach as she acknowledged her feelings out loud.

Grandmother shook her head and patted Maggie's hand again. ''Does he know?''

''I . . . I don't know.'' He had called her *mo chroí, my heart*. She remembered the feel of being in his arms as they danced in a sun-dappled clearing. *It is all I have to offer you. All I have to leave you.*

''Then you must let me—''

''No.''

Grandmother's eyebrows shot up in surprise as Maggie interrupted her.

''Forgive me, Grandmother. I beg you not to interfere in this. Devin has his life to lead, as I have mine. You know it has never been my intention to marry. He, too, has his reasons for not wishing to linger. What we have is almost over.''

The finality of that statement slammed into Maggie's heart, shattering it. Time was so precious when it was nearly gone. But she couldn't let Grandmother see how devastated she felt. Grandmother would try to fix it for her and she couldn't accept that, for herself or for Devin.

If they were ever going to find a way to be together, to stay together, even in the distant future, they would have to find it for themselves.

"If this is my one chance at love, then I will take from it what I can and go on from here."

"Be very wary, Margaret, that in your search for strength and freedom you do not lose the other wondrous opportunities life has to offer you. You are far too much like me for your own good." Grandmother shifted in her chair. "You speak and it is like hearing echoes from the past."

"If that is my worst vice, I am a lucky woman." She kissed her grandmother's cheek. "Now, shall we talk about you for a few minutes?"

Grandmother arched one pale brow. "If you're going to try to lecture me about resting, you'll be wasting your breath."

With that the older woman dissolved into a fit of coughing, retightening the bands of worry that had loosened around Maggie's heart as they spoke.

Maggie waited until the coughing fit had subsided and her grandmother sighed in relief. "It sounds as if you are the one wasting your breath."

Grandmother's intent hazel gaze shot back to her, but Maggie had learned to hold her own beneath the determined glare that had been known to send towering lumberjacks scurrying for cover.

"You cannot run the mill by killing yourself in the process," she offered in a tough but reasonable tone, one she'd learned long ago worked best with her grandmother. "You have pneumonia."

"I did not achieve what I have by coddling myself."

"No, but you had to do it alone. I am here now. I can run things for you until the doctor says you are ready to take control again."

Her grandmother pondered that in silence for a few moments while Maggie waited. "You'll not have Jacob to help you."

A little of the tension eased out of Maggie's shoulders. That sounded suspiciously close to agreement, but a new source of worry crept in. "What do you mean?"

Grandmother sighed again. "He's not feeling too well himself. I guess age is finally beginning to catch up with both of us." For a moment, the older woman looked every one of her sixty-four years.

It was a sobering sight.

"Is he ill?" The bands around Maggie's heart tightened another notch.

"Not in the way you mean." Grandmother shook her head. "He is suffering from rheumatism, especially in his hands. He cannot do all the things he used to do. He always had such capable hands." This last trailed away as though she were lost in thought.

Silence ticked through the parlor as the fire in the hearth hissed, popped, and resettled itself. After a moment, Grandmother blinked and focused her gaze on Maggie once again. "You may want to rethink your decision, Margaret. Without Jacob's help, what you intend to take on is a much larger and more demanding prospect than you imagined."

Maggie lifted her chin. "Perhaps so, but I have never been one to shrink from a challenge."

"No." Grandmother patted her cheek again. "That is entirely true. You have never failed to make me proud of you. I merely want you to completely consider the responsibility you intend to take on."

"I can manage. I'm your granddaughter, after all."

"Indeed you are, my dear, though there has been many a time I wished you had been my daughter. How different things would have been.'' Grandmother smiled and drew Maggie close.

Maggie rested her head on her grandmother's shoulder and for just a moment she was eight years old again, warmer and happier than she had ever been in her life. This was not the first time Grandmother had repeated that wish. And when Maggie was small, she herself had wished for it every night.

"Very well, my dear. Because I can count on you, I'll listen to that youngster Jake Warren and I'll try to do a little less.''

Maggie lifted her head, surprised at the older woman's easy acquiescence. Could this illness be taking more of a toll than she'd realized?

"In the meantime, I'd suggest you change and find out what is keeping that young man. Kate will not wait supper for him.''

Kate Butler had been Grandmother's housekeeper for a very long time. She had become more friend and companion than employee, and in doing so had taken on the forceful nature of her employer, a trait which only served to satisfy Grandmother's need for structure and control. So far as Maggie knew, Kate had never waited supper for anyone.

"Yes, Grandmother. I am in desperate need of some hot water and clean clothes first.'' Maggie kissed her grandmother's cheek again and turned to go. "After that I'll go and check on him.''

"Do that, my dear.'' Grandmother settled against the chair's cushioned back and waited.

Chapter Fifteen

Maggie raced up the wide central staircase, her thoughts churning over her grandmother's words.

Be wary that in your search for strength and freedom you do not lose the other wondrous opportunities life has to offer you.

She wasn't quite sure what to make of that. Did Grandmother mean Devin? Her thoughts spiraled. Whatever wisdom Grandmother had intended to impart seemed to have missed its mark entirely. She must be more tired than she had realized.

Late afternoon sunlight poured through the windows, gracing either side of the cottage foyer, bathing her in warmth. How she loved it here, both outside, amid the grandeur of nature, and inside, with the familiar majesty her grandmother had built with sweat and determination alone.

Maggie had always known deep down inside this was where she belonged, where she intended to be. Now that she was here, with her former life's bridges burning behind her, she was torn by a mix of emotions.

She couldn't stop thinking about her time alone with Devin in the poor excuse for a cabin where they had taken shelter and made love. Nothing had prepared her for the actuality of such intimacy with a man. Not even Grandmother's ancient tales of doomed lovers and ill-fated alliances—Tristan and Isolde, Romeo and Juliet—had prepared her for the incredible bond they had forged. Or so she thought.

He'd held himself aloof from her during the end of the trip. He'd claimed it was part of his job in protecting her, but she wondered. More than once she'd caught him looking at her, stark longing etched in his eyes, or reaching for her, only to halt the touch before it happened.

If this is my only chance at love, I'll take from it what I can and go on from here.

Brave words. She meant them, but would she really be ready to let him go when he said good-bye? The question loosed emptiness inside her.

She didn't have an answer.

She stared aimlessly out the window, her gaze drifting toward the path into the forest that wound its way to the mill and the responsibilities she had come here to oversee. She wanted to shoulder those obligations, needed them now more than ever. The days stretched out ahead of her, long and lonely. She would have her grandmother and her stolen freedom, but when Devin left, an indefinable part of her would leave with him.

The sound of her own forlorn sigh brought her up short.

''Stop this.'' She couldn't stand here and worry about the situation she had gotten herself into. She'd known he was leaving when she let herself care for him, had known it wasn't permanent when he took her in his arms and thrilled her with his kiss.

And when he made love to you?

"Yes, even then," she answered herself. She could not lay the blame for her broken heart on anyone but herself. It was time to pull herself together and begin her life. She left the stairs and walked toward the room at the far end of the spacious upper hallway—her room, on the corner where she could see both the trees and the ocean.

Inside the broad oaken wardrobe, ample changes of clothing hung awaiting her. Grandmother had always provided for her. There had never been any need to pack more changes of clothes than she needed for the trip.

She pulled out a pale yellow cotton gown and spread it on the four-poster bed that dominated the room. Only when she stripped out of her traveling gear and washed up at the basin on the washstand did she begin to feel a tiny bit more in control. She stopped in front of the large oval mirror next to the wardrobe.

How many times had she stood in front of this mirror, wondering about the girl who stared back at her? She could remember her reflection at eight, at twelve, at sixteen. Now the woman who stood before her made her take a second look. In her own deep brown eyes, she could read the changes Devin Reilly had wrought in her life. She could see the shadows of his leaving looming ahead, twisting pain through her.

Was she up to the task she had set for herself?

"I will take from this what I can and go on from here." More a vow than a statement.

She turned from the mirror and the questions dwelling in her own gaze. Grandmother was waiting and Devin would be here only for tonight. The loss spiraled through her as she reached for the gown on the bed. Her hands slid across the satin coverlet and she couldn't help picturing Devin's hands doing the same. She caught back a sigh.

She left the bedroom ten minutes later, holding tight

to her determination not to dwell on his imminent departure. It would leave a hole in her life, a large one, and it would hurt more than anything she had ever experienced. But she was strong. She had enough Worth in her to survive this, to survive practically anything life wanted to throw at her. At least she hoped so.

She walked briskly down the hallway toward the guest room and knocked. Devin opened the door.

Heat spiraled through Maggie, stealing her breath. She could only look at him and blink. His shirt was unbuttoned and untucked, baring his chest straight down to the line of his trousers. His hair was tousled, and she longed to run her fingers through it and smooth it into place. His green-eyed gaze traveled her length, taking in every detail of her freshened appearance and making her long to follow him into the bedroom and satisfy all the yearnings he drew from her.

"Aye, *mo chroí?*" He lifted a brow at her continued silence and leaned against the doorjamb as she gaped at him. *My heart.* The endearment only served to heighten the memories she was trying desperately to get under control.

"I came to make sure you had everything you needed." Somehow the remark she'd intended as an offer of hospitality tightened the yearning inside her. "I mean—"

"I can manage, Maggie. Your friend Jake has supplied me with some of his things." His tone was gentle, but the heat blazing in his gaze twined inside her and cracked the foundations of her determination to let him go. Her desire craved release in his arms. She held it back with an effort.

"Very well. Supper will be ready soon. Kate will not wait for anyone." She turned from him and hurried toward the stairs, struggling against the rapid beating of her heart and the pain she couldn't hide from.

"Nice fellow, that Reilly." Jake's comment drifted up the wide staircase toward her. He met her gaze with a look that would brook no nonsense. "Where did you meet him, and how did he become your escort?"

"Oh . . . I . . ." Maggie halted, wondering if everything she had just been thinking showed on her face. How much should she tell her trusted childhood friend? Every detail of what had passed between her and Devin washed through her mind. There was a time when she would have shared almost everything about her escapades with Jake Warren without hesitation, but those times had passed on a stolen night sheltering under an ancient oak.

"We met when he first arrived in Boston," she said, hoping Jake would drop it at that.

But he had known her too long.

"And?" He tipped his head to one side and leaned casually against the newel post.

She caught back a sigh, willing the heat to stay out of her cheeks. "It's a very long story. Suffice it to say he saved me when my carriage had an accident and then stayed on as a substitute while our coachman, Marcus, recovered from his injuries."

"Mmmmm." Jake studied her face. Was he considering her with the eyes of the youth he had been or the doctor he had become? "I always liked long stories, and I've a feeling this one could be particularly interesting."

"Indeed." Devin's voice sounded behind her, and she blessed his timely appearance for saving her the need to answer further.

"It is far less appealing than you would expect." Devin joined them at the bottom of the stairs and nodded pleasantly toward Jake before continuing. "Miss Brownley and her family have gone out of their way since then to welcome me and make me feel at home."

Maggie almost lost what little control she had managed

thus far beneath his dark regard. Heat crept over her cheeks as Devin's deep green gaze met hers. She'd welcomed him and more, that much was true.

Jake's gaze ran back and forth between the two of them. He had received enough letters from Maggie describing her father's prejudices to remain skeptical. "I'm glad to hear it. What are your plans now, Reilly?"

Maggie's stomach seemed to drop into her toes as Jake voiced her own question. She waited for the answer, not daring to look at Devin, even though she already knew it. Hearing the words would make tomorrow that much more real, more immediate.

"My plans?"

"Yes." Jake nodded. "You strike me as a man with a mission."

"Indeed?" Devin raised a brow.

"Are you staying for supper, Jake?" Maggie inserted the question. She wasn't quite ready to hear Devin's plans. *Coward,* a tiny voice inside her accused, but she ignored it.

Jake shrugged. "Not tonight. Besides my practice with Dr. Michaels, I've been volunteering at a clinic in Somerset. I promised to be there this evening. It's a good thing you've shown up, Reilly. Kate has never been known to hold supper for anyone."

"Kate? I think Maggie muttered some sort of warning about her when she came to check on me just now."

"Grandmother's housekeeper." Maggie supplied. "Kate has been with Grandmother since before she married my grandfather. They make quite a pair."

"I can vouch for that." Jake added with a laugh. "She runs a tight schedule—an admiral could not be so strict—but her dumplings will make you more than glad you followed her demands. I'll come back tomorrow and check on Sylvia."

Maggie couldn't hold back a grin at his irreverence. "You don't call Grandmother by name to her face, do you?"

"Never." He winked at her, a twinkle glinting in his dark brown eyes. Still the same charming Jake she'd always known. "She'd not allow me in the door next time if I tried something like that."

"Jake's father, Jacob, has known Grandmother since before she got married. He's the only person I know who calls her by her given name and gets away with it."

Devin frowned. "What does she prefer to be called?"

"I have been Mrs. Worth for nigh onto forty years," Grandmother offered in a tone that rang with authority and dwarfed Maggie's own mother's attempts at such command. Grandmother stood impatiently in the dining room door, still draped in her purple silk shawl. "Now come in here at once and stop talking about me as if I were not present."

Kate held the door to the dining room open as Maggie, Devin, and Jake approached.

"It is nice to see ye, Miss Margaret." Kate bobbed her head ever so slightly, the twinkle in her eyes belying the staid manner she portrayed in emulation of her mistress.

Devin stopped stock still in his tracks, his eyes widening as he looked at Kate. "It is a touch of hearth and home ye offer, mistress."

"Indeed." Kate's mouth spread in a wide smile. " 'Tis a pleasure to hear a touch of the green in ye as well, Mr. Reilly. It has been far too long since I left Ireland. Perhaps ye'll offer me some news later."

"It would be my pleasure." Devin nodded and then came to stand by Maggie.

"An improvement in the both of you." Grandmother nodded her approval of their freshly scrubbed appearance. Grandmother's throat already did not sound so tight as when she had first spoken. Devin held Maggie's chair for her as Grandmother's astute gaze watched each movement.

"I thought I told you to leave a while back, Jake Warren. And mind you, if I catch you calling me Sylvia again, I'll wash your mouth with lye soap. I don't care how many degrees you try to hide yourself behind." She turned toward Jake as Devin took his seat and fixed him with a quelling stare. "Do you intend to sit down with us?"

"Not tonight, Mrs. Worth." Jake caught Maggie's gaze and managed to slip in another wink. "But I'll be back tomorrow to check on you again."

"Very well. You never listen to me when I tell you to stay away, anyway. You may dine with us tomorrow. Kate will make those crab cakes you are partial to." Definitely a command that time, despite the cough that accompanied it.

"I'd be happy to." Jake bowed ever so slightly to Grandmother and then waved his good-byes from the doorway.

The savory aroma of beef and vegetables drifted through the dining room as Kate brought in a massive tureen and set it on the table. Maggie caught back a sigh as her stomach rumbled appreciatively. No one could make soup to rival Kate Butler's.

"Now, young man, perhaps you would share your plans with me," Grandmother said to Devin while Kate ladled and served.

Maggie's heart sank again and her appetite began to evaporate. She recognized the tone her grandmother had chosen to turn on Devin. It was the same one she used for suppliers when they didn't meet her expectations, or on lumbermen who thought they could get away with doing a lesser job for a woman.

"Plans?" Devin lifted a polite brow, his tone guarded.

"Yes, my granddaughter has told me you mean to go to California—that, in fact, you have delayed your intentions already in order to help her."

Devin's gaze shot to Maggie's for just a second. "Aye, madam, it is my intention to continue on to California."

"For what purpose?"

Devin eyed Grandmother for a moment and Maggie cringed, waiting to see how he would respond to her grandmother's rather formidable directness.

"My purpose, Mrs. Worth, is to help my family."

Kate passed a bowl of soup to Devin.

"The Reilly Ship Works." A statement, not a question.

Devin nodded. "Aye."

"I see. Would you like to tell me what type of dire straits the Reillys have gotten into that they would need you to rush off on a fool's search to California in the unlikely chance of finding gold?"

Maggie grabbed the glass of wine Kate poured and sipped it, avoiding looking at either one of the participants in this pointed conversation. She wished she could disappear straight through the floor.

What on earth was Grandmother up to?

"Perhaps we should say a blessing." Maggie offered into the quiet that awaited Devin's reply.

Grandmother frowned at her. Devin smiled and her heartbeat quickened yet again.

"Perhaps Mr. Reilly would do us the honor."

Devin quirked an eyebrow, but dutifully bent his head. "God bless the loaves and fishes and those who labor to bring them to this table. God bless the meek and suffering who remind us how blessed we truly are. God bless the ones we love, both near and far, and keep us ever close to one another in our hearts when we cannot be together."

Everything inside Maggie melted at his words. She was going to miss him so.

"Well said." Grandmother nodded. "Now back to my question."

Devin took a mouthful of Kate's soup as his green gaze held Grandmother's. He chewed and swallowed in thoughtful silence for a moment while Grandmother waited.

"It pleases me to know you have heard of my family's enterprise," he told Grandmother in a quiet tone that held a dignity no one would ever tear from him. "Reilly Ship Works is something we all believe in very deeply and would give much of ourselves to protect. Every business worth its salt has its highs and lows, as I'm sure you know from your own enterprise."

Grandmother nodded while he sipped from his wine goblet. "Go on."

"What we face now is competition from unexpected sources and a series of setbacks," Devin continued. "Illness has temporarily laid my father low. New tariffs, coupled with changes in Europe's economy, have led to several of our best customers defaulting on payments. Then there is the ongoing problem of finding quality timber and other building supplies."

Pride swelled Maggie's heart as his words rang clear through the dining room. There was integrity, strength of will, and determination in the set of Devin's shoulders and the gaze he held level with her grandmother's.

"I have studied at university in Dublin and worked in the shipyard for a small time. I am doing whatever I can to help. And if that means traveling to California in search of gold that may or may not be there, then that is what I shall do."

Grandmother digested this in silence as her bright gaze narrowed. Maggie could only wonder what she thought of all he had said and the manner in which he presented himself. What new questions was she formulating to force more information from Devin? Grandmother loved nothing better than to keep her quarry off guard, a tactic Maggie's father had always found irritating in the extreme—to Grandmother's delight. Maggie found she was holding her breath in anticipation and forced herself to breathe naturally.

"Then your ultimate goal is to help the shipyard?" Grandmother leaned forward ever so slightly.

Devin nodded. "Aye."

"By any means, or the most suitable and sure?"

"The latter, if possible." He kept his face and tone cordial, but neutral.

"Excellent." Grandmother nodded to herself, pleased with his answer. "And how soon do you plan to leave for California?"

Again the question everyone seemed determined to ask him, the one Maggie would just as soon not face. She swallowed over the tight lump in her throat.

"Tomorrow." Devin's voice was devoid of inflection. The word rang like a death knell.

Maggie stirred her soup, watching the vegetables and beef swirl around like the lost pieces of her heart, uprooted and decimated. She blinked hard to hold back the tears gathering in her eyes. A tightness welled in her throat.

"I see," Grandmother said. "And when you have found your gold, what then, young Mr. Reilly?"

"I'm sorry?"

"Never mind. Better still, what if you never find your gold, but another opportunity seizes you? It has been my experience that young men, regardless of their goals, often find their answers in far different places than they originally expected—in hidden blessings, you might say."

Devin took a second sip of his wine before he answered. "My grandmother always warned us that a blessing missed was a curse indeed."

Grandmother pushed back from the table abruptly.

Maggie realized she had hardly touched her dinner. "Margaret, I'm sorry, but I find I am more tired than I realized. Would you ring for Kate?"

"Of course, Grandmother." Concern tightened Maggie's stomach as she rang for the housekeeper. She'd been so busy mulling over her own loss she had not considered her grandmother's health. "Would you like me to go up with you?"

"No, my dear." Grandmother's smile belied the brisk denial. "Mr. Reilly is our guest. You will still be here after he is gone."

Her glance flicked between the two of them. "Entertain him in my absence."

Maggie held her grandmother's arm as the older woman made her way toward the door. Kate took care of her from there, and Maggie watched the two of them amble toward the stairs.

"She is everything you said she is. And a wee bit more." Devin's amused tones drew her back to the dining room. "I can see why you admire her so. She loves you very much."

"Thank you." Awkwardness settled like a lump in her middle.

"Maggie." The rough timbre of his voice echoed through her, threatening to undo her hard-won control.

"Perhaps you'd like to go into the parlor." She forced the words out. "Or outside for a breath of air?"

"If you like." He pushed away from the table and followed her into the parlor.

She paced over to the front windows and opened them, letting in the cool night air and the fresh scents of the forest and the ocean breezes. Soothing—and yet nothing could fully assuage the turmoil having this man near her wrought over and over again. Nothing except being in his arms.

"Are you all right?" His question came from just behind her, close—but not nearly close enough.

"Yes. I am fine." She didn't think she could bear a close scrutiny of how she was feeling. Not now. Not tonight. She swallowed hard. Beyond everything else he was a good man, a moral man, one any woman would be proud to count on. It hit her suddenly what he must be feeling about everything that had happened between them.

"Maggie—"

"No." She had to stop him before he made a mistake. She could not be responsible for keeping him from completing all the things that meant so much to him. She turned toward him.

Fire and candlelight flickered over him. No man had a right to be that handsome or make her heart and resolve melt just from looking at him.

"What?"

"Please don't try to apologize or talk yourself out of doing what you know you need to do."

"But—"

"Devin." She took a step toward him and then halted herself. If she got too close she would not be able to stop herself from flinging her arms around him and begging him to stay. "Your goals, your family, are paramount. You owe me nothing. I am very like my grandmother— or at least I have always tried to be. What I asked of you, you have already given me."

"What have I given you, lass?"

"My freedom," she whispered.

"Will you ask nothing else of me?" His voice was rough and tight.

I will ask for everything you have to give.

"Only that you do the very best you can when you arrive in California." She smiled. "Grandmother will give you the papers and money you need to arrange passage directly from Portsmouth to Panama. Then a short passage to the Pacific and you will be nearly there.''

He locked his gaze with hers for the space of several minutes, intent and fathomless. Did he struggle to stand back the same way she did, so that all the tomorrows to come would hurt a little less? He sighed. Something shifted in his eyes, and he pressed his lips together.

''Good night, *mo chroí.*'' He cupped her cheek, his thumb tracing a pattern over her lips.

''Good night, Devin.'' She turned and left him standing there in the parlor, feeling his gaze boring into her back with each step and knowing she could not leave it like this.

Tonight would be the last night he would be anywhere near her.

Tomorrow night and all the nights to follow would be empty husks.

In a matter of hours she would have nothing but memories of their time together to keep her warm. Tonight she would not settle for mere phantoms of his touch, his kiss, and the feel of his body against hers, joined with hers. Tonight she would be with him and revel in the feelings the two of them wrought so spectacularly in each other. One last time.

Chapter Sixteen

Maggie paused once more in front of the mirror, nibbling her lip. The gown she wore was thinned to gossamer with age. When Grandmother had given it to her several years before, she'd been entranced with the soft cream silk. It tied in neat little bows at her shoulders, leaving her arms bare.

The garment was more a sheer veil over her body than an attempt at modesty. She turned away from the mirror, gnawed by conflicting desires. She wanted, more than anything, to tempt Devin Reilly beyond the limits of his control. To that end, this nightgown would suffice. This would be her last chance—their last chance together.

Yet all her mother's teachings still resonated deep inside her. Despite her best efforts to be as unlike her mother as possible, she could not completely turn her back on years of ingrained propriety. She'd already given up the one thing a young woman should cling to above all else.

Now she intended to compound that sin by offering herself again.

A shudder crept over her as she pictured her mother's response to her plan. Alberta Brownley would tear her daughter to shreds with her own bare hands rather than accept such behavior.

But Maggie could not escape the one thought that circled consistently through her mind and heart—if there was such a thing as a man and a woman being meant for each other, if fate and a grand design existed in the world, if anything had ever meant anything to anyone, Devin was the one man in the world she would love.

And he was leaving.

It was right, in a way her mother would never be capable of understanding, that she spend this last night in Devin's arms, loving him with everything she had inside her. She grabbed her wrapper from the foot of her bed and shoved her bare arms through the sleeves. She sashed it about her waist before opening the door.

For a moment she hesitated on the threshold, feeling far more nervous than she had the first time they'd made love. That had been a deed of the moment. This time she was going to him with a purpose. She wanted him to make love to her, wanted to enjoy all that could be between them while she still had the chance, wanted to give him everything she had to give. Would he still want her? Or would he think her far too bold?

She forced her fears aside and closed her bedroom door behind her. The house lay quiet and dark.

Would he be asleep?

She moved down the hall toward his room, her feet almost soundless against the floorboards, her heart thudding in her ears like the rhythmic cadence of a hundred drums. She paused at his door and took a deep breath, striving for a calm she was far from feeling.

She knocked and then died a thousand deaths as she waited for him to answer.

The door opened and he stood before her, clad in nothing but the trousers he'd worn earlier. The soft glow of moonlight kissed the back of his shoulders as he stood in the doorway.

"Maggie." Nothing but her name, yet the sound vibrated with the same yearnings burning inside her.

"Devin." His name sighed out of her, husky and low. "May I come in?"

"*Mo chroí*, this is not—"

She moved closer and placed her fingers over his lips, halting him. "Don't tell me to go."

"You should not have come." But he did not send her away. His gaze burned with a welcoming fire. He turned from the door, not asking her in, yet not blocking her entrance.

She stepped into his bedroom and shut the door behind her.

"Maggie, I'm leaving tomorrow." The words came in the same flat tone he'd used earlier.

"I know." *That's why I've come.*

"Then—"

She moved closer, aching to touch him, but uncertain. "I want to be with you while I still can."

He turned back to face her, all male animal in the darkness broken only by the moonlight spilling through the windows. "Don't taunt me, *mo chroí.*"

"I'm not."

"You have done naught else since I met you." Harsh words, but his tone held pain that resonated with her own. "It is bad enough—"

She moved closer still and covered his lips with her fingers, unwilling to hear any recriminations he might express for either one of them.

"Please don't," she whispered, tears stinging her eyes. "What lies between us is more magical and wondrous than anything I'd thought to have in my life. Regardless of whether I ended trapped in a marriage to Jonathan or achieved my freedom here with Grandmother, I never thought to have even a small part of what you have given me."

"Ah, sweet Maggie." His fingers brushed her cheek, catching the single tear that fell. "You are all a man could wish for in his life."

"Then make love to me, Devin Reilly."

"Maggie." He groaned in protest.

She closed the distance between them, shrugging out of her wrapper to stand before him in the sheer veil of her nightgown. "Make love to me because it is what I ask of you. For tonight I am yours and you are mine, and no questions or promises need be asked of either one of us."

His gaze devoured her for long slow seconds as her words hung in the air between them.

She straightened her shoulders and lifted her chin, standing proud before him as she awaited his reply in breathless silence. Her heartbeat drummed in her ears, throbbing with all the passion that sparked between them, all the heartbreak yet to come.

Maggie Brownley's beauty, her pride, her incredible giving heart, tore to shreds any reluctance Devin harbored. The sight of her standing before him in a whisper-thin gown designed to entice undid his resolution to keep his distance and let her find her way amid the trappings of the life she wanted for herself.

Skin-warmed chamomile and ginger, tangy and sweet— the essence of Maggie—wafted through him. All he wanted in life stood before him, merely waiting his acceptance of her gift. But he would leave her on the morrow.

He had to. A fast parting would be less painful in the long run for both of them. Wouldn't it?

He pulled her into his arms, unable to resist the desires raging through him. As his hands slid over her back, molding and testing the soft curves her gown revealed, her gaze locked with his, the rich smoky amber denying him nothing.

The knowledge twisted through him like a knife, leaving a trail of pain even as the swift lightning of The Blessing sizzled over his soul.

"I will be gone." He flung the words at her as he threaded his hands through the thick springy silk of her hair.

"It does not matter." She refused to back away, and instead twined her arms around his neck. "We have tonight, Devin. If that is all we ever have, then it will have to be enough."

"*Mo chroí.*" He surrendered to her, to himself, to The Blessing that demanded all from him and refused to allow either one of them surcease from its requirements.

He covered her lips with his own, sipping her pain and his as their mouths melded together. A long slow kiss, rendered with exquisite care even as the banked fire burning constant inside him surged higher and hotter.

She felt so good in his arms, so perfect. Each bit of her, each curve, each angle and line, fit against him with incredible sweetness. The silk of her gown, the swell of her breasts slid against his chest in exquisite torment.

"Maggie." He groaned her name against her cheek, then pressed a trail of kisses from her brow to her ear and to the soft skin behind it. "I need you."

"Yes, oh yes." Her fingers slid into his hair as he laved her ear with his tongue and then tasted the fresh soft skin of her throat and the delicate line of her collarbone.

She arched her head back, granting him access to each

part of her. Her fingers gripped his shoulders. He kissed the hollow of her throat and felt her pulse beating deep within her. She shivered in his arms, her fingers tightening as he licked a slow pathway from her throat down into the low neckline of the sheer creation she wore.

The upper swells of her breasts, creamy and resilient beneath his lips, beckoned him onward. He kissed every inch of exposed flesh, taunting them both before moving his attentions lower still to the dusky tips of her pebbled nipples.

Her breath rushed out of her in a shuddering gasp as he closed his mouth over one tempting morsel pressing boldly against her gown, begging for his attention.

"Oh, Devin." Her fingers cupped his head, holding him to her breast while she trembled with pleasure. He suckled her thoroughly through the gossamer silk, slowly, teasing her with his teeth, pulling, as her fingers arched against his scalp.

"Aye, Maggie-mine." He lifted his head and allowed his gaze to drift over the incredible woman in his arms, arched and willing and oh so beautiful. The flare of passion in her eyes nearly undid him on the spot.

He scooped her up against him and carried her toward the bed. Moonlight gleamed on the soft green satin coverlet. For tonight, one last night, he would have all of her. He would give her all of himself. That would have to be enough for both of them.

He kissed her then, kissed her as he cradled her in his arms, kissed her with all the passion and love he could summon. Her lips, her tongue, her breath became one with his.

He let her down next to the bed, her satiny curves sliding down his chest and legs in delicious torment. His breath grew harsh with the demands of the passion rising so hot and heavy inside him. He drew back and drank in

her amber eyes, her soft lips, and the passion that added
a delicate flush to her cheeks.

"Mo chroí," he growled and locked his fingers with
her own. He kissed her, worshipping her mouth, sliding
his tongue against hers over and over again. Every inch
of his body wanted her with a painful ache that would
not be denied.

He slid his hands up over her arms as their tongues
mated in a slow, hot rhythm. Catching the ribboned ties
at her shoulders, he undid both with a quick twist. The
silken gown sighed downward over her body and pooled
at her feet.

Each time he looked at her, she was more lovely than
the last. Her beauty took his breath, leaving him dazed
and awestruck for the span of several heartbeats. She
stepped forward into his embrace and kissed him, winding
her arms about his neck and pressing her soft breasts
against his chest.

Flames leaped through him, scorching his soul, searing
his mind, and stirring his heart.

He slid his hands over the smooth golden silk of her
body, her back, her breasts, her hips. He pulled her tighter
to him, cupping her buttocks and letting her feel the full
swollen ache of his need.

"Make love to me," she whispered again, drawing
away from him to lay back on the bed in a wide splash
of moonlight. Light and shadow played enticingly over
her body. Her curls spread beneath her, pillowing her
head. "Make love to me, Devin."

The sound of his name on her lips, of her plea, raged
through him with awesome power. He tore at the fastenings of his trousers and shed them, watching her as her
gaze traveled the length of him from his shoulders on
down to the painful thrust of his manhood.

By God, he wanted to taste every inch of her, stroke

every inch, kiss her until they were both dizzy with want and need and ultimate satisfaction.

He knelt by the bed, sliding his hands over her calves, her thighs, stroking the tender skin of her stomach.

"Devin." She breathed his name as he followed the stroking path of his hands with soft kisses, nipping and tasting her.

"Aye, *mo chroí?*" He touched the downy curls shielding her softness from him.

"Please." She shivered as he continued his quest, pressing his kisses on each knee, nudging them gently apart. "What are you . . . oh!" Her question dissolved as he dipped his fingers between her parted thighs, seeking and finding that most tender part of her and stroking slowly back and forth.

Her legs parted further at his insistence, laying her open to him as she squirmed and whimpered beneath his touch.

"You are beautiful, *mo chroí.*" He kissed the inside of her thigh as his fingers continued to tease her. "So very beautiful."

"Devin." The word was husky and filled with longing.

"Aye." He smiled fiercely against her skin as he dipped his head to taste her sweetness.

"I don't think . . . you should . . . oh! Oh!" Her protest fragmented as he swirled his tongue over the sweet nubbin his fingers had already teased. She squirmed beneath his tongue, cries of pleasure escaping her lips as he licked and then suckled her.

He cupped her lush buttocks, tipping her up to better accommodate each teasing touch of his mouth.

"Oh, please . . . I can't—" And then she shuddered beneath him, crying his name as he tasted the very well of her pleasure.

Her fingers threaded through his hair as her body shivered in the aftermath. "What have you done to me?" She offered a weak chuckle.

"I am loving you, Maggie-mine. Loving you enough to last a lifetime."

The smile died away from her lips. "Then come closer, sir," she coaxed him, "for I've a need to love you as well."

He needed no further urging as he drew himself up beside her. He cupped her breasts, weighing each one and brushing his thumbs over her taut nipples.

"You've had your turn." She told him, placing a hand on his chest and pressing him back against the bedding. "Now I would torment you as well."

She leaned over him, brushing his chest with her breasts, rubbing their tips across his skin while she smiled into his eyes. Then she kissed him, light feathery sighs of her lips against his. Slowly she moved downward over his chest and his belly, burning a path of pure torture with her lips and tongue as she worked her way over his body.

"Will it feel the same for you?" Her breath teased him and he groaned, both at the sensations she evoked and the intimacy of her question.

"Aye." He choked the word out in an agony of patience as she dipped her head toward him. As her lips touched him he could not hold back his groan. So soft, so light— he would not be able to take much more.

"Mo chroí. Sweet Maggie, *mo chroí."* She parted her lips and took the tip of him in her mouth, tasting him carefully and driving him to madness with velvety feel of her mouth enveloping him.

She swirled her tongue around him as her hair drifted over his thighs and stomach. He sucked in his breath, so many sensations rippling through him he could not grasp them all at once.

"Stop, darlin'," he begged as her tongue teased him again. "Oh, Maggie."

But she did not.

She laughed husky and low, the sound moving through him as she tormented him still further, mirroring all the teasing strokes he had unwittingly taught her only moments before, suckling him, laving his length, until he could only groan and surrender to the intimate kiss she bestowed, bucking and straining beneath her touch until lightning cracked in his mind's eye, tearing down every defense he had ever laid claim to.

She drew up beside him, her eyes glittering as moonlight washed over her.

He turned to her and traced his fingers over her cheek. "No woman is supposed to make a man feel like this."

"Like what?"

"As though the earth begins and ends in the this one room." He told her, brushing his lips very softly across hers. "As though I could make love to you again and again and never get enough."

As though my heart is only partially mine, for the rest belongs to you.

"We have all night," she told him as she drew him down for a deeper kiss. "We have all night to try."

Morning came all too quickly.

Maggie slipped away from Devin's room in the pre-dawn hours. She spent a few precious moments memorizing his sleeping face—the way his hair fell over his brow, the strong line of his chin—enjoying for the last time the play of light and shadow across his shoulders and over his chest. She would need all of that combined with her memories of the loving they had shared deep into the night to see her through the long lonely time ahead.

Tears stung her eyes as she closed the door behind her. So final.

She put a hand over her mouth to still the sobs that threatened and hurried back to her own room. A door shut somewhere in the hallway as she closed her own. She could only hope she hadn't disturbed her grandmother. That would be the last thing any of them needed. Grandmother would worry needlessly.

A small ocean of tears later, Maggie dashed cold water over her face, shrugged out of her wrapper, and hurried to don a fresh gown. She'd dallied long enough with her own wants and desires and the sorrow she could do nothing to prevent. It was long past time she got a good grasp on the mill. Having something else to concentrate on would make Devin's parting easier, she told herself, without truly believing it. A glance at the clock on the mantel made her start. She'd spent far too much time in her room and on her appearance.

She scooted down the stairs, her shoes beating a rapid tattoo against the ancient wood. She felt a sudden need to touch the foundation of the things she'd focused herself on for so long. The mill, the forests surrounding Somerset, her life. There was time yet before Kate served breakfast for her to do just that.

She ran through the house and out the back door, heading into the forest without breaking stride. Only the insistent stitch in her side forced her to slow down before she reached the mill. There was a time she'd been able to run the whole way and never stop. But that was when she was a child, before she grew up and came face to face with the knowledge that even achieving your heart's desire did not always bring happiness.

Tears pricked again and she blinked them away. She would not fall apart because Devin was leaving. *She would not.*

She rested her cheek against the tree supporting her, drinking in the smells of balsam and pine, the rich, ancient feel of the forest, searching for the strength that had always been here for her.

These were her roots. She was as proud of the mill as her grandmother was, had spent time there from her earliest memories, and had gleaned what she could from life in Boston in order to prepare herself for the day she would eventually stand beside Grandmother and run the mill.

Now that time was here. She would enjoy it. She would grab the opportunity with both hands. It mattered very little in the grand scheme of things that she had given her heart and her body to a man who could not stay, a man whose life had been pointed in another direction long before he met her. She had never expected him to stay.

Tears dripped over her chin, dropping onto the oak bark cradling her cheek. She closed her eyes and let them come in silence. After countless moments, a feeling of peace invaded her. She opened her eyes and took a slow, deep breath. This is what had drawn her into the forest in the first place, this calm feeling of belonging.

She dashed the tears from her cheeks and continued over the next rise in the path. There below her, spread out above the river, stood the mill. Stacks of newly felled trees and those already trimmed lined the yard in orderly precision. Straight and tall, the wood they produced was highly prized.

Pride swelled within her, catching in her throat. This was home. This was were she belonged. Nothing could change that. She stood there for a long time as the sun rose above the trees.

* * *

Devin was already in the dining room with Grandmother when Maggie returned to the house. He looked up as she entered the room and she wanted to run straight to him and have him gather her into his arms and tell her everything would be all right, that they would find a way. She knew that was a fantasy, but for a moment, he looked ready to do just that. Then lines of worry and exhaustion sketched across his brow, and she knew he had turned aside the impulse.

"Good morning to you both," she managed to say without too much trembling in her voice.

Grandmother was looking a trifle paler than yesterday. Worry clenched Maggie's stomach and she vowed to spend more time concentrating on Grandmother's health and less dwelling on her own broken heart. Truly, she had been much too selfish, thinking only of how much she would miss Devin without sparing enough thought for anything else.

"Margaret." Her grandmother greeted her around a cough. "Are you all right? You're late this morning. That's not like you." That hazel-eyed gaze passed over her appraisingly.

"I'm fine, Grandmother." She kissed the older woman's cheek and hugged her gently.

"Good morning, Devin." She repeated her greeting. Just saying his name burned all manner of heat over Maggie's face, but she lifted her chin and met his dark green gaze anyway.

"Good morning, lass." She would never be able to forget the blazing green of his eyes.

She could feel Devin's gaze on her as she helped herself to toast and coffee from the buffet Kate had set on the sideboard. She had to concentrate to keep her hands from trembling as she poured. The rumble of his conversation with Grandmother passed over her for a moment before breaking into her thoughts.

"I appreciate everything you have been willing to share with me, Mr. Reilly. Perhaps you would like to tour the mill before you make your decision." Grandmother's tone was shaky, but determined.

Decision? Maggie froze at the sideboard. "What decision?"

She turned to face the two of them. Devin sipped his coffee in silence as Grandmother raised an elegant gray eyebrow.

"What decision?" Maggie repeated. Both of them looked entirely too innocent.

"Do sit down, dear, and have your breakfast," Grandmother ordered.

Maggie took her seat immediately. Long years of obeying that stern tone had kicked in before the thought struck her that Grandmother had not answered her question.

Neither had Devin. Something was afloat, but she refused to get her hopes up that it would prove anything beyond a courtesy visit.

She bit her toast and chewed it for a moment, meeting her Grandmother's gaze.

"Will you tour the mill, Mr. Reilly?" Grandmother finally released Maggie from her gaze and returned to her conversation with Devin.

"Aye, Mrs. Worth, I will."

Grandmother settled back in her chair. Maggie knew that pose. She'd seen it often enough. Whatever Grandmother was asking of Devin, she was almost certain she would receive it.

Maggie dared a glance from beneath her lashes, only to find Devin watching her.

"Grandmother—"

"I'm more tired than I thought, Margaret," Grandmother announced. She coughed to underscore the fact, and Maggie winced at the sound. "Ring for Kate, dear. I shall go back to my room and rest as you desired of me now that you are here to see to things."

Far too easy an acquiescence to something Maggie had not even had the chance to propose this day.

"Very well, Grandmother." She rang the bell as Devin offered Grandmother his arm.

"Thank you, young man. I find I have a lot of faith in you."

"Thank you, Mrs. Worth."

Again much more to this conversation. There were undercurrents running just below the surface. Kate met them at the dining room door and assisted Grandmother to the steps. "Send a message to Jacob," Grandmother told the housekeeper. "He must come and take Mr. Reilly through the mill. At once."

"Aye, mum." Kate nodded. "I'll send young Daniel to fetch him."

Maggie placed her hands on her hips and frowned at the three of them. "What have you asked of Devin, Grandmother?"

Grandmother did not pause on her way to the stairs. "Tell her, Mr. Reilly," she called over her shoulder.

Maggie transferred her frowning gaze to Devin, determined to have an answer regardless of how green his eyes were or how she longed to touch her lips to his own.

"She's asked me to stay for the next fortnight and help you get the mill straightened out."

Chapter Seventeen

A savage mix of emotions tore through Maggie so fast it left her lightheaded—wild joy, happiness, and an anger so raw it burned from deep down inside her.

"Help me?" She gaped at him, not sure exactly who she was more angry with, him, Grandmother, or herself for the rising dreams she couldn't stem.

She shouldn't be reacting in this manner, not after she'd forced herself to come to terms with their situation. She'd worked so hard to accept giving him up. This overwhelming feeling of hope and elation smashed against the stalwart fortress she had erected within herself.

"You'll stay to help me?" She could barely hold back the urge to scream at him as everything within her chafed her heart raw. "Why?"

"Because I asked him." Grandmother's voice drifted down the stairs toward them, soft and sweetly stern, but underscored with reason.

Maggie took a long slow breath and turned away from

Devin. The dismay in his expression sent her mind chasing over itself in an effort to think things out and regain her equilibrium.

"What did she offer that would make you delay your dreams of California yet again?" What could Grandmother have offered that she herself had not already given? She turned back to face him, her guilt over her own part in his delays gripping her hard. "You've already deferred them three times, Devin."

His green-eyed gaze bored into hers.

"Three times, because of me. But still you were set on going. What did she offer?" It had to be money. Grandmother had bought her Devin. Devin had sold himself for money when she'd offered him her heart because her heart had not been enough.

He studied her face in silence for the space of several heartbeats, his expression unreadable behind those dark green eyes. "Something we needed."

Her heart tumbled in her chest. *We?*

"What?" She struggled to get the question out.

"Lumber." The word dropped like a stone.

"Mr. Reilly, Mr. Warren is here to see you to the mill." Young Daniel, who'd been sent in search of Jacob, bobbed his head toward Maggie before ducking back out the door.

"That will be Mr. Jacob," Kate called as she descended the stairs.

Maggie wanted to scream in frustration as questions tumbled through her in unrelieved confusion.

"Thank you, Kate." Devin nodded politely to the housekeeper as she passed them. He turned back to Maggie and lifted one dark, silky brow. "Maybe we should save the discussion of why this disturbs you until I return. Or would you prefer to join us?"

A knowing smile curved his lips and made his dimple appear fleetingly on his cheek.

He knew. He knew despite her efforts to hide her turmoil exactly what he was doing to her by agreeing to stay when she had expected him to go after everything that had happened last night.

Her cheeks burned again.

"I have just returned from there, Mr. Reilly." She stressed the formal use of his name, though inside herself, the distance she sought seemed unobtainable. "We will discuss this the moment you return."

"Indeed we shall, Miss Brownley. Indeed we shall." He left her standing in the dining room doorway, her heart pounding with hope and rage in rhythm with the hard click of his boot heels against the floorboards.

She paced a circle around the dining room, trying to pull her thoughts and roiling temper into a semblance of order. Just yesterday, Grandmother had agreed to let her begin to shoulder some of the burdens of running the mill. This morning she'd enticed Devin to stay, exactly as Maggie could have wished, with a purpose that would help him aid his family and allow them to work side by side.

Her objection seemed rooted in their having made this arrangement without her. She needed to focus on that aspect if she was going to make her point without losing everything in the process. She turned to go in search of her grandmother. She might not be able to speak to Devin at the moment, but Grandmother was still upstairs. Regardless of her grandmother's rather formidable personality, Maggie was determined to make her point.

As she gathered her resources, hiked her skirts, and marched toward the staircase, the front door opened. Light spilled across the foyer, only to be cut short by a large shadow.

"Margaret, cover your ankles and come here this

instant.'' Alberta Brownley's disapproving tones washed icy cold dismay through Maggie's veins.

''Mama—''

Her breath left her in a rush as William Brownley marched through the portal past his wife.

''Where is he?''

''Papa—'' She heard the slap before the sting of his hand against her cheek fully registered.

''I don't want to hear anything from you, girl, except the location of that insolent Irish laggard. After all the trouble we went through to arrange your marriage to Jonathan Lawrence, you ran off with a two-bit Irish monkey.'' Papa paced away from her, anger in every rigid movement.

Tears sparked in Maggie's eyes, from pain, loss, and a feeling of hopelessness she couldn't hold at bay. ''I cannot marry Jonathan—''

''Why not?'' Her father turned so quickly she jumped. ''Have you become that filth's trollop? Have you bartered away any value you might have held? I'll have him hanged.''

''No, I—''

Alberta stepped to her husband's side and caught Maggie's chin in her hand. Her mother's cold gray gaze, so different from Grandmother's, perused her with a practiced eye for a moment before releasing her. ''She'll marry Jonathan, husband, trollop or no. She won't be the first bride to present her husband with a ready-made heir.''

Sickness clawed Maggie's stomach at the thought. She could never allow Jonathan to touch her now, not when she and Devin were so close to finding a way to be together. ''No—''

Another slap dropped Maggie to her knees. Pain lit stars behind her eyes. She almost wished her father would hit her hard enough so she could lose consciousness. The present scene was far too horrifying.

"Don't you dare defy me." Her father towered over her. "Ever again."

Anger poured off him in cold, shattering waves. She shuddered.

"William, you cannot present her to the Lawrences with bruises." Mama's reasonable tone chilled Maggie to her core.

"This is as much your fault as it is hers," Father snarled, and Mother stepped back without further comment. "When I think of the years spent on this, only to have the whims of some stupid girl almost bring me to ruination. A man expects better things of his family, Alberta. Better things."

"Yes, William."

Maggie cradled her hot cheek and willed herself not to succumb to the sobs rising in her chest.

"Where is he, Margaret?" Mama leaned down toward her. "There is no use in delaying things with your father. You know that."

"He has done nothing. He's not even here." Maggie managed to whisper, grateful Devin had already left for the mill.

"Nothing!" Her father's snarl cut through her like a knife. "He has run off with my property—my daughter as well as my horses—after I offered him the sanctuary of my home! This is just an example of what happens when you encounter these Irish rounders. I never should have believed you'd stick by your proposal."

Maggie bit her lip. What now?

"Get up and follow your mother to the carriage. We are leaving here at once. I shall send the authorities to deal with Reilly." To hurry things along, Papa grabbed her by her elbow and forced her to her feet.

"Papa, please—"

"You are not taking my granddaughter anywhere without her consent." Grandmother's voice rang through the entryway.

William Brownley turned on his mother-in-law with slow relish. "I see you are quite able to get about. I thought as much when your letter first arrived."

Oozing angry satisfaction, Papa dug his fingers into Maggie's arm so hard she nearly cried out. "Don't even begin to place yourself further in this muddle, Sylvia. Margaret's disgrace is no longer any of your affair."

"Margaret always has been and always will be my affair. She is my granddaughter." Grandmother was not in the least concerned, though Maggie cringed at the way her father's hand bunched into a fist.

"I am head of this family. My decisions are law."

"She is of age." Grandmother inserted with a lift of one silvery eyebrow. "She is more than capable of making her own decisions and directing the course of her own life."

"That matters not one whit to me. I have tolerated your interference and your influence for far longer than a lesser man would have. When I think of the years I've spent mollycoddling you in order to preserve Alberta's interest in that blasted mill—"

"Alberta has never shown the slightest interest in the mill."

"Mother!" Alberta gasped.

"It's true, my dear."

"Of course she hasn't. What proper woman would?" Papa's voice carried bitter derision at the notion.

"Your daughter."

"Whom you have all but ruined." He advanced still further, menace evident in every line of his bulk. "You have no say here, none whatsoever. She is my daughter—

my property. She owes me for the very clothes on her back. She will do what I want her to do, and I will have that Reilly fellow clapped in irons and shipped off to servitude!''

"You cannot." Maggie couldn't hold the words back, drawing her father's menace with her comment.

"You question me, girl?"

"Devin has done nothing wrong."

"You may not consider the sullying of your reputation a wrongdoing. I do. We are now faced with rushing back to Boston and somehow controlling the damage he has already caused. You will marry Jonathan Lawrence, my girl, as quickly as we can manage it." Just saying it seemed to soothe some of her father's ire.

"Besides that, he has stolen good horse flesh. Your Reilly will see a good many months in jail and then spend years as an indentured servant, you can count on that. I've a few friends who will be only too glad to offer me any assistance I need in this matter."

Maggie locked gazes with her father, finding strength from deep inside her. "You cannot accuse him of theft. I took the horses. Hail your threats at me, but leave him out of it."

"Obviously you have forgotten during your sojourn about the countryside just *who* is in charge of this family."

"Papa, I—"

His hand gripped her chin, sending pain along her jawline. Restrained violence shuddered through his muscles. "Alberta, take your daughter out to the carriage."

"But—"

"Not another word, Margaret." He leveled a heartless gaze at her. "You will leave with us now. If you do not, I will have Reilly held on more charges than horse thievery. Do you understand me?"

The trap closed solidly around her. Maggie swallowed as bile rose in her throat.

"Yes."

"Margaret, your choices decide the path of your life. Don't let him bully you into one you'll regret." Grandmother spoke in an urgent tone.

"Cease your prattle, old woman." Anger stiffened her father's posture yet again. "Do not attempt to bait me further, Sylvia. I have had quite enough."

He strode over to stand in front of his mother-in-law. She seemed quite small and frail next to him. "I intend to see to it that you sign the mill over to Jonathan Lawrence as Maggie's lawful husband as soon as possible. It will be a small price to pay to get him to accept damaged goods. You'll cooperate, or you will very likely never see your precious granddaughter again."

The world seemed to tilt beneath Maggie. "You cannot do this. This is not the Middle Ages, when wives were bought and sold!"

"Into the carriage, Margaret." Her father turned back to her with a speed that left her breathless. "You may yet have some impact on my plans only if you do precisely as I say. It will take your cooperation to convince Jonathan and his parents you were away on a mission of mercy all this time. You'll cooperate, too, or Reilly will face years in prison and I'll have your grandmother declared incompetent and have her committed."

Trapped.

Maggie nodded. "I'll come with you."

"No!" Grandmother's voice crackled with fire.

"Take her to the carriage, Alberta." Satisfaction purred through her father's tones.

"Alberta, stop. Do not do this to her."

"Good-bye, Mother." Alberta Brownley did not so

much as meet her mother's eyes as she caught her daughter's wrist in her hand and pulled her toward the door.

"Margaret—"

"I'll be all right, Grandmother. Please don't worry about me. I love you." Maggie managed to get the words out beyond the painful lump welling in her throat. "Tell Devin I hope he finds his gold."

She could only hope he would leave for California as soon as possible. The farther away he went, the less likely her father would have any influence at all.

"Enough of this emotional drivel. Good day, Sylvia." Father slammed the door hard enough to rattle the hinges as he followed them out and hustled them toward the carriage.

"Hello, Miss Margaret." Marcus's gaze met Maggie's in sympathy. She couldn't bear it. Tears pricked her eyes and yet she felt numb—hollow and dead at the same time.

"How are you, Marcus?" She managed in a voice that trembled. Missy and the gelding were tied to the back of the carriage. Her father had accomplished the return of all of his belongings. Hysterical laughter bubbled in her throat.

Better that than the tears that would give her father satisfaction from his dominance of the situation.

"I've been better, Miss." Marcus nodded.

"No more familiarity with the servants. I'll discharge the first one you speak with. It's your mother's laxity in allowing you such free rein with them that began all this." Father handed first Maggie and then her mother into the carriage and shut the door behind them.

"William?" Mother leaned forward. "Aren't you coming with us?"

"I find I've a need for fresh air, my dear. I'll ride for a bit." He told her, then offered Maggie a self-satisfied smile. "Your cooperation will do much to alleviate Devin Reilly's future circumstances, Margaret. I suggest you remember that and spend your time thinking of how best to present yourself as a meek and malleable bride to Jonathan Lawrence."

There was nothing to say to that threat.

"I didn't hear your answer, girl."

"Yes, Papa." She managed to give him the response he wanted only in the hope he would leave her in peace to contemplate the future she thought she had escaped.

"Drive on," her father called to Marcus as he released the gelding's reins and swung up into the saddle. "And don't dawdle. I wish to be back in Boston by tomorrow night."

Maggie slumped back in the seat as the carriage turned away from Grandmother's and the mill and the life she had so longed for. She could still see the older woman standing on the porch, so tall and strong. She had always wished to be strong just like Sylvia Worth. Now, when the trial had come, she was knuckling under, giving up her freedom to satisfy her father's demands.

She had truly accomplished nothing in her race to Maine.

The memory of her hours in Devin's arms rushed into her, igniting all the banked fires that burned on inside her. Yes, she had one treasure to cling to for the rest of her life. She loved Devin Reilly.

"You were . . . intimate with that Irishman, weren't you?"

Her mother's blunt words shocked Maggie back to the carriage with an abrupt thump.

"Don't try to deny it. I am not a fool." Her mother's narrowed gaze traveled her face as Maggie's cheeks burned.

She lifted her chin. "I did not deny it."

"How disgusting." Mama truly looked revolted. "Did he rape you?"

"No, he did not. I love him."

"Oh." Mama scrutinized her yet again. "How unfortunate for you. You will discover in time that love is very unimportant. We shall have to have a long discussion about how you are to proceed with Jonathan."

"I beg your pardon?"

"Well, Margaret, you cannot very well allow your husband to find out you have given yourself so cheaply to the hired help. Think of the scandal broth you would brew. There are ways for you to convince Jonathan he is your first. You will have to work at it, but I'm sure you'll be able to accomplish the task."

The thought of Jonathan's putting his hands on her, touching her in any of the intimate ways Devin had, made her stomach roll.

"This is entirely your own fault, Margaret." Alberta tsked as Maggie put a hand to her lips. "Jonathan is bound to be a randy fellow. I can see it in his eyes when he looks at you. He would not be the least bit surprised to find you breeding a month from now."

Breeding?

Cold reality washed through Maggie. She couldn't even imagine succumbing to Jonathan's advances, let alone accepting him in her bed. In her body.

The image of him perched above her, going sweatily about the business of putting his child inside her, loomed in her thoughts. She shuddered as her stomach rolled again. She had barely withstood the one kiss he'd forced on her. How could she survive a lifetime? She was beginning a nightmare, one with no hope of eventually waking up.

"You'd best quell that rebellious nature of yours, my dear," her mother scolded. "It truly doesn't matter what

you want or don't want. Your father's wishes are paramount here.''

"His wishes have always been paramount.''

"As they should be.''

"Why?''

"He is your father. My husband.''

And that was all there was to it, in her mother's mind.
He was the male, and therefore he should have whatever
he wanted. Once she married Jonathan, her own life would
be exactly the same.

Devin stood beside the office doorway, leaning against
the sun-warmed rail in comfortable silence beside Jacob
Warren. The old foreman had been more than forthright
about the running of the mill, the quality of the timber,
output quantity, various facts and figures that now swam
eagerly in Devin's head.

A huge sprawling edifice, the mill was magnificent,
from its slow-moving waterwheel on down to the saws.
The size somehow fit with his overall impression of how
Sylvia Worth did things. No meek and retiring business
for Maggie's grandmother. She owned an enterprise
Reilly Ship Works would be only too happy to affiliate
themselves with.

Just surveying the stacks of fresh lumber, rife with the
clean scents of oak and cedar, infused him with excitement. His mind reeled with plans and stratagems. This
would truly be a godsend for Quin and for the entire
island. His answer would be a resounding yes to the
proposals Mrs. Worth had offered this morning. More
than yes.

He found his mind focused less on the lumberyard
spread out before him and more on the independent lass
with smoked amber eyes whose happiness had come to

mean more to him than his own. She was the one obstacle in this proposition he had yet to face. How would Maggie deal with the fact he was staying instead of going?

In the wee hours of the night, when he'd held her so close in his arms and watched her sleep, he'd have sworn she would be as pleased as he was, that she would welcome him with open arms. But now?

Her reaction as he'd left this morning had been anything but enthusiastic. He couldn't help but wonder if he'd read her wrong all along. He certainly wouldn't be the first poor fool to misunderstand the workings of a woman's mind. Seamus hovered in his thoughts for a moment, and doubt stung his heart. Was his Maggie cut from the same cloth as Clara?

"So what do you think, young Reilly?" Jacob Warren's deep blue eyes twinkled from beneath his gray frosted eyebrows. "Is she what you want?"

"I'm sorry?" For a moment the other man's meaning escaped Devin entirely.

Then Jacob spread his gnarled hands in a gesture that encompassed the mill he'd spent his life working in.

"Aye, it . . . she . . . is a grand sight, Jacob."

"Indeed she is, indeed she is. Do you think you could spend your life here?"

"Mr. Reilly!" A call echoed up to them from the floor below.

Young Daniel from the house. Something in the boy's expression sent a chill down Devin's spine.

"What is it, Daniel?"

The boy raced up the long flight of stairs to stand, panting for breath, before the two of them. "It's Mrs. Worth. She wants you to come back to the house. Right away."

"Sylvia?" Jacob rested a hand on Daniel's shoulder.

"Yes, sir." Daniel gulped in another breath. "There's

trouble with Miss Margaret. Something about Mrs. Worth's daughter.''

As the boy gulped for air again, Jacob's worried gaze met Devin's. In those steady blue eyes, Devin read the reflection of his own fears. The Brownleys had come for their daughter.

''Go on, boy.'' Jacob told him in a rough voice, understanding without asking exactly what was twisting Devin's insides in a vise. ''Don't let her get away if she is truly what you want. I'll get the cart.''

''Thank you, Jacob.'' Devin turned back to Daniel. ''How long, Daniel? How long have they been up at the house?''

''Oh, no, sir, Mr. Reilly.'' In one thirsty gulp, Daniel swallowed the water Jacob had handed him. ''They're not at the house.''

Dread-filled certainty spread through Devin's middle. He knew they would not have left the retrieval of their daughter to correspondence. ''What do you mean? Where is she?''

''She's left with those folks, Mr. Reilly,'' Daniel explained. ''That's why Mrs. Worth sent me.''

Devin didn't wait for further information as he sped down the steps and made his way through the stacks of lumber and machinery to the cart Jacob had pulled around.

She'd left?

He grabbed the reins from the older man and urged the cart horse to her fastest pace as his mind ran over everything that had passed between them in the last few days. So much, all filling the void deep inside himself that he had never wanted to face. Why would she have left with them after trying so hard to get away, to reach her grandmother?

Had she changed her mind? Did she even now anticipate her marriage to Larry of the damp hands? The thought burned like acid through his gut. That couldn't be. It couldn't be. Not now, when he'd finally recognized she was his Blessing. Truth be told, she was that and much more.

Pain twisted deeper inside him. He loved her. He should have known it from the very beginning, *had* known on some deep, indefinable level even as he had struggled against the knowledge and the feelings he wasn't ready to accept. Now all the times he could have told her and hadn't taken the opportunity rang through his mind.

He leaped from the cart, Jacob not far behind him, and raced up the steps to burst through the door of her grandmother's cottage. Urgency strained his temper with every step as pain drained his heart.

"Where is she?"

Mrs. Worth met them in the foyer. "She is gone, Devin. Hello, Jacob."

"Sylvia." Jacob nodded, tension crackling in the air between them.

"Gone where?" Devin urged, breaking the eye contact between the two older people.

"My daughter, Alberta, and her husband came for her some time ago. They are on their way back to Boston. She is to marry a Jonathan Lawrence in all haste, if my son-in-law has his way."

Pain and anger such as he'd never experienced before dazed Devin, roiling through his stomach and tearing through his soul. She'd left. Gone back to Boston. To marry Larry. Why?

For a moment all the old doubts crowded back into his mind. The weight of Seamus's body against his arms and his own vow that he would never suffer the same fate echoed from the past. But this was Maggie, not Clara.

He caught Sylvia Worth's clear hazel gaze with his own. "Tell me why she left with them."

"Because they threatened you," the old woman told him, without trying to soften the blow.

The words fell like a weight against his shoulders. "What do you mean?"

"William Brownley has many friends in all of what he would consider the right places. He has influence. He has power that cannot be bought, and he is forever seeking to increase it. He told Margaret if she did not leave with them immediately and agree to marry Jonathan, he would have you arrested as a horse thief and see that you were indentured."

Mrs. Worth rubbed a hand over her eyes and released a heavy sigh before continuing. "I'm afraid he has just enough bluster to accomplish the task. He certainly had my granddaughter convinced." She stopped for a moment. "And so she left with them. She has bargained herself into a life she will abhor, rather than see any harm come to you."

"*Diabhal.*" White-hot anger surged.

"Exactly." Mrs. Worth nodded her approval. "Now what do you intend to do about it?"

Chapter Eighteen

"If ya turn down that way after ya pass the Pattees at Mystery Hill, ya can't miss it. Ain't that right, Bill?"

"That's right, Amos. Can't miss it."

Maggie listened as Marcus thanked the two old men at the Crossroads General Store for directions to the nearest smithy. Bill and Amos nodded amiably and went back to their chess game.

Maggie's heart twisted within her.

Pattee and Mystery Hill. She and Devin had spent happy hours there a few days before, yet it seemed like a lifetime ago.

"All I want is the nearest stable where we can have that blasted wheel fixed. Now you're taking us off into the back of beyond. What kind of service will we get there, I ask you?" Papa's disgruntled voice lashed Marcus as the coachman limped back to the carriage. "Why didn't you check this before we left Portsmouth?"

"The ruts in the road this side of Plaistow made the

difference, sir,'' Marcus explained. Again. ''I can try to make it to Andover, but it is a trifle more wobbly than I like to put my faith in.''

''No, blast it. You've gone slow enough this journey home already. We need the thing fixed as quickly as possible. Harrumph.''

Papa's grumbling sounded close to the carriage. He had been alternating between riding the gelding and sitting inside with them on this second day of their journey toward Boston—toward her doom. He left the carriage only after he'd made quite certain she knew he was leaving because he couldn't stand the sight of her. His habitual diatribes meant much less to her now than ever before, as though leaving Devin behind had numbed her to the pain her father so readily inflicted.

''This is a gross miscarriage of your responsibilities, Watson.''

Mama sighed and played with her handkerchief as Papa continued.

''I do not tolerate such negligence in my employ.'' The theme Papa had been stridently pursuing for the last half hour continued. Pointing out that his tirade made the delay worse would only whip his fury further. ''We haven't time for such misdirected handling. I'll dock your wages for this.''

Mama remained oblivious to it all as she perused the pages of the Godey's she'd brought with her. That was a trick Maggie knew she would have to cultivate if she were going to keep any portion of her sanity in her marriage to Jonathan. The ability to shut out Papa's unpleasant orations and downright tantrums had seen Alberta Brownley through most of Maggie's life.

Did she really want to live a lifetime dreading the nights and ignoring the days?

"Yes, sir." Marcus remained unfailingly polite beneath her father's tirade.

Maggie gazed out the side window, watching as they rumbled down the familiar roadway on the loose wheel. She didn't know whether to hope Bernie could get the wheel fixed quickly or to hope for a delay, a reprieve from the sentence she had agreed to. Each mile back toward Boston seemed to drive a greater wedge into her heart, and thoughts of the bleak future she faced started a dull ache throbbing in her temples.

At least she'd have the opportunity to see Abby again, and Harry, Harvey, and the little girls. Her heart twisted. And to envy them the life they shared.

Her gaze sought the turn to Mystery Hill hidden in the trees. She could still feel Devin's hands at her waist, guiding her through the steps, could still hear the music.

She sighed. The carriage gave occasional lurching jolts, signaling the wheel problem was worsening.

"Whoa." Marcus's call to the horses brought her reminiscences up short as he jumped down from his perch. "I'll see to the smith, sir."

Maggie leaned forward, hoping to catch a glimpse of her kindly friends. It would serve no purpose to have her parents know she had been here before. In fact, the reminder that she'd been cavorting in the wilderness with *that man* would only serve to set Papa off on another round of lectures and recriminations.

"Sit up straight, Margaret. You know I abhor it when you slouch."

"Yes, Mama." Ingrained habit had her doing as her mother bid without question. A gleam of satisfaction shone in her mother's eyes. Mama might turn a deaf ear to much of what Papa raged on about, but she had her own need for control to satisfy.

"You see, my dear, you can do everything you need to do when the time arises."

Maggie held back her shudder with an effort. Her mother's detailed description of exactly what she was to do the night of her wedding to Jonathan made her stomach roll.

"What were you looking for out there? These crude people can do nothing to aid your situation."

"I . . . nothing, Mama. I'm tired of sitting. I really would like to take a short walk." Maggie held her breath. She wanted more than that. She wanted to run as far and as fast as she could from the bargain she had struck with her father.

"A walk? Out amidst the wilderness?" Her mother wrinkled her nose and gave a delicate shiver. "I can't see what you think you would accomplish with such a task."

"Merely a bit of exercise. And this is hardly wilderness, Mama."

"Hmmm." Her mother eyed her for a moment before sitting back against the carriage seat with a bored expression on her face. "We'll see what your father has to say about that."

Maggie caught back the angry words that sprang to her lips. She was tired of waiting on Papa's every whim. She'd always known she couldn't live like this, under a man's constant constraints, but after having gained her freedom, however briefly, she chafed at every intrusion.

"Mama, surely Papa won't mind a brief—"

"Won't mind what?" Papa pulled the carriage door open. "What do you scheme about now, girl?"

Maggie took a slow breath and prayed the ire she felt would stay out of her tone as she faced her father's frowning visage.

"I wish to take a short walk, Papa." She held his gaze

with her own, refusing to be cowed and hoping all the anger roiling inside her did not show in her expression.

"Your wishes got us into this debacle in the first place," her father informed her with a cold sneer. He looked around the little settlement surrounding the smithy. "However, I will grant this request, if only to show you I can be amenable—provided you continue to do as you are told. There is little point in your trying to run back to your grandmother's. I still hold you to our bargain. This time I will not be gainsaid."

She nodded, refusing to thank him for something that should have been her own decision, not his. He backed away from the carriage door and she alighted on her own with no help from him. So be it. Her father did not respect her, and that was fine. She had long ago lost respect for him.

"I am taking your mother over to the hostelry for whatever crude refreshments they may offer. Come, Alberta. We will be heading out as soon as the repairs can be effected."

She dared a quick peek into the smithy and caught a glimpse of Bernie Paulson in speculative conversation with Marcus. The urge to go and talk with him fought against the pain of her memories and hopes from her last visit here.

Abby and the children were nowhere in sight, and she dared not risk seeking them out lest she give away her earlier sojourn here. She turned away and started for the path that would take her back toward Mystery Hill.

Everything she had hoped and dreamed for, everything that would have meant anything to her in her life was now part of the past. Perhaps it would be best to just leave it that way.

"Margaret."

She stopped in her tracks at her father's call.

"Do not go far, my dear." His tone carried smug assurance that she wouldn't dare disobey him. She must follow his dictates to the letter in order to save Devin from any possible repercussions. Her throat felt tight, as though bound with an invisible shackle, irrevocably linked to a chain held securely in her father's hands.

"I will not be far, Papa," she answered without looking at him. She wouldn't give him the satisfaction of seeing the tears that blurred her vision. She swiped them away with the back of her hand. After last night, locked in her room in the Portsmouth Inn, she'd been certain she had no tears left.

A light breeze carried the scents of sun-toasted leaves and fresh wood and the sound of children laughing somewhere in the distance. Harvey and Harry, no doubt. The thought of them brought a wistful smile to her lips. Her thoughts drifted toward wondering what Devin had been like as a child, and she prayed with all her heart that Jenna was wrong and she had indeed conceived a black-haired boy with Reilly green eyes.

She reached the edge of the clearing where she had danced in Devin's arms. She could hear the music even now. The plaintive notes of the fiddle wound their sad magic through her. Her heart twisted as pain gripped her and tears stung the backs of her eyes again. She could feel Devin's hands on her own, at her waist, cradling her close.

She closed her eyes and swayed in time with the music in her mind and heart.

"*Mo chroí.*" The words came tight with longing and sorrow as she remembered Devin's explanation of the endearment. *My heart.*

She blew out a harsh breath. How she yearned to hear him say those words again, to hold him one more time. No, not just one more time. Once would not be enough.

She faced the void losing Devin created inside her life, her soul. Had her parents not forced her to leave him, ripped her from her chosen course, she would not have been able to let Devin go without a fight. All the times she had told herself she could let him go for his own sake echoed through her, mocking her.

What lay between them was far too special to lose without fighting to keep it.

Mystery Hill rose before her, echoing old puzzles from the past that might never be solved, crowded with ancient stones that could tell the tales if one knew how to tap into the knowledge stored there.

The effort needed to create such a place was amazing and humbling, achieved so long before these modern times as to be astounding.

Inspiring. Here was an example of something put together out of grit and determination and a belief there was a purpose to the action—more than thirty acres of stone circles and monoliths. Wasn't that what Bernie had said? The overwhelming size of the place dwarfed her own problems into insignificance.

Hill upon hill rippled off into the distance as she drew closer.

Hill upon hill of ancient stones and determination.

Just the idea lifted her spirits—that and the notion Devin might have spent time in just such a place as a boy. Is that where he'd grown his own determination to succeed? Was the highest point on his island a hill such as these? Was that where he would have gone to wait for his brother Quin to find him?

Unreasoning hope hammered in her chest as she lifted her skirts and raced through the trees, up one hillside to the crest, even as hot tears streaked her cheeks. Reaching the top, she was rewarded with a view that spanned the

Pattees' new house as well as the maze of stones that was beyond it.

She gripped her hands together as more tears dripped onto her fingers. "Oh, Devin, if only you could find me."

"Yup. Went on to my nephew's. 'Bout an hour ago, ya reckon, Bill?"

"I reckon, Amos, I reckon."

The answers Devin gathered from the two old codgers at the general store repeated over and over in his head as he urged the brown mare he'd taken from Maggie's grandmother to a faster pace.

A carriage had passed this way, and, according to Bill— or perhaps Amos—it matched the description of the Brownleys' vehicle. A wobbly wheel had forced a detour that was surely part of destiny, sending them to Bernie Paulson's smithy.

He could only pray it was so as hope burgeoned within him that he had at last caught up with them—that he would soon find Maggie.

He was almost afraid to hope. After all the false trails and misdirection, it seemed almost impossible they would have traveled the very same roadway he and Maggie had so recently used, past Pattees' and Mystery Hill.

The memory of holding her in his arms, of dancing with her to drifting music within sight of the ancient stones, twisted inside him, heightening still further the strained sense of urgency that had ridden with him all the way from Somerset.

Losing Maggie had tightened the focus he held within himself to a fine point of clarity. She was part of him in ways that could never be fully explained, a link from which he had no wish to extricate himself.

She was more than his Blessing.

He loved her.

If he could only find her again, he would not hesitate to tell her so.

As the hills and dips that encompassed the area known as Mystery Hill came into view, he knew he had reached the fork in the road that would lead to Bernard Paulson's house and the most likely place to fix a broken carriage wheel.

He turned the mare toward the road and then yanked hard on the reins, wheeling her to a halt as his mind registered the sight his gaze had just flicked past. There in the trees, atop one of the larger rises overlooking Mystery Hill, stood a lone figure, as still as one of the monoliths she viewed.

A painful band tightened around his heart. She didn't need to move or to speak. Even without being able to see her clearly, he knew who she was—had known before he'd really spotted her.

"Maggie." He barely squeezed her name out around the thick lump lodged in his throat.

He slid from the mare's back and raced toward the woman who held his heart so securely in her possession.

"Oh, Devin, if you could only find me." As he reached the top, her words drifted back on a faint breeze carrying the scent of ginger and chamomile and Maggie.

"Mo chroí."

She gasped and stiffened, every line in her graceful back frozen into place.

"I love you, Margaret Sylvia Worth Brownley," he told her, the words ringing straight from his soul as he closed the distance between them. "I cannot let you go."

"Oh, Devin." She turned to him. Tears sparkled over her cheeks, belied by the warm glow in the depths of her smoked amber eyes.

Unable to stand the aching emptiness a moment longer,

he pulled her into his arms. She felt so right against him. This was where she belonged, now and forever. He would do whatever he had to do to make it so.

He covered her lips with his own, capturing her broken laughter as he tasted her kiss, sliding his tongue against hers.

"I didn't leave you . . . I left because—" she started to explain when he at last lifted his head.

"No, Maggie-mine." He covered her soft lips with one finger. "I know why you left. Your father and his influence do not frighten me. My father and brother are not without influence of their own in most ports where Reilly vessels call."

"But—"

What an arrogant fool he'd been not to seek whatever aid he could among his father's associates from the outset of his disastrous landing. But if he had, he might never have gotten past that arrogance to find his destiny twined in this woman's arms.

"You will never marry Jonathan Adams Lawrence III," he said, reveling in the sweet power of holding her, and knowing to the depths of his soul that he needed her as much as his next breath. "You've been mine since that first day on the docks."

She shook her head. "Papa—"

"You must marry me instead, *mo chroí*. I have discovered I need you more than I ever thought possible. You hold my heart. Without you, life is not worth living."

Her smile dazzled him.

"Then, Mr. Reilly, if you would kindly stop talking, you would see that my wishes are the same as yours."

"Indeed?" He lifted a brow at her as her words warmed him clear through.

"Aye," she said, her smile soft. "I need you as well, Devin Reilly. This day and always."

She punctuated her words with a soft kiss that promised him heaven in her arms.

"Then we must go—"

"No." Now it was her turn to stop his words with the brush of her fingers against his mouth.

"We cannot run from my parents like thieves in the night. They will only take that as a sign of weakness. I have another idea."

"And what would that be, lass?"

"Didn't Bernie tell us his brother-in-law was a minister?"

"Aye."

"And is not Bernie one of the town selectmen, well able to move a few political mountains even my father cannot gainsay, given that we have not yet returned to Massachusetts?"

"Aye, again." He wondered where this was leading, but really did not care, so caught was he by the delight sparkling in her eyes.

"Well, my dear Mr. Reilly"—her voice played huskily against his ear—"my father would not dare to attack his own son-in-law for fear of the scandal reflecting back on him. His pride is more dangerous than his ambitions. He might disown me, but he'd never suffer the consequences of putting his son-in-law in prison."

"Miss Brownley, have I ever told you how much I appreciate the keen intellect you possess?" He kissed her temples, her ear, the warm skin of her neck. He buried his fingers in the hair she had gathered at her nape and released the springy softness of her curls, as he had been longing to do through all the hours of searching for her.

She sighed, her arms tightening about his neck. "Mr. Reilly, you may tell me all about it later. In great detail."

He kissed her very softly, loving every inch of this warm incredible woman. His woman.

"Let's go find Bernie."

"My parents are enjoying the comforts of his in-law's dining room. We will need to be careful if we are to accomplish this without their knowledge."

He led the way down the hill and retrieved the mare's reins from where he'd dropped them.

"Hey, you're back again." A young voice halted Devin in the process of swinging up into the saddle.

"Harvey," Maggie greeted the lad. "Where is your brother?"

"Left him at home with Mama and the girls," Harvey answered, frowning. "Sometimes I'm jest too old to be follered around."

"Indeed," Devin agreed, smiling. "You are certainly way too old. So my own brothers informed me quite frequently when they were your age. And in that vein, Harvey, I have a job for you. It's important and secret."

The boy's eyes widened, and he straightened his shoulders. "What is it?"

Half an hour later, Maggie stood beside Devin at the center of the ancient druid stones behind Mystery Hill. The minister, Kenneth Jones, stood before them, managing to look at home amidst the stones and the greenery despite the odd request they had made of him. His sister, Abby, and her children would serve as witnesses.

Devin could only marvel at the feeling of peace that had stolen over him from the moment he'd set foot within the Mystery Hill confines. All of Granny's stories of the druids and the boon they had granted his family so long ago echoed through his head.

For nine unto nine generations.

'Tis a sound once heard that lingers on, a sight once seen and never forgotten, a feeling once felt, always remembered. 'Tis in the blood of all Reillys.

He could almost smell the scent of Granny Reilly's

lavender perfume, feel her nod of acceptance and approval as he embraced once and forever The Blessing and his belief in the tales she told so faithfully.

I haven't missed my Blessing, Granny, he thought, *and I'll remember.*

Devin's gaze held on Maggie as the minister laid the last of his blessings on their heads.

"You may kiss your bride, Mr. Reilly," Mr. Jones said gently.

His bride.

He drew Maggie to him as timeless power rushed through his body. She was now his in the eyes of God and man, and no one, no matter how determined, would ever set them asunder.

"I love you, *mo chroí,*" he whispered against her lips.

"Aye," she whispered back before surrendering herself to his kiss.

"Oh, it was a lovely wedding. Bernie very much wanted to be here, too, but his work at the forge needed his full attention." Abby sniffled into her handkerchief as Devin released his wife's rosy lips. Her two girls clung to her skirts and the boys shifted restlessly beside her.

"Not the usual games you play here, huh, boys?" They rewarded Devin's teasing observation with shy smiles at being caught in their boredom.

"Thank you, Mr. Jones, for coming so quickly." Maggie patted the minister's hand.

"No problem, my dear. Bernie allowed it was a matter of utmost urgency." He scratched his head. "Never held a wedding up here so near Mystery Hill before, but it felt pretty good. Guess those old stories Amos Gandy tells hold more truth than fiction."

"What stories are those?" Devin asked.

"Bernie's Uncle Amos believes these stones are here for some sort of ancient religious purposes," Abby offered with a nervous laugh. "Who knows, he may be right. But I must admit I far prefer church."

Mr. Jones laughed. "Don't worry, Sis. I was not about to suggest we move the weekly services up here."

"Again, we thank both of you." Devin laced his fingers through Maggie's. "And now, my dear wife, we have some unfinished business to attend to."

"You can ride in the cart with us, if you like," Abby offered.

The ride to the settlement was accomplished in too short a time to suit Maggie. She could have stayed on that hill in Devin's arms for ever.

Devin. Her husband. Mrs. Devin Patrick Reilly.

Her fingers laced through his, giving her strength as she gathered her thoughts for the battle to come. She would be strong. She could be strong because of him.

Abby respected their need for silence, keeping herself busy with her children, though she cast several knowing smiles their way as Devin and Maggie smiled and stared long into each other's eyes.

Maggie's stomach churned the closer they got to the stables. Her father would not take this news with anything remotely resembling pleasure. That did not matter anymore. She was Devin's wife now. They would face Papa together.

Devin's wife. He squeezed her fingers as if he agreed with the wonder that floated through her.

They still had problems that needed to be solved: The shipyard. The mill.

Questions about how they would resolve those problems swirled around in Maggie's thoughts, but she came no closer to any answers. However they handled things from now on, they would handle them together.

The cart rumbled to a halt beside her parents' carriage. Devin helped her alight. The feel of his strong fingers about her waist shored up her defenses and offered something to cling to as she anticipated her parents' reaction.

"Devin, I—"

"Unhand my daughter this instant!" Papa's voice cracked through the air.

Devin squeezed her waist, sliding his arm casually about her as he turned to face her father.

"Good day to you, Mr. Brownley," he said. His pleasant tone was belied by the tension running through his arm.

"Good day! *Good day?*" Papa repeated, his face flushing an ugly shade of red. "How dare you greet me with a casual good day, as though we were acquaintances? As though you were my equal?"

Papa seemed far more flummoxed by the idea that Devin would regard him as an equal than by the fact that his former coachman had an arm around his daughter.

"Papa—"

"Don't even speak to me, you little strumpet. Your mother has told me what she suspects of you. Of you both." He fairly spit the words.

Angry heat stung Maggie's cheeks. "Papa—"

"Not another word out of you, missy, or I'll—"

"Mr. Brownley"—Devin cut Papa's tirade off as he pulled her more solidly against his side—"I'll thank you to address your comments and your threats to me, rather than to my wife."

"Address them to you! Why, I'll . . ." Papa's mouth opened and closed for a moment, making him look oddly like a fish gasping for air. "Your *what?*"

"His wife," Maggie said quietly as triumph surged through her. "This is my husband, Papa. Devin Reilly of Reilly Ship Works, Beannacht Island, Ireland."

The minister, Mr. Jones, waved from the cart where

Bernie had gone to greet his family. The Paulsons all waved, a merry contrast to her own family.

"You cannot be married! I'll not allow it. I don't care if he's related to Queen Victoria or the governor himself. You'll not remain married to him!"

"You cannot stop them, William." The velvet-covered steel in those soft tones made Maggie turn toward the smithy.

"Grandmother?"

"Hello, Margaret, darling." Grandmother smiled at her, pride radiating from her like sunlight as she stepped from the shadows with Jacob in her wake. "Mr. Reilly, it is always a pleasure to deal with a man who completes his task so quickly and efficiently."

"Anytime, Grandmother." Devin nodded modestly, a wicked smile spreading over his face.

"What have you done?" Papa's outrage drew every eye. "Sylvia, I see your hand in this! I'll not allow this!"

"It no longer matters what you will or won't allow," Grandmother told him with a slight wave of her hand. "Margaret is of age and she has chosen her own mate. Your blustering holds power no longer, William. Call it a day."

Papa's face went a deep crimson. "You will rue the day you interfered with my family."

"You cannot blame this on anyone but me, Papa," Maggie managed in a clear tone that immediately drew her father's gaze. "This was my decision. Mine and Devin's. I hope someday you will come to understand that."

Deathly silence held as her father's scathing glance passed over her. Finally he arched a brow and straightened his jacket, and the cold veneer Maggie was so familiar with dropped into place. Mama refused to look at her. She could almost hear the ties that had bound her to these two people snapping once and for all.

"Alberta, it is past time for us to leave this wretched place. We have only one daughter now. It is time to turn our thoughts to Lenore."

A pang lanced through Maggie at his cruel words. Devin's arm tightened about her. He was her family now. That was more than enough for her.

"Good-bye, Papa. Good-bye, Mama."

Her father ignored her as he escorted her mother into the carriage without further comment.

Only Marcus's wink of approval provided a touch of warmth as the Brownley carriage wheeled away from Bernard Paulson's smithy and out of her life. She could only hope Nora was up to what her parents had in store for her.

"Mo chroí?" Devin's fingers touched her chin, turning her face up to his.

"I'm all right," she told him, surprised to find she truly meant it. "I always knew there would be a parting of the ways for me and my parents."

"You handled that very well." Grandmother approached them both, Jacob Warren beside her. "I'm so proud of you, Margaret. So very proud."

"Thank you, Grandmother. But how did you get here?"

Grandmother turned a warm smile on Jacob, whose blue eyes twinkled warmly in return. "Jacob provided my escort. He always was good at traveling places in a hurry."

Their gazes locked for the space of several heartbeats, and Maggie realized with something of a shock that there was more between these two than she had ever guessed.

Grandmother sighed. "At any rate, we found you— and in time, too."

"In time?" Devin asked.

"Indeed, young Mr. Reilly. For though you have taken

care of the immediate matters concerning my grand-daughter, there is yet more to discuss.''

''And what might that be, Grandmother?''

''Margaret, you know it has always been my intention to turn the mill over to you.''

''Grandmother—''

Maggie's heart sank. She didn't think she could bear to hear what she feared her grandmother had to say. Not now, when she had pledged herself to Devin and whatever the future held for both of them.

''Don't interrupt, dear,'' Grandmother admonished. ''I have decided to turn the mill over to you now. Oh, don't think I won't keep my hand in. It's taken me too many years to see it where it is to completely lose interest in Worth Lumber now.'' She chuckled. ''I was going to do this before you arrived, because I thought you might need an extra foundation to give you the strength to do what you needed to do to make the break.''

Grandmother appraised her in silence for a moment.

''But you didn't need that at all. You found your own way in the end. Which is far better, I think. However I'm still ready to hand you the mill.''

''But—''

''You and this young Reilly husband you've attached yourself to.''

''Oh, Grandmother.'' Hope and fear swirled in Maggie's stomach. Would Devin be interested in tying himself so completely to a world an ocean away from his family, from all that he had known?

''Actually''—Devin squeezed her side—''I'd be proud to accept such an offer, if my wife approves.''

Confusion tightened the reins on the hopes threatening to leap out of control. ''But what about California?''

''Maggie-mine.'' He turned her to face him. The sparkle lurking in his deep green eyes made her breath hitch. ''I

can accomplish more here with the contacts your grandmother has in place than by running off to California in
search of something that might not be there. And Reilly
Ship Works can transport Worth Lumber to more markets
for a far better profit if we combine our efforts.''

He sent Grandmother a quick wink.

''But what of your gold?'' The last vestige of protest
whispered out of her, flying away on wings of hope.

''I have already found a treasure more precious than
mere metal could ever be.''

''I really do like that boy,'' Grandmother whispered to
Jacob as Maggie's heart swelled within her.

''What have you found?'' She asked him.

''You, *mo chroí*,'' he said in a husky tone. ''You are
more than I ever could have hoped for. You are The
Blessing in my life.''

His words spiraled through her on a bright ray of hope
and promises. ''Oh, Devin.''

She twined her arms around his neck and rewarded her
husband with a kiss that told him all the wondrous feelings
surging inside her heart and welling from the depths of
her soul.

''I love you, Maggie-mine,'' he whispered against her
ear, and she knew all their tomorrows would be spent
together.

As she hugged Devin tight, Jacob leaned toward Grandmother, who was beaming with pride.

''Why were you so determined for them to get married,
Sylvia? I thought you wanted her to be strong, just like
you.''

Grandmother nodded, old pain reflected in the gaze she
leveled at him. ''I still want that for her. But I've learned
a few things late in my life.''

Jacob raised a brow at her. ''And what might that be?''

''That strength comes from within,'' she told him as

something wonderful sparkled in the depths of her hazel eyes. "No one can take it from you unless you allow it. A woman can marry and still be strong, Jacob."

Maggie smiled. The misty gazes the older couple locked revealed a connection too long denied. Then she turned her attention back to the love shining in her husband's green eyes and the glorious future about to claim them both.

"Tell me again, husband," she whispered later that day, as they lay entwined and spent from the passion that had sealed their marriage vows, "what is it you found that is more precious than any mere metal?"

He nuzzled her neck for a delicious moment before meeting her gaze to answer her. "Love, *mo chroí*. Love is more precious than gold."

If you liked REILLY'S GOLD, be sure to look for Elizabeth Keys's next release in the Irish Blessing series, REILLY'S PRIDE, available wherever books are sold in May, 2001.

When Quintin Reilly comes home to Beannacht Island to run Reilly Ship Works, he doesn't expect to meet Siannon Rhodes again. Now a widow with a young son, Siannon proposes a marriage of convenience to Quin, with the promise of badly needed capital for his business—and the hope of fulfilling a love destined by The Blessing . . .

BOOK YOUR PLACE ON OUR WEBSITE
AND MAKE THE
READING CONNECTION!

We've created a customized website just for our very special readers, where you can get the inside scoop on everything that's going on with Zebra, Pinnacle and Kensington books.

When you come online, you'll have the exciting opportunity to:

- View covers of upcoming books
- Read sample chapters
- Learn about our future publishing schedule (listed by publication month *and author*)
- Find out when your favorite authors will be visiting a city near you
- Search for and order backlist books from our online catalog
- Check out author bios and background information
- Send e-mail to your favorite authors
- Meet the Kensington staff online
- Join us in weekly chats with authors, readers and other guests
- Get writing guidelines
- AND MUCH MORE!

Visit our website at
http://www.zebrabooks.com